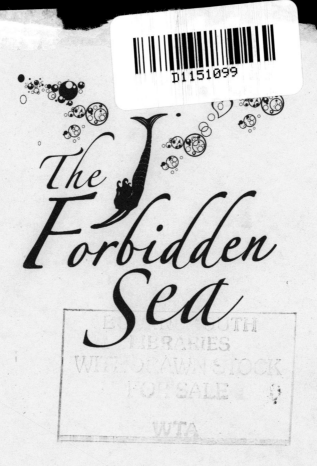

The Forbidden Sea

SHEILA A. NIELSON

The Forbidden Sea

SCHOLASTIC

*To all those dear family and friends who
encouraged and supported a starry-eyed author
as she followed her dreams. (You know who you are.)*

Scholastic Children's Books
An imprint of Scholastic Ltd
Euston House, 24 Eversholt Street
London, NW1 1DB, UK
Registered office: Westfield Road, Southam, Warwickshire, CV47 0RA
SCHOLASTIC and associated logos are trademarks and/or registered trademarks
of Scholastic Inc.

First published in the US by Scholastic Inc, 2010
This edition published in the UK by Scholastic Ltd, 2010
Text copyright © Sheila A. Nielson, 2010
The right of Sheila A. Nielson to be identified as the author of this work
has been asserted by her.

ISBN 978 1407 12099 7

Printed in the UK by CPI Bookmarque, Croydon, Surrey.
Papers used by Scholastic Children's Books are made from wood grown in
sustainable forests.

1 3 5 7 9 10 8 6 4 2

www.scholastic.co.uk/zone

Prologue

One hundred years ago, Lady Lauretta Durran vanished from the shores of Windwaithe Island. Some say Lauretta met her fate while wandering the sparkling shores, as she was wont to do on warm summer days. Others say she was lured from her bed late one night by the enchanting echoes of an eerie melody, which led her to climb out across the rocks at the edge of the ocean. One thing common to all the tales is the mermaid – beautiful as the distant stars, with skin the deep green colour of the darkest fathoms of the ocean. So, they say, through wind and rain, Lauretta Durran made her way to the water's edge, a sacrifice to this creature of the sea.

Then, taking the girl with her, the mermaid disappeared beneath the waves for ever, neither ever to be seen again on the shores of Windwaithe Island.

One

Pelting rain battered against me, stinging my skin and eyes, almost driving me backwards. Forcing myself to continue, I felt my way down the slick rock face one foot at a time. I clung to the cliff face a moment, crying into the dark squall raging around me.

"Cecily! It's Adrianne. Can you hear me?" The force of the storm shoved the words back into my mouth, the desperate cry lost in the roaring of the wind. Had she been even a few feet away, my little sister wouldn't have heard me.

"Cecily!"

Hot frustration burned at my eyes and mingled with the freezing rain. Crying wouldn't do Cecily any good. Neither would huddling against the side of a rock, shivering in my soaked and clinging dress. I needed to find her. Forcing my frozen fingers to uncurl, I began my descent once more.

During good weather it was a short climb to the bottom of the steep shelf that connected the upper road to the beach. I'd clambered down this shortcut to the shore a hundred times. The rocks were slippery with rain now. I tried to think about Cecily's safety and not about how foolhardy I was to risk my life this way.

When Cecily first went missing, I was upset with my sister for making Mama worry and causing us to waste precious time hunting for her – time that was needed for more important tasks. If we wanted to eat at the end of the week, the mountain of mending Mama took in from the villagers had to be done sometime.

I was haunted by the memory of my sister's pale face and wide horrified eyes, as Mama told her I meant to take Lark, our old Irish setter, to the manor to be sold. Lark had been around long before my nine-year-old sister was born. The dog was her closest friend. But things were different now that money and food were scarce. Lark had too large of an appetite to stay. Before Mama could even finish explaining, Cecily bolted to her feet and fled our small cottage, her unbound hair flying free behind her. She had not returned, not even when night fell and a sudden storm blew in from the ocean. A sickening heaviness had settled itself in the pit of my stomach hours ago.

"She must be hiding somewhere in Cormy's Wood," Captain Young had said to the crowd of villagers who'd gathered at his home to search for Cecily. Somehow, Captain Young's eldest son, Denn, convinced the boys his age to help out. I didn't mind Denn, but, as I'd watched Marcus Stebbs and his friends strut about with their arrogant hero airs and false bravado, I'd wished they'd all stayed home.

Time had passed now and I was grateful for even Marcus's help. I didn't care if the mending never got done, as long as Cecily was found safe. The storm raged worse than ever around me. I had to find my little sister as soon as possible.

Cecily wasn't in Cormy's Wood as Captain Young had thought. I'd tried to tell the searchers, but they wouldn't listen to me, a mere girl of fourteen.

"A child of Cecily's tender years would never go to the Rumbles in a storm like this." Captain Young tried to reason with me in his gentle way. "A little girl would be too frightened."

The other searchers agreed and set off for the woods on the west side of the island. Mama, Auntie Minnah and Mrs Young waited at home by the fireside for the news they would bring – whatever it might be.

But I knew my sister. She went to the sea when she was troubled. She said it talked to her, murmuring calming secrets. At a time like this, she would head straight for the Rumbles. During low tide, these massive outcroppings of stone were close enough together that anyone could safely climb across them out to the edge of the sea. When the tide came in, they roared and rumbled as wave upon wave crashed over the rocks, almost covering them with water. The ominous sound they made as the waves pounded against them gave the rocks their name. I knew the place. I often went there myself, letting the ocean soak me with its spray and sing me its song. Sometimes, I even sang back. That was before the hard times. Before Papa died. I didn't sing any more.

Clinging to the rocks, I adjusted my weight long enough to brush back the dripping hair from my forehead. How many times had I cursed my unfashionably short hair in the past months? Now I was grateful for it since I could still see, even with the wild wind blowing soaked strands into my eyes.

I lifted my wet face to the dark sky. "Please help me find Cecily." I prayed the words aloud thinking it would give them more power, but might have saved myself the trouble. Even I couldn't hear my voice above the sudden thunder that crashed over the island at that moment.

Its booming echoes made me jump and lose my footing. My knee came down hard against a jutting stone and pain shot through my whole body. I trembled, all ten fingers burning with the effort of clinging to the side of the cliff. For one moment I wasn't sure I could hold myself. Feeling with my foot, I found a place to jam my wet boot into a crack. If I could only hang on a little longer I might make it to the bottom in one piece. One step downwards – two – then three – and I was there, panting and dripping on the sandy beach spread before the Rumbles.

That's when I heard it. From down the beach, carried on rain and wind – someone was singing.

"Cecily?"

Lightning crackled across the sky. The earth shook beneath me as thunder pitched over the land. Yet the singing continued unbroken. I listened, caught up in the most beautiful and haunting voice I'd ever heard. It was hard to breathe for the aching perfection of the song. Lack of air made me feel strangely lightheaded, like in a dream. The wind died to a sudden lull – only the singing and the hard patter of great, wet drops met my ears. I blinked, trying to see through the curtain of water falling from the black night. Not far ahead, the ocean threw itself against the rocks. A distant flash of lightning showed all but a few of the Rumbles now covered with a wild, heaving sea.

The singing came from there.

"Cecily! Where are you?" I shouted towards the surging swell. The song broke off as if I'd startled the singer into silence. I stood waiting, listening for the slightest sound. Lightning tore at the sky, illuminating everything before me like a spectral stage. I saw the clear, glistening silhouette of a figure sitting on the largest of the Rumble Stones far out in the water. Cecily was trapped! The tide must have come in while she wasn't paying attention.

I broke into a run, scrambling down the beach as fast as I could, and dived into the salt and spray. Cecily would need my help to get back to shore. The children of Windwaithe were required by necessity to learn to swim at an early age. It was the only way to survive in a village whose biggest means of income was fish brought in by boat. But Cecily hated getting wet, and managed one way or another to get out of learning to swim.

The water fought me with a fury. White-capped waves smashed me against wicked sharp rocks hidden beneath the surface. I was covered with painful cuts and bruises by the time I reached the furthest Rumble Stone. I looked to where I'd last seen the figure, but the spot was empty. My heart lurched heavily inside my chest as I imagined my sister washed out to sea. That's when I saw Cecily's drenched form sprawled lifelessly across the flattest part of the rock. Her eyes were closed, her pretty face pale in the flare of lightning that danced on the ocean.

I dragged myself, heavy with water, from the surf, and crawled to her side. She looked so small and pitiful, soaked clear through. I grasped her fingers in mine. They were cold as ice. Pressing my trembling hand to her mouth, I felt her shallow but warm breath flutter against my frozen fingertips. She was still alive.

I couldn't understand. I'd seen her sitting on the rock, heard her singing. Yet, as I looked at my sister's unconscious form, I knew it couldn't have been her. The voice was too perfect, too mature to be Cecily's. Someone else had been there with her, perhaps had pulled her from the water to save her life. Now they were gone.

I looked out over the churning ocean. Had I startled the person when I shouted? Did an unexpected wave wash them out to sea?

Pulling Cecily's limp body closer to mine, I peered out over the water, not sure what to look for.

Something touched my leg. I let out a terrified gasp that was swallowed up in the roaring of wind, rain and tide. Nerves completely rattled, I looked down, forcing myself to meet this new unknown terror.

At first I didn't see her – the woman whose head and shoulders floated in the water not two feet from where my boot lay at the edge of the Rumble Stone. If it were not for her lighter hair, her dark skin would have made her invisible against the surface of the midnight sea. Long fingers of lightning lanced through the clouds above, imprinting every detail of the strange woman against the canvas of my stunned memory. What I saw made me doubt my waking senses.

She was impossibly beautiful, from her delicate pointed ears to her slightly slanted elfin eyes. She wore a strange but lovely garment of shimmering purple that covered her from neck to waist but left the outer curve of her shoulders and upper arms shockingly bare. A collar of fine gold beadwork lay spread across her neck and shoulders like a dew-laden spider's web. An intricate crown of gold encircled her head at the hairline. Her head bore strand upon strand of flowing light green braids, each fastened with a glittering bead at its end. These ropes of hair twisted and writhed, pushed and pulled by the surging surf around her.

I thought at first it must be an odd combination of lightning and reflecting seawater that gave her skin and hair their greenish tint. One of her hands rested on my ankle as she pulled more of herself from the water. I tried to jerk my leg back but her strong grip held me fast. I glanced down at the fingers peeking from beneath a glove-like sleeve that ended just above her elbow. Her fingers were as green as her shoulders and face.

She didn't speak as her golden eyes took in every detail of my face. I gaped back at the stranger, unable to move. What was she doing in the raging water? Where did she come from? I knew everyone on the island, and I could see by looking at her she was no homeless tide drifter. Just as I was about to speak, she gave me the most curious smile – one side of her lips curving upwards. She took her hand from my ankle and settled it on my right wrist. Despite the freezing cold water, her touch was surprisingly warm against my skin. Her grasp was firm but gentle – then she jerked, hard.

I cried out as Cecily slipped from my arms and rolled heavily back on to the wet rock. I tried to catch her, but the woman's grip on my wrist prevented me from reaching my sister. I groped blindly along the rock beneath me with my free hand and found a crevice. I dug my fingers into it.

The unknown woman yanked again, harder this time. I held on tight, to keep myself from toppling into the water with her. Before I could react, she wrapped her other hand around my wrist, to give her a better hold. The winds howled into life, tearing at my clothes and hair.

"Let go of me!" I cried.

She didn't answer. I read no anger or malice on her beautiful, smooth features. She gave my arm a tug, gentler this time. A strangely warm heaviness settled over me. My limbs felt made of stone, and my head reeled for a moment. The howling of the rain and the wind slipped back from me, as if a safe bubble protected me.

A soft moan came from somewhere nearby. Cecily! What happened to Cecily? The thought of my sister's name was enough to break the spell taking hold of me.

Using the stones beneath my left hand for leverage, I jerked against my captor's grasp with all the strength I could muster. My movement was so quick, the woman in the water almost lost her hold on my arm. Once again the icy rain and wind beat against me. The harsh cold instantly sharpened my wits.

The woman tightened her grip, her long nails biting into my skin. A mass of shimmering, golden scales and iridescent fins flashed beneath the lightning-filled sky. They slapped at the surface of the water, dragging me towards the edge of the Rumble Stone. The fingers of my left hand shook under the strain of holding me back.

True panic rose up inside me. This was no mortal woman, but a mermaid! Fearsome and beautiful beyond imagining. A century-old legend breathed to life before my very eyes.

I tried to twist and pull myself free of the creature's grasp. My skin tore beneath her nails but still she wouldn't let go. The terrible winds rose up again and rogue waves pounded against me, pushing me towards the ocean. I clutched at the stone with my aching fingers, my strength almost spent. I thought of kicking at her but knew I needed both legs to brace myself against the rock face. It was hopeless. The power of the sea was on her side. She would take me down into the shadowy waters and drown me just as the mermaids in stories did to sailors of the sea.

"Adrianne?" A male voice shouted its way through the storm. "Adri, where are you?"

The mermaid turned in the direction of the sound. While she was distracted, I slipped my mangled wrist from between her fingers and heaved myself back on to the Rumble Stone, scrambling far from her reach.

She looked at me and smiled her curious smile, as if she were pleased I'd escaped from her.

"Adri!"

It had to be Denn Young. He was the only one who ever called me Adri.

The mermaid nodded at me once before slipping beneath the waves as silent as a shadow, taking the raging wind with her. Even the rain fell gentler as it pattered on my short hair and down my cheeks.

I dragged myself to Cecily's side and drew her tight into my arms. I heard Denn stroking his way through the water towards us. Even though we shared no blood ties, all my life Denn had acted the part of a protective older brother. I should have known he would follow when he noticed me missing from the group of searchers.

Denn's normally red, unruly hair hung in dark, wet ringlets. His brow was furrowed with worry. His handsome face, anxious and pale against the dark waves. He didn't look anything like the mischievous boy I'd grown up with.

"Adri, I thought I saw something moving out here. Are you all right?"

I tried to speak, but no sound came past the swollen mass tangled in my throat. Everything around me was muzzy and dreamlike, even Denn's face. My thoughts slithered away in a useless jumble.

"You must be exhausted. Give me Cecily. I'll swim her to shore and come back for you," Denn said.

I made myself nod. With great care, he took my sister from my limp arms. As I let go, I noticed a throbbing in my wounded wrist. I clutched at it as a thick green mist closed around my vision. Everything around me drew back.

My head reeled drunkenly as I slipped into silent, still darkness.

Two

I drifted along a warm sea, my body gently rocking with the ebb and flow of the tide. A single voice sang far in the distance. Beautiful, but haunting. Seaweed and kelp swayed around me in a slow, hypnotic dance. I felt perfectly comfortable; my lungs needed no air.

"Adrianne?"

I tilted my head back in a slow, lazy movement, trying to find who spoke my name. Above me I saw the surface of the water – shimmering and golden. Through its shifting view, I could see Cecily standing in the sunlight. She looked down into the water, her lovely face tight with worry, eyes searching urgently for something she couldn't seem to find.

"Adrianne?"

My eyelids snapped open. The sunlight of my dream was gone, and in its place were the velvet shadows of night. I lay still for a moment, panting as if I'd been holding my breath for a long time. Instead of the comforting sway of water and seaweed, I felt points of straw digging into the skin along my arms and back through the thin cloth of the pallet I lay on. I recognized the bed as the one I shared with my little sister back at our cottage. I'd almost forgotten what it felt like to sleep on a feathered mattress like the one I once had as a child.

To my surprise, the smoky smell of hearth fire filled the draughty room. In the two years we'd lived in this cottage, this particular fire had never been lit – we couldn't afford the extra wood. Something was wrong.

I could barely make out Cecily's pale, delicate face hovering over me in the light of a flickering candle by the side of the bed. Her large eyes glistened, as if she'd been crying. She looked like a sad little princess from one of Papa's old stories. My little sister had always been the beauty of the family.

"Adrianne?" Cecily whispered. "Are you alive?"

Such an outlandish question made me want to laugh, but I found, to my surprise, I had no strength for it. My body lay as heavy as a sodden blanket around me.

Had it been a dream? Cecily lost, the heaving sea, and the green-skinned mermaid? A trick of a weary mind, perhaps?

"How did I get here?" My voice rasped from a parched throat.

"Denn carried you." Cecily gave me a wobbly smile. "Just like a prince in a story."

Heat rose in my cheeks as I imagined Denn carrying me in his arms all that distance. Such a thought was nonsense, of course. Knowing Denn, he'd probably slung me over his shoulder the whole way, like a limp sack of potatoes. He would never have carried Cora Lynn Dunst that way. He didn't think of *her* as a troublesome younger sister.

"Denn shook me something awful," Cecily continued. "I didn't want to wake up but he made me. Nothing he did would wake you. I cried and cried but you didn't move. I thought you'd died." She put a small hand to her mouth in a childish gesture. "Mama sent me for the healing woman, Mrs Rousay, but she didn't know what was wrong with you."

Knowing how Auntie Minnah felt about Mrs Rousay and their mutual dislike of each other, I was surprised Mama had been so bold. She must have really been worried about me.

"When Mrs Rousay couldn't help you, Mama sent Denn for Doctor Goodwin," Cecily said. "The doctor couldn't wake you, either. He took care of all your cuts and scrapes instead – said they'd heal in no time."

I swallowed hard. Doctor Goodwin? What had Mama been thinking? Didn't she know things were different for us now? How could we possibly afford to pay for the doctor's visit?

"You've been sleeping for ever so long. You even missed church yesterday." Cecily sounded more than a bit envious.

"The Sabbath has been and gone?" I asked in surprise. "How long have I been asleep?"

"Three days," said a smooth voice from the shadowy doorway.

Cecily jumped as a short, stout figure walked out of the darkness into the firelight. Unfortunately, Auntie Minnah was now the only thing I could see clearly in the dark room. Folding her arms lightly across her ample chest, Auntie gazed down at me with a cool, detached expression.

"It's taken you an awfully long time to recover, Adrianne." Auntie's tone was as cold as her face. She rested a hand on Cecily's head. The gentleness of the gesture seemed oddly out of place with the hard look in her eye. "Your little sister recovered within an hour after she was found. That's rather odd, don't you think? Especially since she was out in the storm so much longer than you."

I had learned not to rise to the bait of Auntie Minnah's sly hints, but Cecily had gained no such wisdom. She drew back from Auntie Minnah's touch. "Adrianne's not pretending, Auntie. She really is sick."

Auntie's tones became soft and cajoling in an instant. They always did when she spoke to Cecily, her favourite. "I never said she was pretending, dear one. Whatever would make you accuse your sister of doing something so dishonest as to pretend to be unconscious and leave all her work to be done by her family?" Auntie's gaze slid in my direction. Her features were smooth, but

17

her eyes glittered dangerously. I knew from experience that changing the subject was the best way to deal with one of Auntie's moods.

"Who has been milking Belle?" I asked.

"If you were so concerned about that cow's welfare, you shouldn't have pretended to be ill so long," Auntie said in a careless tone.

I tried to sit up, but my muscles were too slow to respond. It felt like moving through molasses. Inside my heart raced at a fearful pace. I could barely whisper.

"You didn't sell her, did you?"

Auntie lifted her jowly chin, the light from below casting strange, twisted shadows over her round face.

Seeing Auntie wouldn't answer, Cecily spoke up. "Captain Young sent one of his men over to milk Belle while you were sick."

I breathed a silent sigh of relief. I didn't know what we would do without Belle's milk to get us through the winter. Auntie Minnah had never agreed with my decision to keep the cow when all the other stock was sent to be auctioned. I'd put my foot down and refused to sell Belle or the three best laying hens. Auntie complained regularly to Mama about my decision, saying we needed money more than we needed milk and eggs. But I knew she was wrong.

Mama's rustling skirts announced that she had come into the room.

"Adrianne is awake, Mama." Cecily bounced up and down in excitement. It made me dizzy to watch her. Briefly Mama entered the circle of firelight. She looked tired as she placed a steaming bowl of broth on a small wood stool. She settled her thin frame into a chair next to the bed.

"Praise God, you're all right," Mama said reverently. "I was so worried. Mrs Rousay said she'd never seen anything like your condition."

"Funny that even Doctor Goodwin couldn't find anything wrong with her." Auntie turned away from me as she said it, pretending to fuss over something, probably mine, that she'd stumbled over in the darkness.

The only part of Mama I could see were her hands clasped much too tightly in her lap. Auntie Minnah finished her fussing and came to stand before her. When Auntie spoke, her voice was light enough.

"If you'd poisoned that dog six months ago when I first advised you to, none of this would have happened, Giselle. Now we've lost time and money – and Adrianne is *sick*."

Cecily leaped to her feet, wringing her hands before her. With the dim light now falling across one side of her smooth face, she looked strangely older than her nine years.

"You can't poison Lark!" She turned to Mama in desperation. "Lark hasn't done anything wrong. She's a good dog."

"Of course she is," Mama whispered. The light slithered across her as she drew one arm around Cecily's thin shoulders.

"No one will hurt Lark." I was surprised at the firmness of my voice. Auntie Minnah turned to glare at me, the shifting light of the flames falling full upon her harsh face. I pretended not to see her. "I give my word, the dog will not be poisoned."

Cecily gave a shaky sigh of relief.

"Your word?" Auntie Minnah smiled at me with all her crooked teeth, but there was no warmth in the expression. Her tone was icy and cutting. "The noble promise of Adrianne Keynnman is a treasure indeed. Why it's almost as valuable as this grand, draughty old cottage she's managed to land us with. Was it not her 'honourable word' that lost all her father's fortune while her mother recovered from her long illness?"

As Auntie spoke, I noticed Mama sitting there, shoulders hunched, her head bowed low, face lost in shadow – as if it were she, and not I, Auntie shamed with her words. I reached out to take Mama's hand. It trembled beneath my touch.

Stand up to her! I wanted to shout at Mama's still form. *You're the head of this house, not her. She only goes on this way because she knows you're too timid to stop her.*

I knew saying the words aloud would be pointless. Mama had never been able to stand up to Auntie Minnah's stinging darts of sarcasm. She didn't have enough strength inside, and no amount of wishing on my part would give it to her. If someone were to stand up to Auntie, as usual, it would have to be me. Knowing I was too weak to meet her in a head-on battle, I decided a softer approach would be best.

"We should be thankful to Captain Young for his generosity. He has been extremely kind to let us live on his land for so little," I said.

"Kind?" Auntie feigned surprise. "I notice his roof doesn't leak during the rainy season as ours does. Being the kind, devoutly religious man that he is, I'm sure Captain Young would never make his own family live under a thatched roof, as he does so generously to ours."

"If you dislike it so much, you are free to leave anytime you wish." The minute the weary words were out of my mouth I wanted to catch them in my fingers and pull them back. Even to me they sounded harsh and cold. After Papa's death, Auntie Minnah had been forced to leave the comfortable little cottage Papa had rented for her most of her life. As far as we knew, she had no other place to go. But it was too late, the thing could not be unsaid.

With dead calm, Auntie Minnah turned to Mama. As far as she was concerned, I'd ceased to exist. When she spoke, her voice was laden with airy condescension. "Do you see now what I'm talking about, Giselle? Listen to the words of your own daughter. The brown-eyed minx is completely beyond control. Talking back to her elders, wallowing about in dirt and manure, why, she even looks like a boy with her hair hacked off the way she has it now. I worry about her future. Only two more years and she'll be of marriageable age. What man would look at such a girl, much less marry her? You need to take her in hand immediately or she'll be beyond saving."

My heart quivered like a wounded animal as Auntie's cruel words found their mark. What she said was only too true and no one knew it more than I. Ugly, dirty and undesirable – yes, I was all those things – but to hear the words spoken aloud in such a matter-of-fact tone stung my tender soul far more than any whip upon skin.

"I like Adrianne's hair short," Cecily's small voice spoke from the darkness. "The man who cut it gave Adrianne lots of money for her hair, Auntie."

I wanted to hug my adorable sister. It wasn't often that anyone dared to speak in my defence.

Auntie's whole demeanour changed as she turned to Cecily. The shadows on her face softened and her voice soothed in gentler tones as she spoke. "It isn't proper for young ladies to speak to strange men they have not been introduced to, so your sister shouldn't have spoken to the travelling wig maker in the first place. Selling her own hair to such a person was immoral. I pray every day that God will forgive her for her lack of decency. May you never follow her example, my pet."

I glanced in Mama's direction. Her face was still in shadow, but her hands silently twisted her ragged apron between her fingers – tighter and tighter. She knew how badly we needed that money, but she made no move to stop Auntie's attack on my character. I hadn't really expected her to.

Auntie looked down at me, an expression of mocking pity

spreading across her round face. "I don't know what is to become of you, Adrianne, running out in the eyeteeth of a storm like a wild thing. You could have drowned yourself and your little sister with you."

"We wouldn't have drowned," Cecily said. "The mermaid would have saved us."

My sister's words blanketed the room in thick silence as we all stared at her. Something inside my chest shrank back into a tight, hard ball. I dared not breathe. The only sound was that of a log settling in the fire.

"Cecily, what are you saying?" Mama's small voice asked.

My sister's face turned towards me. "Didn't you see her, Adrianne? She was beautiful, with skin the colour of dark jade."

I could not look away from Cecily, my heart hammering against my ribs. Seeing I wasn't going to answer, she turned to Mama, tears rising in her voice.

"There *was* a mermaid. She was in the water, calling me. She even knew my name. Her singing made me sleepy."

"Cecily, be still," Auntie Minnah snapped. "It's wrong to speak of the devil's dark creatures." I'd never heard her use that harsh tone with my little sister, whom she loved almost as much as she hated me.

Cecily gaped at Auntie in disbelief. Mama tried to collect the little girl in her arms, but my sister pulled away, a desperate look on her face. She flung herself at the side of my bed.

"Tell, them, Adrianne. Tell them about the mermaid. *You* saw her. You had to."

Auntie Minnah marched up and pulled Cecily away from me. "Enough. Do you want to bring bad luck to the whole household speaking of such things?" A strange tension had crept into my aunt's voice. Could it be fear? I couldn't see her face now that she had her back to the fire.

"It's time for you to get ready for bed. You'll continue to sleep with your mama and me till Adrianne is better." Auntie rushed Cecily from the room before she could find words to protest. Mama and I were left alone in the dark.

For a long time neither of us spoke. I squeezed her hand tighter in my own. My touch seemed to bring back her strength. With a shaky sigh, she stood up into the light, and squaring her shoulders she looked down at me. "Do you think you can sit up and eat?"

I needed help to get myself propped up on the pillows. Mama spooned broth, which was now lukewarm from sitting by the bedside so long, into my mouth.

"I'm sorry about Cecily," Mama said. "It's all those old stories Papa told her while she was growing up – especially the one about Lady Lauretta and the mermaid. It's put foolish notions in her head and now they won't come out." Mama lowered her voice so Auntie couldn't hear. "I'm not sure there are such things as mermaids."

"Then why do we pay the sea's offering?" I asked, referring to the portion of fish in each catch that was released by the fishermen to appease the mermaids and keep them from harming the men as they worked.

"That's just an old tradition," Mama said, refusing to look me in the face.

Then what was she so nervous about all of a sudden? I could see her eyes flitting about the room as if she were afraid something might be lurking in the shadows.

"Auntie Minnah believes in mermaids – and so did Papa," I said.

The flames crackled in the quiet. Mama reached out, taking both my hands in hers.

"Papa was like a child, Adrianne, always wanting to believe magic was still left in the world. The reading he did made him something of a dreamer. But he knew he must keep his feet on the ground. Cecily must learn this, too."

And so do you. Although she didn't say the words aloud, they echoed in my mind as if she had.

She'd always been against Papa teaching me to read. Girls weren't taught to read on Windwaithe Island, because it supposedly made them fanciful and headstrong. Because Papa had no sons, he chose to teach me against Mama's wishes.

"If there are no mermaids, what really happened to Lady Lauretta?" I asked. She, at least, had been real.

Legend said that one hundred years ago, a powerful mermaid used her voice to cast a spell of ancient magic over the heart of Lady Lauretta, convincing the young woman to come away with her into the ocean and marry the Sea Queen's son.

Lady Lauretta agreed, but asked to return to her father's manor one last time to say goodbye to her family. The mermaid placed a mark upon the girl's wrist as a sign of their agreement. When Lauretta's father saw the mermaid's mark upon his daughter's wrist, he feared for her. Refusing to let her go, he locked her in her room with maids to watch over her and make certain she wasn't drawn back to the sea.

When Lauretta did not return, the mermaid became angry and drove the fish from the waters around the island so the fisherman could catch nothing in their nets. Then she called up a terrible storm to rage over the island, destroying many crops and homes.

While the mermaid's anger played havoc upon the island, her spell over Lauretta strengthened. The young woman begged her father, day and night, to let her go to the mermaid and fulfill her promise to marry the Sea Prince. Torn between love for his child and concern for those who lived on his island, Lord Durran finally saw he had no choice but to sacrifice his daughter to her fate.

"Why would Lady Lauretta's father tell everyone his daughter had been stolen by a mermaid if it were not true?" I pressed Mama.

"Perhaps his daughter was drowned in the sea or captured by wicked seamen," Mama said hesitantly. "Sometimes when people are sorrowing they pretend things aren't as bad as they seem.

The pretending becomes so real they can't tell it apart from the truth before long."

Mama wouldn't look at me as she spoke these last words. I could see she was still ashamed of her own behaviour those first few months after Papa died.

I looked away from her and gazed at the flickering candle next to the bed.

Had I really seen a mermaid? Cecily claimed to have seen one, too. We couldn't both have dreamed the same thing, could we? My body felt cold around me as my uncertainty grew.

"You'd better rest now, Adrianne," Mama said. She took hold of my wrist to help me lie down in bed. Searing hot pain shot through my arm. I cried out, trying to pull away.

"What is it?" Mama gently drew my arm closer to her, examining it – then gasped.

There in the firelight, I could see them – ugly red marks marring the surface of my right wrist. The welts were so large they looked like giant worms burrowed beneath my flesh. Each one ran in a straight line down the length of my lower arm, stopping at my hand. Mama turned my arm slowly, revealing that the marks had been scratched into the back of my wrist as well.

"They weren't anywhere near this bad when the doctor was here," Mama said in alarm. "How did you get these, Adrianne?"

No matter how hard I tried, I couldn't rid myself of the

memory of sharp nails digging into my flesh. My silence grew in the shadows around us.

A troubled look crept over Mama's flickering features.

"Adrianne," Mama spoke without looking me in the eyes. "Did something – strange happen to you down at the Rumbles? You know you can tell me. I will believe whatever you say."

The words were brave, but her voice had the high uncertain sound of a frightened child. She knew. I could see it in her wide, unblinking eyes. Like every other person born and raised on Windwaithe Island, a part of her believed in fairy creatures like mermaids, no matter how much she chose to pretend she didn't. The sea and all its mysteries had been a part of our lives and the lives of our forefathers for generations.

But I could never tell her the truth. Mama was as fragile as china inside. Too much strain could cause her to shatter. I remembered only too well what happened after Papa's funeral. Those long months of – illness. I'd seen then how weak she truly was.

"The night at the Rumbles is so foggy, Mama," I said, as truthfully as I could. "I must have hurt myself on the rocks while rescuing Cecily."

I saw the relief wash over her face and knew I'd done right by keeping the rest from her. Even I wasn't sure exactly what had happened to me out on the Rumbles. Could the mermaid have been a figment of my own imagination?

What would a real mermaid be doing out at the Rumbles?

How could she know Cecily's name?

Most of all, what would such a creature want with my little sister?

Three

I came into the front of the house around noon. Savoury smells led my nose over to the hearth, where I breathed in the warm delicious smell of rabbit stew simmering over the fire. Cecily sat on a three-legged stool in the corner, daintily eating from a steaming bowl. Usually she was out hunting shells for her collection this time of day. I'd been too sick to stop her from going near the water those first few days, and it now seemed pointless to do so when there was no sign of a mermaid after so much time. I wanted to just forget the whole incident ever happened. Perhaps it never had.

My stomach growled loudly. I lifted the dipper from the pot, ready to take a taste.

"Oh no you don't." Auntie Minnah's wooden spoon gave me

a smart rap across my bandaged wrist. The welts beneath the layers of cloth were still as raw as the day I'd first discovered them. I flinched with pain and dropped the dipper into the pot. Hot stew splashed down the front of my skirt. Ignoring the stain, I clutched at my throbbing arm.

"All I wanted was a taste," I said.

"If everyone in this house took a taste of the stew before it finished cooking, there wouldn't be any left for supper," Auntie said.

I glanced at Cecily. She tried to hide her bowl in the folds of her skirt. What Auntie Minnah really meant was there wasn't enough for *me* to have a taste.

"Supper is a long way off. What should I eat till then?" I asked.

Auntie Minnah turned her back on me, picked up a pot and scoured it with a vengeance I'd rarely seen, even in her.

"There's a little porridge left over from breakfast," she said, just when I'd decided she didn't mean to answer.

I moved to the table and grimaced down at the mess still sitting out from morning. Porridge was bad enough when fresh, but as cold hunks of grey mass sitting all morning in the bottom of a pan, it was unbearable. I'd have to go hungry – but I was used to it. Sometimes there just wasn't enough food for a midday meal.

Auntie Minnah lifted the now-clean pot from the washtub, scrutinizing it for a moment; then she began scrubbing it all over again like the devil himself might be hiding in its black surface. I knew it couldn't possibly still be dirty. Something had Auntie in a fluster, and she was taking it out on the poor pot. I gave Cecily a questioning look. She shrugged.

"Is there anything I can help with this morning, Auntie Minnah?" I asked.

Having finished her furious second scrubbing, Auntie splashed the pot back into the hot water in the washtub. It struck the bottom with a loud clatter. Usually she was so careful about everything she did. Something was definitely wrong.

"There's always the tower of mending from town. Nothing *you'd* be of any help with," Auntie Minnah said in a cool voice.

It was true, of course. I'd tried and tried to improve my sewing skills now that our livelihood depended on them, but I soon discovered I couldn't sew a straight stitch to save my life. Any mending and sewing I tried my hand at usually ended up ruined beyond repair. This deficiency in my skills was a thorn in Auntie's side.

"Some people came by this morning, Adrianne." Cecily's words startled me from my thoughts.

I turned to her in surprise. "What people?"

"Tide drifters," Cecily said, using the name our village gave those poor folk who regularly came in on trade boats, hoping to start a new life on Windwaithe. But our small island didn't have enough jobs or trust in outsiders to give them a chance.

They usually ended up setting out for friendlier shores with the next tide.

"It was a mother and two little girls. The girls looked like twins – maybe two or three years old." I watched Cecily grip her empty bowl tight with both hands. "They were so thin and dirty. One had little clean streaks on her cheeks, as if she'd been crying. They wanted food. But Auntie said—"

"I refuse to fill the mouths of beggars with food that barely fills the mouths of my own kin," Auntie Minnah said.

Cecily bowed her head in silence. It was only out of the kindness of Captain Young and his family that we had not yet been reduced to being tide drifters ourselves. Papa and Captain Young were as close as any real brothers growing up. When the captain saw the trouble we were in after Papa's death, he let us come live on the land under his stewardship, as if we were his own blood. If it had not been for the Youngs, I don't think anyone else on the island would have cared what became of us.

Mama came into the room, winding her long, blonde hair into a coil on top of her head in preparation for scrubbing the wooden floors. I was surprised to see her wearing Grandmama's golden locket around her neck. The locket was the one thing of value we still owned. Mama hadn't allowed it to be sold with the rest of her jewellery. Papa had given it to Mama on their wedding day. The memories it held were far more precious than the metal it was fashioned from. I couldn't help but wonder why Mama chose to wear it when she would be indoors doing housework.

The locket had first belonged to Great-Grandmama, who had, in turn, given it to my grandmama when she was a girl. People said Grandmama was the kindest, gentlest soul on the island when she was alive. She had a heart of gold and a will of iron – just like her mother before her. Having been widowed at a young age, Grandmama raised her children alone, often getting by with nothing but the sheer force of her determination. My own memories of her were dim, but the few I still had were of a cheerful, laughing woman. Though she had little, no family on the island went uncared for while she had a hand to lend. Even Auntie Minnah's voice lowered with reverence when she spoke of her.

Grandmama would *never* have turned the tide drifters away.

"Where shall we begin?" Mama asked, as she looked around at the warped and knotted boards that made up our dusty floor.

"Before you do anything else, I think you'd better read the letter Marc Tiernay brought by this morning," Auntie Minnah said as she pulled a folded paper from one of her massive pockets. She held it gravely before us. "It's from Lord Durran."

We fell into a horrified silence. A letter from the lord of Windwaithe Island was no small matter. That accounted for Auntie Minnah's sudden pot-scrubbing frenzy.

Mama stared at the letter without moving. "It can't be the tax yet. We still have four months before it comes due."

"The lord of the island can request taxes be paid whenever

he wants. It's his land we are living on," Auntie Minnah said. "Captain Young is only the steward."

Hesitantly, as if it might bite her, Mama reached out and took the letter, then handed it to me. Auntie Minnah sniffed in disdain. My ability to read irritated her, even though I read the frequent letters from Auntie's childhood friend Laura Mills, a now-wealthy widow who lived on the mainland, more often than I read anything else for our family.

I broke the seal and unfolded the letter. Though I am a steady reader, I am also slow. It took some time to work out the meaning of the proper language used by Lord Durran.

"What does it say, Adrianne? Is it the tax?" Mama asked in a hoarse whisper.

"You're needed up at the manor this evening, to help finish sewing some last-minute things for the trousseau of the bride of young Lord Graham," I said. "It's just for this one night, but the money you earn for your time will be deducted from the balance of the tax still owed."

"God be praised," Mama breathed an audible sigh of relief. "Lord Durran only wants me to help with sewing wedding clothes."

"They want you to come after supper."

In silence, Auntie Minnah turned back to the washtub. She did not inflict any more abuse on the hapless pots.

I put the letter on the table. My movement caught Mama's attention. She took a good look at me for the first time and noticed the old pair of outdoor boots I wore. A concerned crease appeared between her brows.

"You're not planning to go out today, are you, Adrianne? You've barely recovered from your illness. You ought to give it more time before you walk any distance alone."

"I've rested for three days already, Mama," I said. "Six, if you count the three days I was unconscious. We can't keep relying on the Youngs for help. Besides, it's high time I made my trip to the manor-house kennels."

A sharp cry came from the corner where Cecily sat. It felt like a fist was clutched tight around my heart. I forced myself not to look in my little sister's direction. It would be hard enough for me to part with our sweet old dog without seeing Cecily's stricken face in my mind as I did it.

I lifted my chin, forcing my voice to remain deep and firm. "She needs to be sold. There's no use putting it off any longer. We can't keep a dog any more."

My sister began sniffling. I ground my teeth together, forcing my face to remain hard. I didn't want to do this any more than she wanted me to. I would gladly have let someone else do the wretched deed, but Mama was too soft-hearted and Auntie Minnah's answer would be poison. So the job fell to me – like all unpleasant things these days.

Mama sat silent and still a long time, gazing at her hands tucked tight in front of her. I willed her to look up and tell me she would do it.

Without lifting her gaze, Mama spoke. "Take the dog and do what you have to."

Sobbing, Cecily bolted into our bedroom and slammed the wooden door behind her. No one made a move to follow her.

Without a word, I turned and walked to the front door. I paused to touch the iron horseshoe nailed into the mantel of the door's wooden frame. It had come from Regiment, Papa's favourite horse. My fingertips lingered at the U-shaped bottom where all the luck was supposed to collect. I whispered a quick prayer for safety in my travels before stepping from the house.

I blinked back the blinding sunlight. My eyes hurt after being in the dim interior of the house for so long. A stiff sea breeze stirred the air. Although I could not see the ocean, obscured as it was by trees at the east end of the garden, I could hear its pounding roar and smell its tangy sweetness in the air around me. The distant chime of church bells rang out over the island. A gull cried mournfully somewhere out of sight.

To the south lay the fishing docks and lighthouse. To the north was a great slope, on the top of which sat the squat little Rousay cottage – about a half mile to the west was the Youngs' sprawling homestead.

Our own humble cottage was tiny. Hewn from great blocks of stone, its thatched roof was covered with a thick blanket of moss that gave the house the look of an overgrown mushroom. The cottage was divided into two parts, the kitchen and the back bedroom. When we'd first come to live there, Captain Young had ordered the back room divided in two so Cecily and I would have a tiny bedroom of our own. Mama and Auntie Minnah shared the other.

The wind blew short strands of tangled hair into my eyes. I brushed them aside while taking in a deep and satisfying breath of air. It felt good to be out again.

"Lark! Here, Lark," I called out over the yard.

An answering bark came from the direction of the vegetable garden. The red setter came trotting through the rows of tomatoes, waving her jaunty tail. I took her silky head in my hands. Despite her good breeding, she didn't look like the kind of dog they kept in the manor kennels. Her fur was matted with thistles and burrs, her paws and muzzle splattered with dried mud. She'd probably been tracking rabbits all morning.

There was no help for it now. I couldn't put off the job any longer. Cecily had suffered enough. Whistling the dog to my side, I began the long, winding trek up to the manor. The Manor Road twisted and wandered, bending this way and that, rambling its way over grassy hill and dale. I often wondered if the town drunk had built it those many centuries ago.

Lark investigated everything ahead, cautiously sniffing among some underbrush here and gravely sticking her snout down a moist, earthy rabbit hole there. I felt like a traitor as I watched her. All her life, Lark had roamed wherever she wished. I tried not to think about how she would feel locked up in a kennel with the other manor dogs.

Despite the dancing sunshine, the road was packed and muddy beneath my boots. I was glad to see new grass pushing up through the golden earth. If it were not for the unpleasant task before me, I might have enjoyed the beauty of the day.

I came around a bend and saw, sitting a good distance off the main road, the various brick chimneys and part of the tiled roof of our old home peeping over the tops of the trees. Even Cora Lynn Dunst, who liked to brag about the size of her father's cottage whenever she could, would have had to admit her home was a shack in comparison.

I paused a moment, looking towards the cosy dormer window on the second floor – my old room. Seeing it now, so empty and dark, caused gossamer strands of sadness to drift over me like webs caught in the wind. Papa had loved this house. He'd overseen its building with meticulous care. Our life there had been a happy one.

How often as children had Denn and I played blind man's buff in the stable or caught milk-white moths by dusky twilight? I could almost hear our childish laughter, echoing down from the apple orchard behind the house. The memories were so perfect – for a moment, I thought I heard Papa's prized gelding, Regiment, whickering impatiently from the direction of the stable, demanding I bring him oats at once.

But it was only a bird crying somewhere among the trees, and my home stood lonely and abandoned, as it had since the day we'd left it two years before. Out of respect for my father's memory, Lord Durran bought it when our debts became too great, but he never used the house himself.

I shivered under the shadow of things that would never be again.

Don't let the few harsh things of life blot out your happiness in everything else, Adrianne.

Papa's oft-repeated words came back to me. But the bad things loomed up so large these days, clamouring and biting, demanding my worry and frustration all the time.

I gazed up into the sky. "Give me strength. I could use any help you're willing to offer about now," I prayed.

I worked so hard to keep everything from falling apart. At times I felt stretched as thin as the leather on my old boots. I glared down at the holes worn through the toes. They looked like hungry little mouths waiting for someone to feed them. Not that I ever looked nice these days. My best dresses had long since been taken apart so Mama could make up new ones for Cecily, who grew like a weed.

Lark froze, growling low in her throat. I almost walked into her. There, just off the path, stood a young woman, maybe five years older than myself, with two small girls sitting at her feet. The children's clothes were in tatters, and the woman's face was pale and gaunt. She clutched a thin shawl around her shoulders. Though the day was warm, she trembled like an old woman.

Cecily's tide drifters. The very sight of them made my stomach twist. They were pitiful indeed. They had not yet caught sight of me as I stood in the middle of the road wondering if I should cut through Cormy's Wood to avoid passing them. I had nothing to give them, even if I wanted to.

One of the little girls coughed, a horrible rattling sound from deep inside her small chest. She cried as if it hurt her. The woman picked her up and cradled her tight, cooing soft comforting words into her daughter's hair. Something about the fierce tenderness of the gesture drove away my fear of her.

I strode forward again, Lark following. As I drew closer, the woman looked up. Her eyes were like dark, dead coals left in the fireplace long after the fire has gone out. I saw her eyeing my short hair and patched, dirty skirt. She could see for herself I would be of no help to her, and remained silent as I walked past. Long after I turned another of the road's winding bends, the woman's sad, pleading eyes haunted me.

"Let us never come to that," I prayed. "Let me find a way to keep my family from such hard times."

But what about the woman and her two little girls? Who would look after them?

With a tired sigh, I glanced upwards into the heavens. "Look after the tide drifters. They need your help more than our family does."

Four

I heard their loud laughter before I saw them. Lark perked up her ears and looked back at me expectantly. Ahead of us stood Marcus Stebbs and his friends, loitering right in the middle of the road I needed to take.

The Roscoe brothers, Lester Gibbons, and several others of Marcus's faithful lackeys were there as well. Probably taking a break from checking the crab traps close to shore. I'd never be able to slip past without one of them spotting me. My first thought was to come back after they returned to their work.

The memory of Papa's firm voice spoke in my mind. *If you let fear control what you do, you'll never get anything done, Adrianne girl.*

With Lark at my heels, I walked on, hoping they would ignore me. But Marcus stepped in my way, forcing me to stop short in the centre of the group.

"Well, look what we have here," Marcus drawled in a lazy voice. His friends gave him deep laughs of encouragement. "I've never seen a boy wearing a skirt before."

I'd grown used to the boys taunting me about my short hair, but it still made me flush. I tried again to slip past, but Marcus blocked me – shaking his sandy blond head at me as if I were a naughty child.

"We were talking about the wedding feast of Lord Graham up at the manor," Marcus said. "Only one week left. You'd better ask a partner soon, Adrianne, or all the *girls* will be taken."

The boys rocked with laughter. One boy tottered right on to the ground.

"Excuse me," I said, stepping around Marcus. He took a firm hold of my arm and yanked me back.

"Where do you think you're going? Lord Durran has no use for boys who wear dresses. You go on home now, *Master* Adrianne."

I glared at Marcus. What did the village girls see in him? They called him the handsomest boy in the village, but his small black eyes and slightly upturned nose made him look piggish to me. The strong smell of salty sea and fish hung upon him from working the traps that morning. The stench made me feel nauseated.

"Would you mind unhanding me, good sir?" I gave him my fiercest, unblinking scowl.

My bravado amused him. "Good sir? Listen to the refined lady speak." His voice changed into a high-pitched mockery of my own. "Unhand me, good sir. I am a fancy toff and don't want you to soil my silken gown with your dirty hands." While pretending to show everyone how dirty and thin my homespun skirt was, he yanked it up much higher than was proper, a wicked leer on his cocky face.

That's when I kicked him – right where the knee joint meets the kneecap. Marcus howled in pain. Lark bounded around us, barking like a mad thing. I tried to make a dash for it. Before I could get far, the Roscoe brothers seized my arms and hauled me back, struggling. Since both of them were built like oxen, I didn't stand a chance. Lark paced around us growling low in her throat, but no one paid her the least attention. Marcus stuck his red face right up into mine, his foul breath puffing into my nostrils.

"I'll teach you to kick me, Adrianne Keynnman." He looked around at his friends, a cunning expression on his face. "What do you say, fellas? Shall we cool her temper in the ocean?" The boys grinned and chuckled knowingly to one another.

I stopped struggling, resigned to the inevitable. It wouldn't be the first time I'd been heaved into the tide. They'd started doing it to me on a regular basis now that I'd become poor. They usually threw me in, laughed a great deal at my expense, then left me to climb out of the water on my own. Getting wet was a small price to pay if it meant I'd be free of them.

"Maybe we can feed her to the giant fish Lester saw this morning," someone at the back of the group called out. Rowdy laughter followed.

Lester Gibbons's face turned redder than a lobster. "By the heavens, I swear it wasn't my imagination, but the largest fish I've ever seen. As large as any man. It swam right under my boat. I tried to catch it, but the fish was so strong it tore my net in two. It might have tipped me into the water and killed me."

"Or maybe you fell asleep and didn't want your father to take a leather strap to you when he found you didn't bring in any catch," Marcus said.

"More than likely, I'd say. Probably cut his own net to make it look like he told the truth," one of the younger boys said boldly.

"It *was* a fish," Lester said with a visible shudder. "All gold, green and purple – like nothing I've ever seen. I rowed for shore as fast as I could after it broke free. Thought it might come after me for netting it."

"Hey, look at Adrianne," someone cried.

They all turned. My face must have been a sight. As soon as Lester spoke the words "gold, green and purple" I'd felt all the blood drain from my features.

"Look at that." Marcus laughed. "Adrianne's afraid of Lester's fish. I say we throw her in the tide and let it have her for supper."

All the boys cheered.

Like a wild animal, I kicked, clawed, and tore at anything I could get my hands on – mostly the two Roscoe brothers holding me. My bandaged wrist burned with pain under the tight grip of the brother holding my right arm. He gouged his fingers into my wound deeper and deeper the more I struggled – till tears of pain stung at my eyes. Still I fought. I would not be thrown willingly to the mermaid's mercy.

Lark could take no more. With a snarl, she lunged at the Roscoe holding my bandaged arm and bit into his backside. In the confusion that followed, I managed to twist my other arm free and bolted up the path. Marcus was on me before I could get three steps. He wrapped his arms around my body from behind, pinning me fast.

"Where do you think you're going, Adrianne?" he growled in my ear. "You've got an appointment with a monster fish."

"Marcus Benjamin Stebbs, as I live and breathe," a voice spoke from outside the circle of boys.

Heavy silence fell. Even Lark stopped barking. We all turned to find Denn Young looking out at us from under his roguishly tilted hat. He waved a lazy hand in our direction, his green eyes glowing with mirth.

"Will you look at the boldness of him? Hugging and courting a young lady right out in public. It's practically indecent. What would his poor mother think?"

The boys took one look at Marcus and me wrapped together

in the middle of the road and roared with laughter. Marcus leaped away from me, his lips twisted in disgust.

Hot shame burned up my neck and into my cheeks. I glared at Denn. Marcus wasn't too pleased with him either.

"I'd sooner kiss a cow than court an ugly boy like her!" Marcus spat.

Rage choked my throat, forcing back the angry words I wanted to utter. I could only stand, fists clenched, and listen to him continue.

"And I'll fight anyone who dares to think different, Denn Young!"

Denn sauntered towards Marcus and gave him a hearty slap on the back while opening his eyes wide in mock surprise. "Fighting and courting all in the same day? Not many young men would have the strength for it, my friend." He raised an eyebrow.

Something about Denn's cocky grin and his good-natured teasing kept people from getting angry with him for long. Even Marcus could not keep himself from smiling over the left-handed compliment.

"You have it all wrong," he said, getting into the mood of the banter. He gave a flourished gesture in my direction. "It is you, Mr Young, who deserves the pleasure of courting such a desirable young lady."

Denn gave me a wink as if we shared some silly secret. Mortified, I ground my teeth, determined not to play along with his farce.

"Indeed, such a fine lady would never give a homely lad like me a second glance." Denn pulled off his cap and ran his fingers through his curly red hair, pretending to be as vain as a peacock. The boys all chuckled appreciatively. Denn replaced his cap and turned to the group.

"Still, I'll have to ask you men to show more respect and not manhandle my true love. I might have to duel someone for her honour." Denn struck a fighting stance, pulling down the front of his cap and throwing fake punches into the air.

The group laughed all the more. Everyone knew Denn no more thought of courting me than he did his own little sister, Hannah. It was an act, to distract them from throwing me into the ocean. As if I were a little girl who needed his rescuing. Still fooling, Denn made a fancy bow in my direction and offered me his arm.

"Might I see you home, charming lady?"

I looked him straight in the eye. "Rot till you are dead."

I stepped past him as if he didn't exist. Lark glanced in confusion at Denn before trotting reluctantly after me. I suppose it was a shocking way to treat a boy who had saved my life not five days before, but there are times Denn Young pushed me past endurance.

The boys hooted and slapped at each other with delight as I tried to walk through the crowd. Denn's laughter rang out loudest of all. Despite his red hair, Denn was hard to offend. Having been a witness to a couple of his true tempers in my lifetime, I figured it was probably just as well.

Before I could get five paces from the pack of howling boys, three figures rounded the bend in the road ahead. Laughter turned to hushed silence. I stopped, wishing I could vanish.

I looked at the ground – hating myself for giving in to the weakness I felt whenever Cora Lynn Dunst and her sisters were anywhere near. I couldn't stand to look, to see their generous curves, their tiny waists, or their fancy, spotless frocks. All the things I would never have. My face burned with the shame of how shabby and thin I must look next to them. They were the kind of girls that boys went out of their way to be nice to. At fifteen, Cora Lynn was the most beautiful girl on the island. Marcus and his gang would never think of treating her and her fourteen-year-old twin sisters the way they treated me.

Just look up, I commanded myself. For once in your life, Adrianne Keynnman, look them in the eye as an equal. But it was useless. Force of habit was too ingrained to be overcome by mere brave words.

The three Dunst girls didn't even glance in my direction as they walked by. After they passed, I was able to lift my gaze and watch them head straight for Marcus and his crowd.

Go now, I told myself firmly. No one will notice if you slip away. You don't want to see this. Not again.

Still my feet refused to move. I could not turn away any more than a moth from a flame.

The boys doffed their hats and grinned like idiotic children as the girls approached. The twins, Heather and Rose, fell back, giggling and whispering to each other. Not flustered in the least, Cora Lynn minced on – as smooth as you please – her cornflower-blue eyes boldly looking out at the young men from under long blonde lashes. Self-assurance, like I'd never known in my drab existence, was written in every graceful movement she made.

"What mischief are you boys up to now?" Cora Lynn asked in a rich, playful voice. "I could hear the ruckus you were making half a mile up the road."

"I-it was Denn and M-Marcus, Miss." Lester stumbled over the words as he spoke, his face and neck a mottled red colour.

Cora Lynn didn't even glance in Lester's direction, but stepped up to Denn and Marcus, who stood together in the centre of the group. She circled the two boys, flouncing her skirts and giving them coy smiles. Marcus and Denn's attention never left her. Marcus looked ready to drool out of the corner of his slack jaw at any moment. Watching the spectacle was enough to make a decent young woman sick to her stomach.

"Mr Young and Mr Stebbs? I should have guessed the two of you would be at the bottom of this. What do you have to say for yourselves?" Cora Lynn stopped before them, her hands on her hips.

"We're sorry if we disturbed you, Miss Dunst," Denn said,

removing his cap. I couldn't think of a single time he'd done that for me. "We promise to behave in a more gentlemanlike fashion; now we know there are young ladies about."

It should have come as no surprise that Denn didn't think of me as a young lady, but his words still left a hollow ache in the middle of my stomach. I dug at the spot with the knuckle of my thumb, as if I could convince myself it was hunger pains and nothing more. I had once believed Denn would come to his senses about Cora Lynn. I knew better now. Did that stop me from sticking around to watch every wretched time? Of course not. That would have been the sensible thing to do.

"Are you two gentlemen attending the wedding feast next week?" Cora Lynn's question addressed both boys, but her eyes were riveted to Denn.

"We most certainly are," Marcus said, stepping between them. "It's the duty of all Lord Durran's tenants to attend the marriage of his son."

Cora Lynn cocked her head ever so slightly to one side so she could see Denn around Marcus. "I heard there's to be dancing."

"Mac Tiller says he'll be fiddling for it," Denn said, moving closer to Cora Lynn. "He plays the liveliest tunes on the island." I'd never seen Denn so courtly. He seemed like a different person as he spoke to Cora Lynn, his face solemn, his soft green eyes looking deep into hers.

"But Denn won't be there," Marcus was quick to add. "He's

going to sail with his father on his trip to the coastlands in two days."

Denn's father was the captain of Lord Durran's fleet of schooners. He often sailed down the coast of the mainland, delivering the island's fish, transporting goods, and ferrying passengers from port to port. Many times, Denn went along to learn his father's trade.

Cora Lynn pouted prettily for Denn's benefit. "That's too bad. Are you sure he wouldn't let you stay this once? After all, Lord Graham will one day be the master of this island. It seems only fitting to attend his celebration."

"They say a real fortune-teller will be there to tell fortunes," said Heather – or Rose. I could never tell which was which.

"We're going to ask her about our future husbands," said the other twin with a giggle.

"How interesting," Marcus said. His eyes turned in my direction. Unlike Denn, he hadn't forgotten I was there. "I wonder what a fortune-teller tells the girls who won't be getting husbands. Do you think she lies to them?"

Heather and Rose gasped. Cora Lynn's face turned a rosy pink. "Marcus Stebbs! Are you saying I'm not going to be married?"

"Oh, I didn't mean you, Miss Dunst." Marcus hastily turned his attention back to Cora Lynn.

She placed two pretty hands on her beautifully rounded hips. "Well, I certainly hope you weren't talking about my sisters."

Heather and Rose glared at Marcus from both sides as he tried to stutter out a good explanation.

I'd tortured myself quite enough for one day. Whistling softly for Lark, I left the group and headed up the road. Not even Denn noticed me go.

Five

The pasture on the south side of Thestledown Manor is probably the grandest piece of land on the whole island. These five rich, green acres housed Lord Durran's horses, animals of the finest breeds you can buy with gold or trade, most of them shipped in from places far overseas.

I stood along the pasture fence watching the mares graze docilely as their foals gambolled about them like lambs. Right in the middle stood a magnificent stallion of the darkest bay. His mane fell in shiny black masses over his muscled neck. An almost forgotten thrill shivered through my spine.

"Dartemore." I whispered his name just to hear the sound of it. He'd always been my favourite.

Guilt shifted inside me like a creeping shadow, making my

stomach clench tight. Was I breaking my promise by even being here? Why should I not look at the horses or enjoy talking to them the way I had once? Being near horses wasn't the same as riding them. What was wrong with admiring Dartemore from a distance? It had been so long since I'd last seen him. Surely never riding again was enough of a punishment to pay for what I'd done two years before.

I forced my attention back to Dartemore, refusing to let my mind dwell on that part of my life. Who would have believed this gorgeous stallion could have been such a gangly colt when Papa first brought him to the manor six years ago? He'd given Papa and the other stable workers no end of trouble with his stubborn spirit. No one had been able to break him to saddle. If he took a disliking to you, the only thing you could do was stay as far out of his way as possible.

Lark sniffed the air, bored with sitting behind a fence post watching the horses. She sauntered off in the direction of the grove and disappeared between the trees, tracking rabbits no doubt. I hardly noticed her go.

Dartemore snorted and wheeled about suddenly, nostrils flaring out, as he caught my scent on a shifting breeze. His sharp ears swivelled forward with interest.

I told myself to relax. He could not possibly remember me after all this time.

He inhaled again, one ear flicking back and forth as if he were trying to figure where he'd caught my scent before. With an excited toss of his head, he trotted in my direction. The sight of him made me catch my breath – with his neck arched and his feet held high, he was a king coming to acknowledge one of his humble subjects. He'd remembered me after all.

I put out my sweaty hand to touch him and saw that it shook. I hesitated. Dartemore crossed the distance for me, touching my fingertips with his velvety soft muzzle, his warm breath tingling against my skin. He explored the scent of my bandaged wrist with flaring nostrils. The heat and smell of such a large creature awakened memories inside me – memories that made me shudder.

Don't think about what happened to Papa, I told myself sternly. Petting a horse can't hurt anything. No one was asking me to ride – no one wanted me to ride again. Dartemore nuzzled my cheek gently. I gave out a long, weary sigh and looked at the herd scattered across the pasture before me. There was such a hollow place inside me, a part that missed them all so much. But I could not go back. I could not betray Papa.

Lord Durran valued his horses more than anything else he owned. He loved them because his beautiful young wife had loved them. She died during the birth of their son, Lord Graham. Our neighbour, Mrs Rousay, once told me about Lady Durran. Her husband worshipped the ground she walked on and let her do whatever she wished, much to the dismay of the proper but loyal tenants of Windwaithe.

"She rode astride, like a man, dear," Mrs Rousay once revealed to me with an amused chuckle. "She was fearless, jumping her mounts over anything standing still long enough for her to gallop up to it. The whole island went into mourning when she died, Lord Durran most of all. He's never quite recovered, poor man. There was once a time His Lordship would have laughed at most anything. Now look at him."

I could not imagine the solemn, stone-faced Lord Durran ever smiling at anything, much less laughing.

After his wife's death, horses became his life, as if being near them brought him nearer to her. He spared no expense when it came to them. Lord Durran's love of his horses was the reason we'd been able to live in a big house with so many servants. Papa was the best horse master Lord Durran ever had, and he'd paid him accordingly.

Dartemore took a mouthful of my hair and tried to rip it out by the roots. The pain startled me. "Ouch! Let go, you stupid beast." I tried to be stern, but I couldn't keep myself from laughing.

Dartemore pushed his muzzle into my arms, wanting me to scratch him behind the ears the way I used to when he was a colt. He'd never been skittish with me the way he was with everyone else. Even Papa.

"Horses are like that sometimes," Papa once told me. "They make a bond to one person and want nothing to do with anyone else."

In those days, I was the only one who could bring Dartemore

in from the pasture. Nothing amused Papa more than the sight of his tiny daughter leading a giant stallion none of the stablemen could get close to.

"That stallion will kill Adrianne one of these days," Mama complained. "I heard what happened to Reigg Wickliff when he tried to ride the beast – broke three of his ribs and sprained his ankle worse than anything Doctor Goodwin has ever seen."

"Reigg Wickliff shouldn't have tried to ride Dartemore in the first place," Papa said, scowling over the memory. "I'd strictly forbidden him from doing so. As for Adrianne, she's better with horses than any man in the stables. I couldn't get along without her."

"The stables are no place for a girl, Richard." Lines of concern settled along Mama's brow.

Papa winked at me over her head. "Lord Durran doesn't mind her working with the horses, and his word is law around here."

It was true enough. Lord Durran had given permission for me to be in the stables.

His Lordship came almost daily to watch Papa work. I avoided his attention by staying back and keeping as quiet as a mouse whenever he was around. But one day, when I was a little younger than Cecily, I'd been so busy holding a nervous filly while Papa shoed her, I didn't even notice Lord Durran till he laid a gentle hand on the horse's neck to calm her.

He looked down at me with his stone-grey eyes. He was an

imposing figure up close, with his long coattails and shiny black boots. Silvery wisps sprinkled his thick, brown hair and the lines at the corners of his eyes looked as if they might have once known laughter. But he didn't laugh as he stared at me that day. I dropped my gaze and curled my toes inside my boots to brace myself against the embarrassment.

"Your daughter is good with horses," he said to Papa. I could still feel the weight of his attention on me.

"She is, indeed." Papa patted me on the shoulder. "She has a gift."

"Does she now?" Lord Durran's deep voice was a thoughtful murmur. "Can she ride?"

I glanced up in surprise. Girls were never taught to ride. Papa rubbed at his bearded chin. "I admit, I've thought about teaching her. But I'm not sure my wife would approve."

Lord Durran nodded in understanding, his eyes still studying me. "If your wife agrees, you have my permission to use my son's old pony to teach her."

Before Papa could recover from his surprise and thank him, Lord Durran nodded at us both and strode away.

"Papa?" I whispered when he'd gone. "Is there something wrong with the way I look? Lord Durran glowered at me so severely just now."

Papa rested a hand on my head. "You reminded him of his wife, I think. She had a gift with horses like you do, and her hair was long and dark, like yours."

I was jerked rudely back to the present when Dartemore snorted against my shoulder. Something warm and wet splattered across my skin and dribbled down the neck of my dress.

"Dartemore!" I cried, trying to clean myself with a sleeve. "Have you no manners? You don't sneeze all over a lady like that. It's revolting!"

He snorted again in answer. This time I managed to stay out of the spray. I glanced in the direction of the grove, wondering where Lark had got to while I daydreamed.

Dartemore's angry squeal was my only warning. The stallion reared up, striking at the air with his hooves. I drew back from the fence, frightened by the sudden change in him. His ears were pinned tight to the sides of his head; the whites of his eyes flashed as he bared his teeth and snapped.

Beefy fingers clamped down on to my shoulder from behind, making me cry out in pain. Roughly jerked around, I found myself staring into the pudgy face of Master Reigg Wickliff. His bloodshot eyes were narrow, and deep lines furrowed into his shiny bald forehead. His lips were parted, yellow teeth clenched, showing off a generous gap in the front. I made a vain attempt to wiggle out of his iron grip.

"What do you think you are doing here, bothering His Lordship's horses and scaring them silly?" Droplets of his spittle showered across my face, making me want to gag.

"He was fine till you came along," I cried.

He shook me so hard my teeth rattled. "Don't you talk to me that way, you little hussy. I'm the horse master now, not your father. And if I say you're bothering the horses, you're bothering the horses. Now get out of here before I take a whip to you."

Dartemore screamed again, throwing his full weight against the fence between us. Its wooden posts groaned dangerously.

Master Wickliff shoved me out of the way and faced the stallion's fury. He shook his fist at Dartemore, yelling foul oaths at the top of his lungs.

I took up my skirts and ran, my boots ripping and snapping through the tall grass. Lark, who'd heard the commotion and come back to investigate, saw me tearing away from the scene and loped after me. I didn't stop till I reached the manor road where I bent, doubled over, trying to catch my wind. Panting, Lark nudged me with her wet nose.

"I hate that man," I told the dog between ragged breaths. "Papa was a far better horse master than him. You only have to see the way Dartemore acted to know how he's been treated." Lark's tail drooped a little at the sharp tone of my voice. She waved it in a limp but hopeful sort of way. I patted her head.

"It's not fair," I said. "Not fair that a good-for-nothing lout like him should be walking around as healthy as a horse while a good man like Papa had to—" I couldn't finish the thought.

For some reason I thought of the young tide-drifter mother I'd seen on the road earlier. Who was I to say what was fair and what was not?

As I looked down, my gaze met Lark's sympathetic brown eyes, still unaware of how I planned to betray her. A large fist took up all the room inside my chest these days. It grew so tight at times I thought it would squeeze the breath right out of me. I laid a gentle hand on the dog's head. Gathering my tattered courage around me, I straightened my back and started towards the manor house once more.

There didn't seem to be anyone at the gatehouse, so I went and found Master Peck working in the kennels myself. The hunting hounds set to baying and leaped about in their cages as Lark and I approached. This set off the setters at the far end of the kennels till the whole valley seemed to be filled with their noise. The closer I came to Master Peck, the heavier and slower my steps grew. He had not seen me since Papa's funeral, and the shame of how ragged and skinny I now looked was almost too much for me. I scolded myself for my pride. What did it matter? I was there to sell a dog and nothing more. I would never have to speak to him again.

Upon catching sight of me, the kennel master grinned in greeting and put down the water bucket in his hand. A man in his late twenties, he had smooth fair skin and hair so blond it was almost white. It stuck out this way and that, like a spiky thistle.

"Adrianne. I've not seen you for a while." He eyed my bandaged wrist. "Feeling better these days?"

"I've come to see you about Lark," I said, ignoring his kind enquiry.

"She's not ill, is she?" His pale gaze turned towards the dog with concern.

"I've come to sell her to you."

He looked at me and scratched his head in confusion. I rushed on.

"She's a good dog, bred right here in these kennels. She was given to my father as a present from Lord Durran himself. We can't—" I found saying the words aloud harder than I'd imagined. "We can't afford to keep her. But she's well trained and her bloodlines are pure. She's a little dirty now, but once she's cleaned up a bit – I could come back and bathe her myself. It wouldn't be any trouble."

"Adrianne." Master Peck's voice was soft and sad.

I hurried on in desperation, pretending not to hear.

"You won't find a better dog on the island or anywhere else for that matter. She's as gentle as a lamb and as faithful as any dog can be. I'm sure she'll get along with the others."

Master Peck didn't speak, but the pity shone in his pale blue eyes.

I knew what it meant. With a sinking heart, I stared at the ground. "Take her. We don't need money for her."

The other dogs continued to bark. Master Peck gave a long, drawn-out sigh.

"I can't take her, Adrianne."

A sharp uneasiness bit into the pit of my stomach as Master Peck continued.

"She's past prime breeding age, and she hasn't been trained the same way the other dogs have. Besides, the kennels are overflowing now. Three females whelped just this week."

The strength leaked out of my body through the soles of my feet, leaving me cold and trembling. What a fool I'd been. Of course they didn't need another dog in the manor kennels. How naïve I'd been, thinking this plan of mine would work. I had built up my family's hopes that somehow I could pull it all off and make everything come out all right. No matter how hard I tried, in the end, I was still nothing but a useless creature.

I turned away from Master Peck as hot, wet tears spilled down my cheek. I'd come so far, why did I have to act like a child now? I managed to keep myself from sobbing, clenching my teeth together by sheer force.

"You might try selling her to someone in the village, or to one of the travelling merchants at the docks," Master Peck said in a lighter tone. "She's an excellent dog. Someone is sure to want her."

I didn't bother answering him. My voice would have given me away. I patted my hand against my thigh. Lark walked obediently to my side. Sensing my upset, the dog licked my fingers with her warm tongue. I trudged away without a word.

"If anyone comes looking for a hunting dog, I'll send them up your way," Master Peck called to my retreating back. They were empty words and both of us knew it.

I didn't know what to do next. If I couldn't even give Lark away, only one option was left.

Auntie Minnah's way.

Six

I threw another pile of cow dung into the wheelbarrow. The smell clung to my clothes and skin, almost as thick and foul as the putrid stuff clumped to the bottom of my boots. I dug the end of the pitchfork deep into the muck, lifting it away with a sickening slurp.

I concentrated on breathing through my mouth as I carried the dark steaming pile to the wheelbarrow. How had Papa managed to do it, day after day, month after month? After a year, I was used to the hard work, but I didn't think I'd ever get used to the smell.

Restless, Belle bellowed at me from where I had tied her outside the stall.

"How any cow can turn perfectly good hay into this wretched

mess overnight is beyond me," I said. She flicked one large ear and continued to chew placidly at her cud. What did she care? She didn't have to clean it up - that's what I was for.

I set down the pitchfork, resting my weight on the end of it. My dress was drenched in sweat and my skirt stained dark with dirt and grime. Belle smelled better than I did. Thank heaven cleaning the stall was the last of my morning chores. After I finished, I could wash up and take a short break before I started on the afternoon chores.

I gave a long, drawn-out sigh as I used a finger, stiff with dirt, to push a tendril of short hair behind my sweaty ear and was surprised when it stayed put. Soon it would grow past the bottom of my earlobes. I tried to think of myself with hair as long as it had once been, but imagination failed me. Dirt, rags, and shabby short hair - it seemed it would always be that way for me.

"Even Papa would have trouble recognizing me now," I said to Belle. "It's a good thing he can't see me."

The barn door flew open, smashing against the opposite wall. I about jumped through the stall rails as Belle bawled in alarm. Denn peeped sheepishly inside the open door. He carried a lumpy, burlap sack over his left shoulder, holding on to it with both hands.

"Sorry. I didn't mean to kick it so hard. My hands are full." Denn turned his back a moment to kick the door closed behind him.

I tried to smooth down my mussed-up hair and brush the loose dirt from my skirt before giving it up as a lost cause. It *would* be Denn who caught me looking like a stable hand and reeking like a privy. Not that he cared what I looked like. I let my hands drop to my sides as he turned in my direction again. Better to brazen it out, as usual.

"Is it true you're selling Lark?"

I considered not answering, but realized it was pointless. By now, the whole island probably knew my family couldn't afford to keep a dog.

"It's true enough." I picked up the pitchfork and stuck it deep into the floor of the stall.

Denn shifted under his heavy load. "You know, I've been thinking of getting myself a hunting dog. It would be safer for Mama and the little ones when Papa and I make deliveries to the ports along the mainland. We sometimes sail for weeks at a time, and I'd feel much better with a dog around to protect them."

Protection? The Youngs' house didn't need a dog for protection – not with all the servants they employed.

"I can't sell Lark to you, Denn," I said.

Denn's green eyes moved to meet my own. "If you won't take money for Lark, maybe I could work off her price."

Charity. The taste of it made my mouth sour. How much more would my family require of the good people of Windwaithe before they grew as tired of us as they were of the tide drifters? Denn didn't need a dog any more than Master Peck did. Still, I could not refuse his offer. It would only be a matter of time before Auntie Minnah took things into her own hands and poisoned Lark herself.

"Take her." The voice that came from my mouth sounded like a tired old woman's. "She's out behind the garden with Cecily."

"I sent Hannah and Trey in that direction. I think I'll let them visit for a while. I'll pick up Lark on my way home." Denn slid the sack from his shoulder and hung it on a nail on the wall. "This sack of potatoes can be the first payment. I'll come tomorrow to start working off the rest."

I looked up in surprise. "Aren't you sailing out with your father in the morning?"

"Papa and I talked it over. He felt that it would be discourteous for all the men in our family to slight Lord Durran by going off and not attending his son's wedding."

I was pretty sure Denn's desire to dance with Cora Lynn at the wedding feast might also have something to do with the decision, but I kept my opinion to myself.

Denn pulled off his cap and resettled it on his mass of red curls as he looked around the barn. "So, Master Adri, you look like you could use some help. Where shall I begin?"

Denn sometimes called me "Master" to tease me about my role as "man of the house" now that Papa was gone. Usually I didn't mind his teasing like I did the other boys'. There was no sting in it. But now it reminded me of how he'd behaved the day before.

"I'd get a lot more done if you'd get out of my way and let me work." I swung the blunt end of my pitchfork in his direction. He stepped easily out of its path, smiling at me.

"Did you come with a purpose, or is it your purpose to annoy me this fine morning?" I asked.

"Whew-wee! Are we ever in a lather today? What's the matter, Adrianne? Got a bee in your shift?"

"My shift would be none of your business, Mr Young. And neither would my battles with Marcus." I swept past him, stabbing the pitchfork deep into the floor of Belle's stall.

Denn folded his arms across his chest and lifted his chin. "Don't tell me you're still on about yesterday?"

I whirled on him. "How could you make fun of me in front of every boy on the island?"

"I was trying to stop you from getting yourself dunked in the tide – again."

"Next time, don't do me any favours." I heaved a pile of muck towards the wheelbarrow, just missing Denn in the process. He dodged backwards, grinning like an idiot.

"Come on, Adri. Didn't you see Marcus's red face? I don't think he'll try to throw you into the sea anytime in the near future. He'd be accused of mooning over you again." He batted his eyelashes a couple of times for emphasis.

I gave a snort and pretended to be busy. Before I knew what

he meant to do, Denn pulled the pitchfork from my hands and began mucking Belle's stall himself. My muscles were too sore for me to protest.

"Are you and your family going to attend Lord Graham's wedding feast?" Denn asked, as if I weren't mad at him.

"Cecily begged Mama day and night till she promised to take her."

"What about you?" Denn asked.

"Why should I go?"

"They say it'll be quite a feast – and there'll be dancing afterwards."

"And who is going to ask me to dance?"

"Hannah has already made me promise to take a couple of turns with her. I suppose I could fit you in, too." He winked at me as he threw another pile into the wheelbarrow.

It was my turn to fold my arms across my chest. "I'm sure you'll be far too busy trying to get Miss Cora Lynn Dunst's attention."

Denn shuffled his feet and pulled his cap down close over his reddening face with one hand. "Oh well—" He broke off, not knowing what to say.

I shook my head. "What do you see in her anyway?"

"I should think the answer to that question would be obvious."

"There is more to marriage than good looks."

Denn blinked at me, startled. "Who said anything about marriage?"

"You expect me to believe you only want to look at Cora Lynn Dunst for the rest of her life? One more year and she'll be sixteen – marriageable age."

"Not all girls marry so young." Denn scooped another load into the lopsided wheelbarrow.

On Windwaithe, boys were not considered old enough to marry till eighteen. Denn still had two years to go before he would be allowed to make an offer for anyone's hand.

"With her looks, she's not going to last past her sixteenth birthday," I said. "I pity the man who gets *her* fancy hide."

Denn laughed. "And what is wrong with a man wanting to marry a girl who's easy to look at?" He would not look at me as he spoke.

"You'll find out for yourself after you've been married to a ninny for thirty years."

"Ouch!" Denn said. "You're in quite a mood today. What has Miss Dunst ever done to you?"

I bit my bottom lip hard. Cora Lynn had never done anything to me. Most of the time she ignored my existence, except when Denn was around. She fawned over me something awful then, patting me on the head and calling me "adorable" and "sweet" as if I were a mere child. I didn't like the way she made me feel when I was around her – like a dirty beetle not worthy of being crushed beneath her kid boots. I hated myself for this weakness. I could only hope that someday, when Cecily got older, she'd give Cora Lynn the competition she deserved.

Denn paused in his work to give me a questioning look. I'd been silent too long.

"The boys all act like such idiots around her," I said. "It's annoying."

Denn gave me an amused smile. "It's not something they can help. You'll understand someday, Adrianne. When you're older."

Scorching rage burned through my veins like molten lead. "I understand *now*, Denn Young! And if you boys think it so fine to act like drunken fools when she's around, by all means go ahead and do whatever you please. She'll have all of you dancing on puppet strings while I laugh at the lot of you. Especially when she pitches you for Marcus Stebbs."

Denn stopped working and gave me a long, hard look. Immediately ashamed of losing my temper, I kicked at the muddy floor, not daring to look at him. He stabbed the pitchfork into the moist dirt, grasped my shoulders and gave them a small shake, as if I were a misbehaving child.

"What is the matter with you, Adrianne?" His exasperation had completely wiped all traces of a smile from his face. It didn't look natural, somehow. "Something's not right, but how can any of us help you if you won't say what it is?" he said.

I stared up into his handsome face. I wanted to throw my arms around him and tell him the horrible things tearing at my heart.

Denn had never been sentimental himself, but he had often let me hug him when I was little, even asking me for one in exchange for this or that favour as a silly joke. With the boldness of an innocent child, I'd sometimes sneaked in a childish kiss on his cheek when he wasn't expecting it. The last time he'd teased me for a hug I'd been thirteen and told him I was too old for such nonsense. He'd never asked for one again. My refusal hurt him, I think, but I knew it wouldn't be right any more. My feelings for him had changed too much.

"Adrianne?" Denn shook me to attention again, but his voice had turned gentle with concern.

I looked away from him, afraid my true feelings might show on my face. He could do nothing for me. No one could. I stared at the ground in silence.

"You haven't been yourself lately," Denn said. "You're so quiet and solemn all the time. I don't think I've heard you laugh for months. You have such a pretty laugh. It would be a shame if you stopped using it altogether."

So, he had noticed. How could Denn be so quick about some things and so thick about others? Were all boys such a contradiction?

I drew myself up to my full height. I barely came to Denn's shoulder. "I don't have time for foolishness these days. Too much needs doing."

"You sound like your Auntie Minnah talking," he said with a humourless chuckle.

His comment made me queasy inside; my whole world rocked like an unsteady boat.

"I'm nothing like Auntie Minnah," I whispered.

"Thank heaven for that," Denn said, but his words didn't make me feel better.

Was I like Auntie Minnah? Cross and short-tempered with everyone around me because of the troubles in my life? I thought back to the way I'd treated Denn since he entered the barn. I felt sick with shame.

Denn turned serious again. "I know it's hard for you, Adrianne. Your aunt isn't the easiest woman to get along with. Personally, I don't know how you manage. You're much braver than I would be, given the circumstances."

"I'm not brave." My words came out stiff. I thought about the day Papa died. I hadn't been brave then.

"I don't know any other eight-year-old girls brave enough to climb to the top of Mr Tipton's old oak like you did all those years ago, do you remember?" Denn said with a returning smile.

I snorted. "I only made it halfway up before I fell."

"It's a good thing I caught you." Denn pulled down on the brim of his cap as if accepting his due.

"Caught me?" I blurted. "You didn't catch me. I fell on top of you by accident."

Denn grinned. "I'll bet you would have broken your neck, too, if I hadn't been there to cushion your fall. Knocked the breath clean out of me."

My lips twitched against my will. "Give me that." I made a grab for the pitchfork still stuck in the earth. Denn snatched it up quick.

"No, you don't. You've got a hurt wrist, remember?" Denn nodded in the direction of my bandage and held the pitchfork out of reach.

"It's only the surface skin that's hurt. I can do work with it." I grabbed at it again.

A small struggle ensued, but Denn had a better hold and jerked the pitchfork free of my grasp. His eyes twinkled as he waved a hand in my direction with the pretended daintiness of a fine lady. His tone was high and annoyed – mockingly like my own.

"Go elsewhere, good madam. You're distracting me from my work this fine day."

I couldn't help it. I laughed out loud. He did sound an awful lot like I had, not five minutes ago.

"Ah, there it is. The beautiful bell-like laugh we've all missed so much." I could see Denn was pleased with his success. He reached out and ruffled my short hair with his rough, brown hand. His warm fingers tickled my scalp and made my skin tingle, even after he lifted them away.

"You know, I think I like your hair better short," Denn said, giving me an appraising look. "It makes you look – I don't know – older."

But not old enough.

I was no fool. No matter how much time passed or how much I grew, I would never be anything like Cora Lynn. I was plain and poor and, as far as Denn and all the other people living on this island were concerned, that meant I would never be worth anything.

For the second time, the barn door flew back, crashing hard against the wall. Trey, Hannah and Cecily tumbled into the barn, Lark dancing at their heels. Belle bawled in fear.

"Careful!" I cried, rushing to the cow's side to calm her. If she got too worked up she might not allow herself to be milked.

"Denn, we want to go rowing. Can you take us?" asked Trey in a breathless voice. He looked like a miniature version of his older brother, with his curly hair smashed under a battered hat. But unlike Denn, his freckles ran riot over his whole face, as if someone had splashed him with strong tea as a baby.

"We've got things to do right now," Denn said, pausing in his work.

"Pleeeeease?" Hannah grabbed hold of her brother's arm and gave him her most charming smile. I've never seen anyone with eyes as expressive as Hannah's, nor eyelashes anywhere near as long and silken. If it had not been for her frizzy blonde hair and overlarge front teeth, she might have been a real beauty, like Cecily.

Denn gave the children a long, considering look.

"Come on, Denn," Trey said. "We could all go. Mama will let us take both the boats if you come. It'll be fun."

All eyes were on Denn. He turned in my direction. His green gaze scrutinized my face so closely I pretended to fuss over Belle to cover my confusion.

"Maybe it *would* be good for us to take a break – to get out in the sunshine for a while," Denn said.

It was me he meant to get out into the sunshine, and I wanted nothing to do with it.

"You four go along. I've still got too much to do here," I said.

"You've been working all morning. There can't be *that* much left to do," Cecily said in the saucy grown-up tone she gets whenever Trey Young is around. I shot her a stern look and she stared down at her boots, her downcast, long lashes making her look more adorable than ever.

"I can't go till the work here is done," I said.

Denn grinned, picked up the pitchfork, scooped up the last pile of manure and threw it on to the wheelbarrow. He untied Belle and led her back into her stall. "All done, Master Adri," he said. "Any other excuses you need me to get rid of for you?"

"I – I can't go out looking like this."

"You look ravishing. Come on!" Denn grabbed my hand in his and pulled me towards the barn door. Lark rushed past us to lead the way as Cecily, Trey and Hannah tore after us, cheering heartily.

Seven

I staggered out of the barn into the sunlight. A brisk wind caught my skirts and ruffled my hair. The fresh air went to Denn's russet red head. He let out a whoop of joy as he raced down the path towards the lagoon. Instead of letting go of my hand, he held it tighter, forcing me to run to keep up with him. I liked the feel of his fingers, warm and strong against my own. He looked back and laughed with me as he pulled me along even faster. Cecily and Hannah giggled as they ran, hardly able to keep up, but Trey was like the wind, sweeping past us down the hill with Lark loping lazily at his side.

A blaze of bright ocean shimmered before us. The sight of it, so vast and endless, brought me out of my exhilaration with a jolt. I dug my heels into the ground – Denn's hand was yanked from mine. His momentum took him a few more steps before he stopped to look back.

Cecily and Hannah flew up to my side, still laughing breathlessly. When they saw my face they fell silent. Even Lark trotted back to give me a curious look, her head cocked to one side.

"Adri? What's the matter?" Denn asked.

"We can't go rowing on the water," I said.

Denn squinted his eyes as if studying me. I wondered if my face looked as tense as I felt. How could I have forgotten? Even in those glorious moments when Denn's hand was in mine, how could I have forgotten the mermaid? If Lester told the truth, she might still be out there, somewhere.

"Why can't we go rowing?" Hannah glanced at me, then Denn, her eyebrows working like knitting needles.

"Lester said he saw something strange swimming close to shore yesterday. It might be dangerous," I said.

Denn started to laugh. "Don't tell me you believe in Lester's monster fish. Lester wouldn't know fact from fancy if it bit him on the backside."

"I didn't say it was a monster." Heat rose into my cheeks. "But it might be something dangerous – like a shark. They do come close to shore this time of year."

"Believe me, there isn't a shark in all the oceans who would dare tangle with Adrianne Keynnman," Denn said. "Besides, you can't stay away from the water. It's our lifeblood on Windwaithe."

He was right, of course. Life on the island was connected to the sea in every way. No one could stay away from it for long without the entire community taking note of the fact. Was it possible I'd imagined that night at the Rumbles? Was the mermaid the product of a hard knock to the head while swimming out to save Cecily in stormy waters? None of the other fishermen had seen a mermaid lingering about the island. Was I really ready to start believing in the existence of fairy-tale creatures on Lester's say-so? As for Cecily, her head was so full of Papa's stories she probably saw mermaids in her dreams every night.

In the sparkling sunshine of a gorgeous summer day, it seemed foolish of me to have even considered the idea. After all, what would a real mermaid possibly want with two poor island girls?

"All right. Let's go," I said.

The Young family kept their boats beached near a large lagoon to the east of their land. Denn and I had often fished there, pulling in herring, cod, and sometimes crabs. The children ran right up to the water's edge. Lark plunged in, spraying everyone in her wake. It had to be a good sign that the old setter felt nothing to fear from the water.

After a short argument about whether or not my wrist was well enough for rowing, we decided Denn, Hannah and Trey would ride in the larger boat, while Cecily and I rode in the smaller. Because she was sopping wet and covered with sand, Lark had to stay ashore, much to Cecily's distress. The dog watched us shove away from the beach, her ears drooping dejectedly at the sides of her head. Cecily called out encouraging words to her, promising to return soon.

With much giggling and splashing, we rowed out on to the water. At first, I found myself checking over my shoulder every few minutes, searching for a flash of green or gold. I saw nothing – only blue waves lapping lazily under the boats.

The lagoon was the safest place for rowing because of its calm waters. At low tide you could look down into the reefs below and see the rainbow-coloured anemones and scuttling crabs living there.

"We should have brought our nets," Trey said, pointing to a large school of fish beneath us.

I manoeuvred the boat so Cecily could see over the port side. We watched the fish swim past in silence. The Windwaithe church bell tolled the hour far in the distance.

"How about a race?" Denn asked, sculling his boat beside ours.

"I'm no fool, Denn. You'd outstrip us in a moment," I said.

"My boat is bigger and carries more passengers than yours."

"Come on, Adrianne. Let's race," Trey said, bouncing the whole boat in his enthusiasm.

"You can do it, Adrianne. I know you can." Cecily looked at me with wide, pleading eyes. I sighed, knowing it was no use to fight against this particular pack of fools when they got ideas into their heads.

Seeing I was about to give in, Denn pointed out across the water. "First one to touch that outcropping of rock at the other end of the lagoon wins. Ready?"

"GO!" Hannah shouted. Denn and I dug in our oars amid much cheering and shouting from our passengers.

I pulled into the lead for the first few strokes, but after that Denn's craft quickly nosed ahead. No matter how hard I rowed with my tired arms, the distance between us grew. Soon the gap was so big, I couldn't help but pull up my oars and laugh.

"Come on, Adrianne. Don't give up. You can do it!" my sister cried.

Her hopeless encouragement made me laugh harder. Cecily started to giggle with me, and before long we were both rocking the boat with our laughter, drifting helplessly over the gentle waves of the lagoon. All the while, Denn got further and further ahead of us.

Lark began barking like mad from the shore. Our boat gave a violent lurch, listing a few feet to the left as if shoved off course by an unseen current. We stopped laughing and I almost dropped one of the oars in surprise. Cecily and I stared at each other, waiting for the boat to steady itself. My sister's eyes were as round as wagon wheels. Lark's alarmed cries echoed out to us across the water. I glanced in the dog's direction. Her tiny form leaped about in an agitated fashion, her barks directed to where we sat drifting.

"What was that?" Cecily asked in a small voice.

"We must have hit a submerged rock," I said, trying not to think about what it might really be.

"Hey, you two lazy swabs. Are you going to give up that easy?" We could barely hear Denn's voice over Lark's barking as he yelled across the distance. They'd almost reached the other side of the lagoon.

There was a soft scraping sound and the timbers of the boat shuddered beneath us, as if something large were running its way along the bottom.

Cecily turned white and clutched at the gunwale with both hands.

I bent to look over the side. A school of silvery fish flitted under our bow. I could see the blurry coloured masses of anemones deep under the water. A sudden movement caught my eye. A large pale green mass of seaweed was caught beneath our hull. The seaweed drifted and swayed under us like long coils of rope. I peered closer and saw it was neither seaweed nor rope, but masses of braids – each with a tiny gold bead attached to the end.

I sat back hard with a gasp. The blood rushed from my face so fast I felt faint.

"What is it? What did you see?" Cecily's voice was high with fear.

"We've got to get back to shore." I tried to sound calm but was too frightened to manage it.

"Adri? Is something wrong?" Denn called out in concern across the water. He'd stopped rowing.

Right behind Cecily I saw, to my horror, a glistening, gold tail rise slowly out of the ocean. Fanning itself out to full size, it slapped down, spraying water everywhere.

Startled by the sound, Cecily leaped to her feet. "Shark!" she screamed.

I dropped the oar, putting out a hand towards her, as if somehow I could stop the inevitable from happening. The whole world tilted dangerously beneath us as my sister struggled for balance. The next thing I knew we were thrown into the shocking cold water, the overturned boat slamming its full weight on top of us.

I knew only blind confusion as the icy water washed over my body. I struggled and kicked, eyes closed tight, trying to climb back to the surface. My boots filled with water, and my clothes grew heavy around me, dragging me down.

Bands of heat pulsed along the welts on my wrist, radiating up and out into my whole body, pushing back the freezing cold. The pain was so fierce my eyes snapped open and salt water flooded into them. I squeezed them shut again, waiting for the tearing pain to begin – but nothing happened. An odd feeling came over me; a warm tingling sensation spread through my body, settling deep inside the centre of my chest. It drove all the cold from my body as if I were burning up with fever. Something was happening to me, something frightening. I stopped kicking, drifting downwards in blind darkness for the space of several racing heartbeats before finally opening my eyes.

At first the world around me was nothing but a blur – then, to my amazement, everything came into crystal-clear focus. I felt as if I floated not under water, but in the air. What I saw astounded me.

Cecily drifted face down, just above my head. Her eyes were closed, her pretty face deathly white. An angry red mark marred the left side of her forehead where the edge of the boat had struck her.

Panic rose within me. I kicked and clawed at the water, trying to climb towards her, but found myself being sucked down further.

With a flashing flicker, the mermaid came out of nowhere, cutting through the water as if she had no more substance than a minnow. She caught Cecily in her arms, turning my sister's face upwards.

They made a strange sight, the beautiful Windwaithe Mermaid and my pale little sister, her hair streaming out in the water like fine brown silk. For one moment I thought the mermaid meant to save Cecily's life by taking her those last few feet to the surface. But she continued to float in place, holding my sister under the water, looking down into her face with the serenity of a mother cradling a baby. Cecily looked so vulnerable, as if she were sleeping rather than drowning before my eyes.

Stark reason seized my thoughts. I kicked off first one boot, then the other, and let them drop away to the ocean floor. With a new lightness, I pumped my legs with all my might and crawled towards the mermaid.

I reached out my hand and tangled my fingers deep into the ropes of her long, green braids and yanked – hard. Her head snapped back, her mouth open in a silent cry. But I heard it, searing through my mind like a blast of scalding steam.

Cecily slipped from the mermaid's arms as the creature reached up to clutch her head, thrashing her tail in an attempt to knock me loose. I released my hold and the mermaid swam away from me, writhing about to rid herself of the pain.

I reached out and wrapped my arms around Cecily's still form. She'd been under the water far too long. How strange that my own lungs had only just begun to feel the need for breath. I kicked, pumping hard for the surface.

I gave out a great gasp as I broke into the open air. Cecily didn't cough, but made a gurgling sigh – water came gushing up from somewhere deep inside her chest. I supported her, letting the water run out over my arm.

I glanced around me, frantic with fear for Cecily's life. Denn and the others rowed hard towards us. I tried to drift in their direction.

Under my breath I murmured prayers to keep the mermaid away long enough for us to reach the boat.

"Adrianne! What happened?" Trey called out as the boat pulled alongside us.

"Get Cecily in. Quickly!" I cried.

Denn must have sensed something was wrong from the tone of my voice. He turned the oars over to Trey, bent over the side and hauled Cecily up next to him. I placed both hands on the gunwale, ready to pull myself aboard as well. I noticed for the first time my bandage was missing. The angry welts stood out against the pale skin of my wrist, swollen and pulsing red.

I hesitated too long. Beneath the water, I felt the mermaid's warm fingers wrap around my ankle. I let out a gasp that made Denn turn in my direction. The mermaid tightened her grip and pulled, almost causing me to lose my hold. I kicked blindly at her with my free foot but missed. Her braids slithered along the bare skin of my calf.

Denn saw me struggle and clutched at me, his green eyes wide with awakening fear. "Adrianne? What is it? What's the matter?"

"She's – got – my – leg," I gasped out between panicked breaths.

I'd never seen Denn move so fast. He wrapped his arms around my upper body and pulled with all his might. I could feel him trembling as the mermaid fought back.

Somewhere in the back of my mind, I heard Hannah sobbing and Trey shouting encouragement to Denn. I was aware of Lark barking in the distance, but all I could focus on was the feel of strong, burning fingers clutching my ankle beneath the water. I waited for the mermaid's nails to dig into my flesh as they had before – drawing me down into the water for ever – but it never

Winton Library

Wimborne Road
Winton
BH9 2EN
Tel 01202 528139

Borrowed Items 29/05/2021 12:18

XXXXX2687

Item Title	Due Date
* forbidden sea	19/06/2021
* Killer ball at Honeychurch Hall	19/06/2021

---

* Indicates items borrowed today

@BCPLibraries
www.bpcouncil.gov.uk/libraries
Email: BCPLibraries@bpcouncil.gov.uk

happened. One moment the fingers were there, the next they were gone. Hannah gave a terrified scream as I came up out of the water so fast Denn fell back against the opposite gunwale. The whole dinghy teetered and almost capsized. I clambered the rest of the way in, scooted over to Cecily and lifted her to me. More water flowed from her mouth and nose. I turned her on her side and pounded her hard in the middle of the back. She didn't cough, but breathed out one last trickle of water before I heard her draw air. Only then did I turn my attention to the danger lurking in the water.

"Is she still there? Do you see her? She might try to overturn the boat," I cried, still half in a panic.

Denn ignored my question and bent to examine my bare leg with shaking hands. The skin was smooth and unmarred, but it tingled as if the mermaid's fingers still clung there unseen.

Trey peered over the side of the boat. "I don't see anything! It must have swum away."

I looked over the side myself. Nothing but clear blue water and shadowy rocks drifted below us.

Denn took hold of my hand and tried to pull it towards him. "What happened to your wrist?" The welts were worse than ever, looking like raw, red boils running the length of my arm.

"Nothing. I'm all right." I jerked away from him and clutched Cecily closer to me.

Denn ran his fingers through his curly hair. His voice was almost a whisper when he spoke. "You were under the water so long. I thought – I thought you'd. . ." He couldn't finish.

Now that I thought about it, I had been under a long time. I knew of fishermen on Windwaithe who could hold their breath for great periods of time, but I'd never had that particular talent.

"It was lucky you were wearing those boots," Denn said, gaining some strength in his voice. "Its teeth couldn't get through the thick leather." His gaze darted nervously towards my wrist.

Teeth? I stared at him, uncomprehending.

"It must have been a big one to come after someone your size," Trey was almost shouting with excitement. "Sharks don't normally attack people like that, especially this close to shore."

A shark? They thought I'd been attacked by a shark? How could they not have seen the mermaid?

Cecily moaned and fluttered her eyes. "Adrianne?" she whimpered in confusion.

I clutched her tighter in my arms and looked Denn right in the eye. "Get us back to land. Now."

My low, even voice could have been my father's. It had the same no-nonsense edge to it his always had when he meant business. Without a word, Denn nodded and settled back to his place at the oars to row for shore. I kept a watchful eye, but the mermaid was gone.

We were a sombre group as we pulled up to the beach. Denn carried Cecily, who was conscious but weak. I tried to comfort the hysterically sobbing Hannah, while treading gingerly over the rocks and sand in my bare feet.

Lark gave us an anxious greeting, nosing and inspecting each of us in turn, as if she needed to reassure herself we were safe. She turned to look at the lagoon. Her slender muzzle pointed in the air and one paw lifted, as if she sensed something that couldn't be seen.

I, too, watched the lazy waves rising and falling across the length of the horizon. I knew the mermaid was out there, watching and waiting for another chance to take my sister's life.

Eight

When Cecily awoke the next morning, she quickly discovered that Denn had taken Lark away the night before, and she took to her bed screaming like a banshee over it. The wailing that reverberated through our small cottage for the most part of an hour attested to the miraculous recovery of my sister's waterlogged lungs like nothing else could. Mama and Auntie Minnah spent the whole morning trying to comfort her. When Mama suggested going down to the shore as a distraction, Cecily bawled in terror, saying a shark might attack her like it had me. While Mama tried to think of something else to suggest, I wrapped my wrist in a fresh new bandage, put on a ridiculously large pair of Papa's old boots, and stumbled out to the barn to do my chores.

All morning I thought about what had happened. I wasn't

sure what Denn had told Mama and Auntie Minnah, but neither of them had asked me any questions about my missing boots. It was the Windwaithe Mermaid, not sharks, that I thought about as I worked.

She was a clever creature – fast, too. I still could not believe she'd attacked me in daylight and managed to slip away without anyone seeing her. Why was she so intent on taking Cecily? There had been a mermaid in the tale of Lady Lauretta, but that had taken place over a hundred years ago. She fitted the description, but surely it couldn't be the same mermaid – a distant relative perhaps? I shook my head in frustration as I searched absently for eggs in the chicken coop. Papa's old boots clumped along, making me feel more awkward than usual. This mermaid could not possibly be after the same thing as Lady Lauretta's mermaid. Cecily was only nine, too young to make *anyone* a bride, much less a fabled Sea Prince.

I'd heard tales about mermaids using their voices to lure sailors to their doom, smashing their boats against the wicked-sharp rocks and reefs beneath the dark surface of the sea. Did all mermaids enjoy killing people for fun?

I picked up a clod of dirt and pitched it against the coop wall. The three chickens squawked in panic and fluttered about.

Who cared what the mermaid wanted? She'd almost killed my sister and me twice now and that was enough. I figured this mermaid couldn't come on to the land to accomplish whatever she had planned or she would have done it by now. Keeping

Cecily away from the ocean wouldn't be too hard now that she feared sharks lurked there. I could never allow my little sister to go anywhere near the water again. Not while the mermaid might still be out there.

Outside I heard barking. Lark sounded happy to be back. If she had returned, so had Denn – to check on Cecily, no doubt. Wiping sweat from my forehead, I lifted the almost-empty basket of eggs. I'd only found one.

As I went into the house, I passed Cecily tearfully welcoming Lark on the front doorstep.

"I come bearing gifts," Denn greeted me as I walked into the cottage. He placed in my hand a handkerchief with a large strawberry tart wrapped in it. It was still warm. My mouth watered.

Although strawberries grew all over the island, for some reason the Youngs' wild strawberry patch grew extra big, delicious berries that couldn't be matched by any others. My stomach rumbled, but I decided to save the treat for my noon meal. I wouldn't get much else to eat. I saw Auntie Minnah frown over the gift. She caught me watching and turned back to her mending, her face blank. I gently placed the wrapped tart in my front apron pocket where it would be safely out of sight.

"Adrianne," Auntie Minnah said without looking up. "We're almost out of thread again. You'd better make a trip to the market."

"How can I go to the market when I don't have any boots?"

"You should have thought of that before you decided to be so careless with the ones you had," Auntie said in a matter-of-fact voice.

As if I could have done anything to stop a very determined mermaid from attempting to drown Cecily.

"The weather is nice these days," Denn said, removing his hat and dusting it against his leg. "All the village children go barefoot this time of year. You could, too."

Auntie Minnah sat up straight. "She most certainly will not. It would be indecent for a girl of Adrianne's age. I'm surprised at you, Denn Young."

Denn shrugged. The moment Auntie returned to her work he wiggled his eyebrows at me behind her back. I had to smother the smile twitching at my lips.

"You'll wear your father's boots till we can afford to get you some new ones," Auntie said. "Though heaven knows when that will be."

I stared at Auntie. Surely she didn't really mean for me to walk all the way to town in Papa's awful boots. She knew I couldn't wear the only decent pair of slippers I had left – they'd be ruined before I got halfway to the village.

Auntie Minnah went on with her work, refusing to even glance at the disbelieving look on my face. I understood only too well what was really behind this request. The whole village was meant to witness my shame.

"I'll go, Miss Keynnman," Denn spoke up suddenly. "I need

to go to the village anyway. Mama wants me to bring her some things."

"Don't you have servants to do the marketing for you?" Auntie Minnah's tone was decidedly unpleasant. Denn chose to ignore it.

"With Papa away, the servants are needed at home," he said lightly enough, but I could see him twisting his cap between his fingers more tightly than necessary.

"You may accompany Adrianne." Auntie's tone was cold and final. Denn bit his bottom lip, as if he were afraid he might say something he would regret. I could almost see his temper beginning to simmer under that red thatch of hair.

"I'll just tell Mama we're going," I said. Auntie's lips pressed themselves into a disapproving slash. She hated when I reminded her that she wasn't the head of the family.

Before I could take a step, Mama came out of the bedroom carrying a basket of mending.

"Adrianne and Denn are going to the village to pick up some more thread, we're almost out." Auntie Minnah's voice had a nasty edge to it. Mama slowed, looking uncertainly from me to Auntie. Gaining no clues from either of our faces, she went to the table against the wall where two fresh loaves of bread had been set to cool that morning.

"You must take some food with you," Mama said. She cut off two thick slices and held them out to me. Auntie frowned. As far as she was concerned, any food going into my mouth was a waste.

"The second piece is for Denn," Mama said, avoiding Auntie's dark glare. "You both must have something to eat. The village square is a long walk from here."

Her words were an excuse. Knowing how dearly we needed food, Denn would never eat any of our bread and Mama knew it. She often complained about how thin I'd become, and how worried she was about my health. It was difficult to keep on weight when working so hard on only two scant meals a day.

I took the bread and stuffed it into the deep pocket of my apron, next to the tart. I hardly knew what to do with such an unexpected feast.

From a dusty shelf, Mama took down the small wooden box that held every cent we'd managed to save so far that year. The tax money. From the box Mama pulled a single copper coin and handed it to me with a weak smile.

"We'd better get going," I said to Denn. He settled his cap back on his head and nodded politely to Mama. He didn't even give Auntie a second glance as he turned to go.

Papa's ill-fitting boots made loud, clumping sounds as I followed Denn to the door. My cheeks burned with the thought of the spectacle I'd make as I plodded into town with boots five times too big for me. Mama looked down at my feet and her eyes grew wide – an expression that reminded me of Cecily.

"Adrianne, you can't go to the village in those," she said, properly horrified.

A charged silence came from the corner where Auntie Minnah sat. Mama hadn't noticed it yet. If she had, she would never have dared to say a word.

"I have nothing else to wear," I said.

"Don't be a goose, Adrianne." I was surprised Mama couldn't feel Auntie Minnah's glare burning into her back. "You can wear my old work boots into town. They might be a little large for you, but they'll be better than those awkward things."

I reached quickly for the boots where they sat by the dusty cupboard, knowing I had to leave before Auntie could interfere. Denn turned his satisfied smile away from Auntie Minnah as we headed for the door. He reached out and brushed his fingers against the iron horseshoe as we passed between the sagging wooden doorposts. I couldn't help but wonder what luck Denn hoped to get from this trip.

"I'll go get what you need, Adrianne. You stay out here and eat your food," Denn said the moment we reached the village shop.

He disappeared inside before I could even form an argument in my head. He also managed to forget to ask for the money Mama had given me for the thread. Probably meant to pay for the purchase himself, the noble idiot. In frustration, I blew a puff of air up into the fringe of hair that lay across my sweaty forehead. How was I supposed to get over my silly feelings for Denn when he was so stinking thoughtful all the time?

There was no point in going in after him. He'd ignore me till the transaction was complete. But what was I to do with myself till he returned? I slipped my hand into the pocket of my apron and clumsily fingered the round shape of the tart tucked inside its handkerchief. My mouth watered as I thought about how wonderful and fresh the tart and crispy bread would taste. Unfortunately, it was still too early to eat just yet. With a sigh of regret, I pulled my hand from the pocket and fiddled with a loose bit of bandage on my wrist to distract myself while I looked around.

Across the cobbled street I noticed a familiar figure and froze – my heart beating like the wings of a caged bird. Cora Lynn Dunst stood before the baker's cart, making a purchase.

I shrank back against the shop wall, holding my breath. I prayed silently that she wouldn't notice me. If she did, she would come over and pretend to talk to me till Denn came back. Once again, I'd have to walk home alone.

Mr Rendall, the baker, handed Cora Lynn her full basket, and she thanked him prettily before turning to cross the street. Though she hadn't seen me yet, she headed straight in my direction. I pressed myself tighter against the wall, trying to flatten myself into the rough-hewn stone. Almost as if my prayers were heard, a woman stepped in front of Cora Lynn, stopping her dead in the middle of the road. Fear rippled across Cora Lynn's beautiful features as she took a hesitant step backwards. Even from behind, I recognized the bony figure and tattered clothes of the woman who had stopped her. It was the tide drifter

I'd met on the road the day I took Lark to be sold.

Her voice was shrill as she spoke to Cora Lynn. "Please, miss. Have you some food to spare for a desperate mother?"

"I have nothing," Cora Lynn said. The ragged little mother's gaze darted onto the basket Cora Lynn held tight in her hand. Three large loaves poked from the top, so fresh they still steamed. Cora Lynn attempted to hide the basket behind her skirt.

"I have nothing for you. Go away." Cora Lynn tried to walk past, but the woman followed her like a starved puppy.

"Please, you do not understand. My children have gone without food for two days. I ask nothing for myself. Just enough to feed my little ones." As I watched, the woman's face cracked, tears welling up in her large, dark eyes. She caught ahold of Cora Lynn's sleeve, sinking her fingers deep into the expensive fabric.

Cora Lynn let out a sharp cry, her face filled with disgust and fear, but the woman held her fast.

"Please! They are starving – they will die! Have mercy!" The woman shrieked, hysteria taking over her reason. She reached out a soiled hand towards the basket of bread.

Pale-faced, Cora Lynn tried to pull away. The woman clawed at her like a wild thing. Any moment, Cora Lynn would regain her wits enough to scream. The constable would come, and who knew what might happen to the miserable creature after that?

I rushed across the road and pulled the tide drifter's groping hands from Cora Lynn. The woman stared at me, startled from her momentary madness.

"It's all right, good mother. Everything will be fine." I reached into my pocket and brought out the two slices of bread meant for my lunch. The smell of it made my stomach growl in protest. I forced myself to place them in her trembling hand. "Here is food. Take it – and this, too." I pulled out the strawberry tart and held it, waiting for her to accept the gift. She looked deep into my face, then down at my tattered skirts. Her lips parted, but no sound left her empty mouth.

"Go on, it's yours now." I kept my words gentle and soothing. She nodded, lips quavering, as she took the tart from my waiting hand.

"May God bless you for your kind deeds." The woman's voice was a hoarse murmur now. She looked me straight in the eye. "If prayers are indeed carried to the ears of God, He will hear of you, young mistress." She rushed back to where her tiny daughters waited for her by the side of the road.

"It's OK now. She's gone." I spoke for Cora Lynn's benefit, but did not turn around.

There was no answer, but the older girl's ragged breathing told me she was still standing somewhere behind me. I turned, my gaze settling somewhere near Cora Lynn's immaculate boots.

Not a sound came from Miss Dunst. Even her harsh breathing had stopped.

For the first time I looked up directly into Cora Lynn's face.

She looked nothing like the flirtatious, self-assured girl I'd always hated. She was more like a frightened little girl, gripping the basket of bread with both clenched hands, her face paler than I'd ever seen it. She looked like Cecily always did when she was about to burst into tears.

"The woman meant you no harm. She was only hungry," I said in what I meant to be a reassuring tone.

Cora Lynn shook her head, looking down, someplace in the dirt near my feet. "She's a madwoman. The constable should put her away."

I was stunned by her sharp tone. Hadn't she seen the way the woman's flesh hung upon her bones? Hadn't she noticed the haunted look in the mother's eyes? Couldn't she understand the horrible, ugly fear that came when one was worried about someone they loved not getting what they needed?

I stared into Cora Lynn's beautiful face. Her normally rosy cheeks were now a furious red, and her gaze flitted here and there, focusing everywhere but on me. A kind of knowing grew inside me, spreading through my body till I almost shook.

Cora Lynn knew no more about what it was like to be hungry than I had before Papa was taken from us. But she did know that by letting me give the woman my small slices of bread while she stood there with three giant loaves, she had done something very selfish indeed. This knowledge shamed her so much she could not raise her eyes to meet mine. Without thinking, I laid my bandaged hand on Cora Lynn's arm to comfort her. She jerked away from my touch, as if I were little better than the tide drifter woman herself.

Denn came stepping out of the shop at that moment, a goofy grin on his face and a spool of thread in his hand. When he saw the distressed Cora Lynn, his smile faded. With a sob, she shoved past me and threw herself at Denn, clutching at the front of his shirt.

"Oh, Denn! It was simply awful. That madwoman tried to rob me." Dissolving into tears, Cora Lynn buried her face in his chest.

I stared as Denn wrapped his arms around Cora Lynn's shaking shoulders. He spoke soft words, his fingers stroking her long, strawberry blonde hair. It looked like Denn's silent wish for good luck had been granted after all. My eyes stung and the world blurred before me. I turned and hurried away as fast as I could.

I did not have enough strength to look back.

Nine

I stumbled along the path, blinded by my own tears. I used the back of the bandage on my wrist to wipe at my eyes. What a complete and utter fool I was. How many times did I have to learn the same painful lesson? Why wouldn't that place deep inside my secret heart give up its last hidden hope? I was nothing. A poor ragamuffin in overlarge boots with a family who relied on the charity of the Youngs to exist from day to day. Why would Denn Young notice me when girls like Cora Lynn were so eager for his attention?

"He'll never see you as anything more than a sister. Never, never, never," I scolded myself under my breath. "Crying changes nothing. It didn't change Papa's death or Mama's illness. It doesn't matter how many tears you shed or how hard you

work, you will always be skinny, dirty Adrianne Keynnman –
a nothing."

It was about this time I realized I'd forgotten to get the thread
from Denn. Going home to face Auntie Minnah was almost
unthinkable. Going back to face Denn and Cora Lynn was even
worse.

I took a shaky breath and looked up at the sky. One more
stubborn tear spilled down my cheek. "I don't understand why
you didn't take me that day, instead of Papa," I whispered. "It
would have been so easy for you to make it my horse instead of
his. Everyone would have been so much happier."

I jumped as an angry yell startled me from my reverie. For
one moment, I actually thought God Himself had decided to
shout down His displeasure over my ingratitude. The crack of a
whip tore through the air, followed by a bellow of pain. The
sound had come from just out of sight, in a nearby thicket of
trees. Heart pounding in my chest, I ran towards the sound, my
legs pumping. I broke through the trees and froze, one finger
jammed between my teeth so I wouldn't cry out.

There stood Master Wickliff, a wicked-looking crop in his
hand. As I watched, he brought it down hard on the trembling
hide of a horse he held firmly by the bridle. It screamed again.

"I'll teach you to dump me off, you lousy piece of horseflesh!"
he yelled. The gelding tried to rear back in fear, and Master
Wickliff snapped the reins. The bit tore viciously at the animal's
sensitive mouth, forcing it to come back down on all fours. I

recognized the horse at once. Midnight, the sweet-natured mount Papa had often let me ride during my lessons. Never could I imagine him doing anything worthy of such treatment.

In a fury, I flew across the clearing, the tall grass dragging at my skirts as I ran.

Master Wickliff carried on at Midnight, swearing so loudly, he didn't notice me till it was too late. I snatched the reins out of his hand and backed quickly out of reach. Midnight reared and came down just inches from me. I felt the ground shudder beneath the impact of his massive weight. Instinctively, I put a steadying hand on his neck. He snorted, breathing in my scent, then threw his head, white foam dripping from his glossy black neck and chest. His eyes were ringed with fear but he managed to hold himself together beneath my touch.

Master Wickliff's steel gaze cut my own. "Just what do you think you are doing?"

The man was easily twice my size and was built like a bear. I was pretty sure the middle-aged horse master had more respect for his horses than he did for a young girl. Judging by his treatment of Midnight, that meant very little respect indeed.

I stood my full height and lifted my chin. "You have no right to beat one of Lord Durran's horses. My father never would have allowed them to be treated in such a cruel fashion."

Master Wickliff showed all his yellow teeth when he snarled at me. "How dare you talk to your better in such a way. You give me those reins right now or you'll feel for it." He stuck out his thick hand. Midnight skittered away in panic.

Knowing I couldn't possibly keep the horse master from taking Midnight back by force, I threw the reins over the horse's neck and gave him a smart slap on the flank. Midnight bolted away, kicking up dirt and rocks in my face. Master Wickliff made a frantic lunge to stop the gelding and ended up flat on his face in the tall grass. I whirled about to make my escape, but the horse master grabbed my ankle and dumped me on to the ground beside him. Struggling to his feet, he yanked me up with him by my arm, his beefy fingers digging into my skin.

"Your father thought he was high and mighty, too. Always looking down his nose at me. I'll teach you to get in my way!" He lifted his crop. I tensed, waiting for the first blow to fall – determined not to cry out, no matter how badly it stung.

Master Wickliff's attention caught on something behind me. He dropped the arm holding the crop and began to hastily brush me off with it instead. "There, there, young miss, you'll be all right now." His voice changed from wild fury to dripping sweet honey in the span of a heartbeat.

I turned in surprise. Lord Durran himself rode into the clearing on a dark bay. "Wickliff, what happened? I heard a commotion."

"So sorry, my lord." He was all meekness as he bowed his head towards His Lordship. "The girl begged me to let her lead the black gelding, but she spooked him into running off. I wouldn't normally have allowed it, but I thought I owed it to her father, him being the old horse master and all. Everything's fine now."

He let go of my arm and gave me a smile. Behind it, his eyes were as hard and cold as granite. "You go on now, dear. I'll catch Midnight and bring him in. But you'd better not pester me to work with the horses any more, if you can't keep control of them any better than that."

I glared at him, refusing to speak.

"I said, run along now." Master Wickliff gave me a none-too-gentle shove in the direction of the road. I shot him a withering look but took off before he could tell His Lordship any more lies about me. I'd just reached the main road when I heard a voice.

"Wait one moment, please."

I felt my heart sink deep into the pit of my stomach as I recognized the voice of Lord Durran. Was I going to get in trouble for Master Wickliff's lie? Would my whole family be thrown off the island in disgrace because of something I didn't do? I prayed like I'd never prayed before that His Lordship would not decide to make an example of me to the rest of the island.

Lord Durran urged his mount up to my side. The mare stamped her hoof with spirit. I recognized the crooked blaze running the length of her forehead, and knew her to be a young filly my father helped break a little more than two years before.

Lord Durran sat very still and examined me – taking in my red-rimmed eyes, my overlarge boots, and mussed hair in a glance. He pursed his lips as if preparing to say something. The thrumming of insects rose out of the grass around us. I fidgeted in place. Finally he spoke.

"I'm glad to see you working with the horses again. It's been a long time."

I didn't know how to answer. Hadn't Master Wickliff just told him I was responsible for losing one of his horses? He didn't sound angry. I forced myself to look up. His attention was not on me but on Master Wickliff as he disappeared over a rise in the land, still searching for Midnight. Something about the way His Lordship sat, so still and unmoving in the saddle, made me wonder if he didn't altogether believe Master Wickliff's story. Lord Durran turned back to me.

"How is your mother faring?" I'd forgotten how piercing his gaze could be, probing deep into my own. I looked away.

"My family is well, thank you, my lord." I gave him a clumsy curtsy, staring doggedly at the ground.

"And you?" He glanced at my bandage. I was sure, village gossip being what it was, he had long since heard the story of my rescue of Cecily the night she disappeared.

I slipped my wrist behind my back. "It's only a scratch, my lord. Nothing really."

He nodded thoughtfully. "Do you still ride these days? You showed great promise in your lessons. One of the best seats I've ever seen. I'd hate to see such talent wasted."

The significance of his words made my scalp prickle. When had he ever seen me ride? As far as I knew, it had always been just my father and me during my lessons and private rides. I ground the heel of Mama's boot nervously into the dirt.

"My mother doesn't think it's a proper pastime for a girl my age, my lord."

"Ahhh."

Something about the sound of his reply made me think he was disappointed by my answer. Was it possible he had an inkling of what really kept me from riding the horses I loved? He finally seemed to notice how uncomfortable I was. His voice was soft when he spoke. "You may go. Give your mother my regards."

I gave him another hurried curtsy and bolted up the road, not daring to look back. I heard him murmur to his mount and the sound of hoofbeats as the horse and rider pounded away in the direction of the manor.

I turned just in time to see his dark form disappear over the same rise Master Wickliff had climbed not a minute before.

"I promised I would never ride again," I whispered, as if somehow saying the words would make them true. I looked up into the sky. "Do you hear me? I will never ride again."

So why was there such a mass of discomfort writhing about in the pit of my stomach? I could almost imagine the black clouds of uncertainty moving in from the ocean of life to enshroud my future. I looked up, half expecting to see real clouds gathering. Only sunshine and blueness filled the endless sky above me. A speckled young seagull banked in the air, screaming its cry into the wind. Something about the restless sound made my heart feel strange, as if part of me were drifting out to sea with the soaring bird.

Come.

The voice was like a whisper on the breeze. The leaves on the trees shivered as if disturbed by unseen ripples of power. I whirled about in a circle, half expecting Marcus Stebbs to pop up out of some nearby bushes, laughing at my reaction to his joke. But I was alone – completely alone. Even the insects had gone silent around me.

Again the whisper came, stronger this time. The hair rose at the nape of my neck. The force of the words filled me with unspeakable horror.

Come to me.

"No!" I shouted at the deserted landscape like a lunatic. "Neither I, nor my sister, will come to you. Leave us be!"

Dull pain burned along my scarred wrist. I gingerly rubbed at the welts beneath the cloth with my fingertips. Why wouldn't they heal properly? Was it possible these marks were linked to the Windwaithe Mermaid's magic? Perhaps they would only go away if she did.

I was pretty sure she meant to stay for a while, at least till she finished the task she had come to do.

Ten

The sound of the ocean roared in my ears. Water flowed all around me, rippling in waves through my short hair. I saw the surface above my head, glittering and shifting like golden flames. I half expected to see Cecily standing in the sunlight as she had been in my last dream of her, but she was nowhere to be found this time. An uneasy feeling crawled across my skin. Where was my sister?

Come.

The voice was soft, yet it echoed inside me like a shout. I saw no sign of a living person nearby, only rock formations and swaying sea fronds.

Come to me.

What have you done with Cecily? my thoughts shouted back.

A school of fish darted past as if fleeing a predator. Ropes of green seaweed drifted close, brushing my cheek. I strained to see beyond the haze into the deeper water. Only darkness lay there, stretching off into a bottomless ocean. She was there. I could feel the weight of her gaze heavy upon me – watching.

My wrist began to burn, like a fresh wound torn anew. I clutched at it.

COME.

The command was so powerful the tide drew back from the land – dragging me towards the open sea.

"NO!"

I sat up in bed with a gasp. Only a dream, I told myself with relief. Cecily was safe. I reached through the darkness to touch my sister sleeping beside me. Her spot was cold and empty.

My heart thundered inside my chest. The voice of my fading dream echoed in my head.

Come to me . . . to me.

I leaped out of bed – still caught in a nightmare that was only too real. My bare feet slapping the wooden floorboards, I knew I had to catch Cecily before she got to the Rumbles!

Rushing into the front of the house, I stopped dead, surprised by the sight before me. In her white dressing gown, Cecily sat among the shadows like a pale ghost. By the dim light of one small candle, I could see I'd startled her in the act of eating a slice of day-old bread. Realizing she'd been caught, my sister stuffed the rest into her mouth as fast as she could. Cheeks bulging, she blinked up at me, trying to look innocent, but failing miserably.

My relief was so great I couldn't muster enough anger to scold her for her deception. I almost smiled as I put both hands on my hips.

"Do you know what will happen when Auntie Minnah finds that bread missing tomorrow?" I whispered under my breath.

With her mouth so full, Cecily could only blink and lift her shoulders in a shrug.

"She'll think I stole it."

Cecily swallowed as much of the bread as she could, and talked through the rest. "I couldn't sleep, and I was hungry."

"We're all hungry," I said softly. "The more you eat, the less the rest of us get."

Cecily looked away, tears welling in her eyes. I reached out and stroked her hair. It wasn't her fault she couldn't understand why she never got enough to eat. Like me, she'd been spoiled by the good life we'd lived while Papa was alive.

"Why couldn't you sleep?"

Cecily chewed at the mass in her mouth before gulping the rest of it down. "You were kicking and talking in your sleep."

"What did I say?"

She paused as if afraid to tell me. My heart fluttered like a nervous bird.

I took my sister's chin in my hand. "You can tell me. I won't get mad – promise."

She whispered so softly I had to strain to hear her. "The words you said were strange. I couldn't understand them. It scared me, Adrianne."

I pulled up a stool next to Cecily and put my arm around her. Though the room was warm, she shivered.

"All people talk that way when they sleep," I said. "It's nothing to be afraid of. Do you know what Papa used to say when I was scared of the dark? He said there were enough real things to be frightened of without letting our imagination make up more."

Cecily sat silent a moment before glancing up. "Do you remember what Papa looked like, Adrianne?"

"Of course."

She turned her face into the candlelight. Her slender brows worked worriedly together.

"The day I ran away, I sat on the Rumbles and tried to remember what Papa looked like. I could picture him – so tall and strong – but when I tried to remember his face, there was nothing."

I stroked her cheek with my fingers. "It's to be expected. You were young when he died. But you remember what he was like, don't you? How he used to swing you around above his head when he came home every night? And sometimes, he let you win when he raced you to the gate."

"Yes." Cecily's eyes looked distant, as if she were reaching back in her mind for the memories. "I do remember that."

"That's all that matters. What someone is like is much more important than the way they look." Even as I uttered the words, I could not help wondering if they were true. The way that Cora Lynn looked seemed to be the only thing that mattered to Denn.

We both sat quietly for a while, thinking our own thoughts. When Cecily spoke, her voice was full of un-childlike gravity.

"The night of the storm – I did see a mermaid, Adrianne."

My stomach clenched, as if preparing itself against a strike. For the first time, I noticed how much the firelight flickering on the walls of the cottage resembled the shifting light in my underwater dream. A dull burning crept up my right wrist.

Cecily's voice sounded far away as she spoke. "She was so pretty, even prettier than Cora Lynn Dunst. She had a gold crown on her head, like a princess. When she sang, it made me want to cry – even though I liked it. Isn't that funny?"

When I didn't say anything, Cecily went on.

"She knew your name. She said you would come to look for me before long. How did she know that, Adrianne? How did she know you'd be the one to find me?"

I shivered and put a protective arm around my sister. "If you ever see the mermaid again or hear her singing, run straight home and tell me. Don't go anywhere near the sea. That way she can't hurt you."

A ripple of confusion crossed Cecily's young features. "She didn't want to hurt me," she said. "She was a good mermaid."

She'd tried to drown both of us in the sea – hardly an act of goodness. I pulled my sister closer to me.

"Promise me you won't go near the water, anyway," I said.

"I'll never go near the water again – not with sharks out there." Cecily shivered delicately, before glancing up at me. "You believe me about the mermaid, though, don't you, Adrianne?"

I looked straight into her eyes. "I believe you."

Cecily smiled and put her arms around my waist, returning the hug. Fierce emotion squeezed my heart. I held my sister tight to my chest. I would never let the Windwaithe Mermaid get my sister in her clutches again. Never!

Cecily snuggled deep into my strong embrace. "I'm glad you didn't die with Papa," Cecily whispered.

My body stiffened. I tried not to think back – to remember that awful day – but the memories galloped beyond control. It could have been me who died that day. If the rabbit had only run beneath my horse instead of Papa's.

Those first few moments, I didn't know Papa had fallen. I was too busy gaining control of my own mount – the gelding was spooked up the hill a good distance by the rabbit's flurry of movement. Only after I calmed the horse enough to circle back did I find Papa lying at the bottom of a steep embankment, so pale and still. I tried to scream, but nothing came out of my constricted throat. The world turned dark, whirling around me. When I awoke, I found myself in my own room with Doctor

Goodwin beside me. My family's whole life had changed while I lay sleeping.

The doctor said it wasn't my fault. Even if I hadn't fainted, I wouldn't have been able to help Papa. He was killed instantly when he landed on his neck. But I couldn't help but feel I should have done something. If only I'd run for help. If only I'd refused to go riding with Papa that day or never tried to learn to ride in the first place. If only, if only, if only.

"I'm sorry Auntie was so upset about the forgotten thread." Cecily's soft voice drew me back from where my thoughts had wandered. Seeing her concerned expression, I realized she'd attributed my sudden sadness to a different source. "It wasn't right for her to say those awful things about you."

"Auntie is right," I said. "I am a dithering idiot who can't be trusted to finish a simple task."

"Don't say that." Cecily took my hand in hers. "I think you're the best sister anyone could have. I want to be just like you when I grow older."

I looked down at her. She grinned at me, so fresh and pretty. She would never be anything like me when she was older – thank heavens.

"Back to bed with you, Cecily. You need your rest."

"Are you coming, too?"

"In a while."

My little sister nodded once before padding barefoot back to our bed. I sat in the shadows a long time, knowing there would be no sleep waiting on my pillow this night.

I snuffed out the candle stub and went to the cottage door. Quietly opening it, I looked out into the night. The darkness was alive with the sounds of insects and the milky light of the round, waxing moon. The evening was cooler than usual. I folded my arms, trying to hold in the warmth of my own body. I could see one distant point of light winking merrily at the top of the closest hill. It looked like someone was up late in the Rousay cottage. Salty winds drifted lazily in from the ocean. Just out of sight, the waves murmured like many distant voices.

That's when I heard it. Haunting, sweet notes – without words I could understand – floating over the night from the direction of the shore.

A shudder ran through my body, but I continued to sit as still as one in a trance – listening to the call of the Windwaithe Mermaid.

Eleven

"Are you all right, Mama?" I found her leaning against the table, a hand pressed to her forehead. My words made her look up, blinking in a daze. She tried to smile but winced instead.

"It's nothing. Just a headache. It will pass in time."

"Maybe you'd better sit down." I put an arm around Mama's shoulders, helping her to a chair, and was surprised by the heat rising from her.

"Mama, you're burning up with fever," I said. "To bed, right now."

Mama opened her mouth to protest but shut it again. Sagging against me, she allowed herself to be led back to her room. I called Auntie Minnah in from the garden. She stood over Mama's bed with her hands on her hips.

"It's only the first day of the new week, and already we're in trouble. I told you this would happen if you didn't stop wearing yourself down, Giselle." Her voice held no hint of sympathy.

"Should I go get Doctor Goodwin?" asked Cecily, who had followed Auntie into the room.

"No." Mama paled with the effort of talking. "We haven't paid him for his last visit to see Adrianne."

Auntie Minnah's glare made the guilt twist in my gut. Auntie put an arm around Cecily's shoulder.

"We're not in any circumstance these days to be calling doctors every time someone gets a headache," Auntie explained to her gently.

"I could go ask Mrs Rousay to help. She's nursed more people back to health than Doctor Goodwin has," I said. "We could give her some of Belle's milk in return."

Auntie Minnah cut me off with a look. "Mrs Rousay is a widow as poor as we are. She hardly needs to be running up and down the hill from her house to ours every time we get sick."

I personally thought Mrs Rousay wouldn't mind some extra milk for her fast-growing little girl – but I kept my opinion silent. Auntie's real reason for not wanting Mrs Rousay to come was one of pride. She and Mrs Rousay rarely saw eye to eye on how things should be done – especially when it came to how Auntie treated me. Because of it, they had never got on together.

"But what if Mama gets worse?" Cecily asked in a small voice.

"We'll just have to take care of her ourselves," Auntie Minnah said.

By evening Mama grew sicker. Auntie Minnah and I took turns looking after her. Between my shifts I tried to get as many of my chores done as possible. As the sun set in the blazing red sky, Denn showed up on our doorstep with the forgotten spool of thread in his hand and not a sign of a smile on his face. I invited him inside for a moment to talk.

"You disappeared before I could give the thread to you that day," Denn said. "Where did you go, anyway? I got away as quick as I could without being rude and tried to catch up to you. I never so much as caught a glimpse of you along the road. Did you run all the way home on purpose?" Something in the sharpness of his voice made me wonder if I had hurt his feelings by rushing off without telling him.

"It looked like you'd be busy for a while," I said.

"I came into town to help *you* that day." Denn sounded like he was about to lose his patience again. "What have you got against letting people help you – or is it just me you don't like?"

I fiddled with the frayed hem of my work apron so I wouldn't have to look him in the eye. "I didn't mean it that way. I'm truly grateful to you and your family for all the help you give us. We'd never make it without your kindness."

Denn kicked at a knot in the floor with the toe of his boot, his jaw jutting in disapproval. "You say that as if my family were nothing more than interfering strangers, forcing charity on you."

"No, it's not like that," I said hastily.

"What is it like?" Denn let the full power of his green eyes settle on me. "You're always angry with me these days. You used to tell me things, but not any more. I can't figure out what you want from me, Adrianne."

It was my turn to look at the knot in the floor, willing myself not to cry. The oppressive heat of the closed cottage seemed worse than it usually was this time of day. I wiped at my perspiring brow with the back of my bandage.

"It's not you, Denn," I finally said. "I'm not the same person I was. Too much has gone wrong, no one can put it right any more – not even you. Time is running out for me."

I was startled by my own words. Till that moment, I hadn't realized I still felt I might be in danger. The flesh along my marked wrist crawled uneasily, like worms shifting beneath my skin.

Denn's green eyes narrowed. "What do you mean, 'time is running out'? Has Lord Durran said something about the tax coming due early?"

I shook my head.

"Why would you say such a thing?"

For one wild moment, I thought of telling him about the Windwaithe Mermaid. How she haunted Cecily and me like an evil shadow, following us wherever we went – waiting for the chance to drown us. Would Denn believe me? Would he be able to help?

I opened my mouth to speak.

"Denn!"

Cecily came running into the room and threw her arms tight around his middle. Although he hugged her back, Denn's gaze followed me as I turned to finish the tub of washing I'd been working on before he came.

"Mama is really sick," Cecily said breathlessly, looking up at Denn. His attention finally drifted to her as he took in this news.

"Sick?"

"She's got a bad fever, a cough deep inside her chest. Auntie says she's been working too hard."

Denn looked at me. "When did this happen?"

"This morning," I said.

"Auntie says it will be awhile before Mama gets better. But she has to get better before the wedding feast, because she promised to take me. She will be better before then, won't she, Adrianne?"

The feast was only four days off. It was not likely she'd be well enough to walk all the way to the manor by then.

But when I looked into Cecily's expectant face I found myself saying instead, "Perhaps she will. We'll do our best to make her better."

"You must need help in the barn," Denn said. "I'll go out right now, so you can stay with your mother."

I nodded. He hesitated for a moment, as if he wanted to say

something more to me before he went. His eyes darted to Cecily, who stood watching us with great interest etched on her young, curious face. He shut his mouth again and tugged on the front of his cap before heading outside.

"I wish you'd marry Denn," Cecily said as soon as he left. "Then he would be my real brother."

Her words startled me out of the stupor I'd fallen into. I stared at her in shock.

"Don't you dare say anything so ridiculous again. Especially where Denn can hear you."

"What's so ridiculous? He's only two years older than you. Besides, how could he hear me – he's halfway to the barn."

"Denn will choose his own bride without any help from you and me, thank you very much. Besides, I don't plan to get married. I'm needed far too much here at home."

Cecily cocked her head to one side and gave me a mischievous smile. "Trey says Denn will probably marry that idiot Cora Lynn Dunst. She has more 'goods in the shop window' than you do."

"Cecily Giselle Keynnman!" I exclaimed in horror.

"Well, that's what Trey said." Cecily's cheeks blushed a delicate pink. "And she does. Ask Denn if you don't believe me."

"I most certainly will not ask Denn any such thing. And you shouldn't be talking about those things, especially with that scalawag Trey Young. I have half a mind to box that boy's ears next I see him."

Cecily gave a careless shrug, her eyes dancing merrily. "Trey also said you were the nicest girl on the island and Denn's a fool if he chooses Cora Lynn over you."

"Enough!" I stamped my foot. She leaped out of my reach, giggling all the more as I chased her out the front door and down towards the garden. Panting and sweaty, I gave up the pursuit when she scooted under the fence and ran across the fields in the direction of the Youngs' house. That was fine by me, so long as she didn't go anywhere near the ocean.

With a tired sigh, I turned and went back into the warm house to finish my washing.

Later, Auntie Minnah made herb tea to bring down Mama's fever – murmuring all kinds of blessings over it before pouring it into the big brown teapot. I placed a steaming cup in Mama's hand and stayed to make sure she drank every last drop.

As she sipped the dark liquid, I noticed she wore Grandmama's locket around her neck. The golden necklace was almost lost in the folds of her thin cotton nightdress.

"Would you like me to put your locket away for you, Mama? It might get broken if you sleep with it on," I said.

Mama slowly shook her head, as if every little movement hurt her.

"I know you'll think I'm silly, but the locket gives me comfort when I wear it. Your grandmama was a strong woman. Grandpapa died before your papa was born, and she had to raise her family alone. I don't know how she did it."

For one moment I thought Mama would cry. Swallowing hard, she was able to continue. "As you know, I am not a strong woman, Adrianne. When I wear the locket, I can feel a little of her strength flowing into me – making me stronger."

Mama gingerly took my hand in hers. "You have that effect on me, too. Sometimes, I fancy if I hold you tight enough, some of your courage will seep into me and help me not to be so weak."

I hesitated only a fraction of a second. "You're not weak," I said.

Mama looked me in the eye. She'd heard the pause. Her lower lip began to tremble. She did not have to speak. I knew her thoughts were of those first months after Papa's death. Her eyes begged me to forgive her, but she still could not bring herself to speak of it out loud.

I forced myself to smile at her. I refused to let her see the pain the memories of those days still caused; the horrible, gnawing emptiness I'd suffered knowing my own mother had betrayed me when I needed her most. I forced myself to say the words she needed to hear.

"I lost all our savings, not you." I couldn't believe what it cost to say the words aloud. "You were so ill. If I'd only thought things through better. I should have known how foolish it would be to keep paying servants without Papa to bring in more money. I should have let them go right at the first instead of going on for months that way."

One lone tear rolled down Mama's cheek.

Shame scorched through me. I hadn't known what to do after Papa died. I was a pampered twelve-year-old girl raised with servants to do everything for me. What did I know about budgeting a household or arranging financial affairs? Yet I'd been forced to do it all alone, with no one to guide me. My blundering had cost us everything.

When the day of reckoning came, I took the blame for everything that happened – and Mama let me.

I'd never told a soul the rest of what happened during those first three months. I would take that secret to my grave.

Twelve

Four days later, Mama's fever dropped to normal, but Auntie Minnah said she was still too weak to attend the wedding feast. I could tell she was secretly pleased over this turn of events. As far as Auntie was concerned, dances were nothing more than gathering places for sin.

Much to Auntie's horror, when Cecily learned she would not be allowed to attend the feast by herself, she flew into quite a state – beating the floor and wailing to the thatched roof. Finally my sister threw herself down beside Mama's bed.

"Can't I go with Trey and Hannah?" she begged.

"The Youngs have been asked to go up to the manor early. You have not, so you cannot go with them," Mama said.

"Couldn't Adrianne take me?" Cecily turned to me, hope

shining in her big brown eyes. How did she manage to look so beautiful with her eyes full of tears? I would have been red all over, my nose swollen to twice its normal size.

"I haven't got a dress, Cecily, and I can't show up to a wedding feast dressed in work clothes," I said.

"You could wear my second-best dress," Mama said. "It wouldn't take much to stitch the sides a bit and take up the hem. You'd look very pretty in that rich blue colour."

I thought about what it would be like to stand around watching Denn cosy up to Cora Lynn all evening. "I don't want to go," I said.

Despite the fact she didn't really want Cecily to attend the dance, Auntie had never been able to pass up a chance to take a dig at me. "Did you ever hear of such selfishness, thinking only of her own feelings," she said as she wrapped a protective arm around Cecily's shoulder.

I wanted to snap back and tell her to take Cecily herself while I stayed home with Mama, but I knew it would only make her angry. She didn't want to go to the feast any more than I did.

"May I go by myself? Everyone else will be travelling the road to the manor, so I won't be alone," Cecily said.

"No, you may not," Mama said.

"It's not fair!" Cecily said, more tears welling in her eyes.

How many times had I uttered those exact words over the past two years? Even over the past few days. Cecily looked up at me – her hands clasped together, her face full of pleading.

"Please take me, Adrianne. Please."

I closed my eyes and thought about all the things Cecily had given up. Even Lark had been sacrificed in the end. The least I could do was suffer through one evening of discomfort for her in return.

"All right. I'll take you."

Cecily clapped her hands and danced about me in pure glee. "Thank you, Adrianne! Thank you, thank you, thank you."

"Come, Cecily," Auntie Minnah said, with a resigned sigh. "I'm going to help you bathe and get ready for tonight."

Cecily skipped happily away, Auntie's hand clutched tight in her own.

Mama turned to me. "Go to the chest against the wall and get out my blue dress. We'll fit it to you, and while I fix it, you can bathe yourself in the kitchen tub. Don't forget to scrub your hair. I want you to look your very best."

I knew it would be a useless effort. Dirt or no dirt, I was still the same skinny, drab creature underneath. No one was going to talk to me, much less ask me to dance. I would be Cecily's chaperone and nothing more. But I did as Mama asked. Shivering and wet, I presented myself at her bedside and let her curl rags in my already-too-short hair. Cecily and Auntie Minnah talked and laughed in the other room, while Mama worked on me in slow silence, not wanting to exert herself too much.

"We'll leave your bandage off just for tonight," Mama said as I tried on the dress. "The sleeve will fit better that way."

Mama had stitched and tucked it just right, hiding how thin I'd become beneath its flowing folds. The dress was nicer than anything I'd owned in a long time.

After my hair dried, Mama took out the rags, brushed through my unruly hair and tied a blue ribbon with a small bow on the top. She had me step back so she could survey her work.

After looking me over carefully, she smiled. "You look nice," she said.

I gazed into the only mirror we owned. Cracked and hazy, it stood against the far wall of Mama's room. Something about the midnight blue of the dress brought out the pink in my tan cheeks and made my eyes look dark and mysterious. My short hair did seem a little curlier and softer as it feathered over my brow. I gave my reflection a surprised smile. For once, I looked pretty.

Cecily burst into the room and instantly shattered the illusion. The heaviness of truth struck me like a clenched fist. Beside my sister's rosy bloom, I was a dowdy weed.

"Mama, Mama, look at me!" Cecily said.

Auntie Minnah had left Cecily's hair long in the back, with flowers tucked into a braid plaited across the crown of her head. Her cheeks were flushed with excitement and her heart-shaped face was elfin and charming. The green dress that had once been mine billowed around her as she spun in a graceful circle. Her eyes shone with delight.

"How do I look, Mama? Do I look like a princess?" Cecily asked.

Auntie Minnah followed behind her, a small smile on her lips, obviously pleased with her work. Cecily spun around prettily, her skirts twirling about her ankles. Auntie's gaze darted in my direction, watching my reaction. I couldn't help but wonder if she'd sent my sister in at that moment on purpose.

Mama laughed. "I have a surprise for you, Cecily," she whispered, holding out her hand towards my little sister. Something caught the firelight and glimmered in her palm. Cecily crept closer, eyes full of curiosity.

I took a step nearer to get a better look. Mama held Grandmama's locket. She'd taken it from around her neck when I wasn't looking.

Mama reached up and draped the necklace around Cecily's slender shoulders. My sister was almost dancing with suppressed excitement.

"I think Grandmama would have wanted you to wear it tonight. And someday, when you're a little older, it will be yours," Mama said to her.

Cecily whirled about. "You mean to keep?"

Not looking in my direction, Mama nodded.

Something slithery and cold constricted inside me. I knew why Mama promised the locket to Cecily instead of me. There was only one necklace and Cecily would have made a fuss if I'd been the one to receive it – crying a flood of tears like she always did when she didn't get her way. Mama couldn't handle Cecily's tantrums. It was easier to deny me because I would remain silent. I always did.

I lowered my gaze, trying not to wonder what would happen if I did decide to make a fuss this time. I could stamp my feet, scream and throw myself on the floor – then what would Mama do? Such a tantrum might win me the locket. But after behaving in such a way, would I ever be able to look at it again without feeling ashamed of myself?

My eyes fell upon Auntie Minnah standing near the doorway. She was as still as stone, watching Mama and Cecily. Her face pale, her lips pulled tight, her eyes stricken with some emotion I couldn't put a name to.

Something about her pained expression made my heart ache with sympathy. Did Auntie also have memories connected to the locket? Why had *Papa* inherited the necklace, when Auntie Minnah was not only the oldest, but also the only girl? What would she have done if I'd been the one who'd received the locket? Auntie glanced in my direction. I quickly turned away, pretending I hadn't noticed her moment of weakness.

"We'd better get going," I said. All I wanted was for this evening to be over and done with.

Mama kissed us both from her bed. Cecily hugged her over and over, happiness spilling all about her. She even hugged me – but not Auntie Minnah, who followed us to the door in grim silence.

We carried our slippers so they wouldn't get ruined on the trip over to the manor. Mama had said I might keep wearing her old work boots until we could afford to buy me more, so I put them on.

"We'll probably be back early," I said to Auntie Minnah as I stepped out of the house down into the grass.

Auntie Minnah didn't answer as she watched Cecily heedlessly skip across the yard towards the main road. Cecily hadn't even thought of thanking Auntie for doing so much work. I knew how much my sister's love meant to my aunt – at times it seemed to be the only thing that mattered to her any more. The pain and longing I saw written on Auntie's face made my chest tighten uncomfortably inside me, but I didn't know what to do. She would be offended if I forced Cecily to come back. Hesitantly, I turned to follow my sister. The door shut softly behind me.

Thirteen

Moths fluttered about the decorative lanterns twinkling here and there along the path from the gatehouse to the manor. The wedding feast was laid out under the open sky, just at the bottom of the orchard. Everywhere we turned, tables stood heaped with platters of meat, barrels of cider and trays of delicate pastries. A group of fiddlers coaxed merry tunes from their instruments while light-footed dancers twirled and leaped about in tight circles beneath the star-laden sky. I felt dizzy just watching them.

Cecily and I sat on a wooden bench beneath an old oak tree to change out of our work boots into our best slippers. Cecily was so excited she got one of her bootlaces in a knot and made me work it free with what was left of my ragged nails. We stowed our boots beneath the tree and went to join the throngs of people making their way towards the tables of food. I noticed the Roscoe brothers standing in the shadows of some bushes, their plates filled with gluttonous amounts of mutton. Their heads together, they whispered and sent wide-eyed stares in my direction. When I cut them down with a look, they quickly turned away in embarrassment. I couldn't help but wonder what they were on about this time. Had Marcus Stebbs started some nasty new gossip about me?

Cecily gave my sleeve a tug. "Look, it's Trey and Hannah, over by the banquet table."

I turned to look and found myself only a few inches from Lester Gibbons's mottled, red face. I jumped back from him, one hand clutched against my startled heart.

"Lester, you idiot. Are you trying to give me palpitations?" I demanded.

Lester's open mouth worked in silence. I waited but no words came forth.

"Um, was there something you wanted, Lester?" I asked.

"Adr – I – I gah – yu – yu." It was as if his tongue were tied in thick knots.

"It's – nice – to see you too, Lester," I said slowly. "But I really think Cecily and I should get some food before it's all gone. Uh, bye."

Lester opened his mouth and gurgled like a newborn babe. Cecily stared up at him, absolutely fascinated with whatever infirmity had stricken him. I grabbed my sister's hand and dragged her with me towards the long banquet tables, leaving Lester spluttering behind us.

"What in the name of all that is holy ails the boy?" I demanded of the dusky sky above.

"I think he wanted to ask you to dance," Cecily said.

I whirled on her in irritation. "Why would Lester Gibbons want to ask me to dance?"

Cecily looked me over appraisingly before giving a mystified shrug.

"What a bunch of nonsense," I said under my breath.

"Did you see his ears? They were as red as lobsters," Cecily said with great irreverence. She stared at something off to my left. "I think the Roscoe brothers are following us."

As I turned around, I caught only the briefest sight of two hulking shadows in the act of diving behind a nearby tree.

"Maybe they want to ask you to dance, too," Cecily said with a giggle.

"Or maybe they plan to dump a plate of mutton down the front of my dress."

I glanced down the table and saw Denn's younger brother and sister stuffing their faces with pie as fast as they could. Mrs Young stood nearby, laughing merrily with a friend from the village. She looked perfectly elegant in her new green silk dress, with her hair arranged in thick red swirls at the top of her head. Her cheeks were as round and rosy as apples. She noticed me standing there, and waved enthusiastically in my direction before continuing her conversation. Denn was nowhere to be seen.

"Why don't you join Trey and Hannah, Cecily? I'm sure they know all the best dishes by now."

She flashed me a grin and raced off to meet the Youngs. Mrs Young greeted Cecily with a motherly hug before Trey and Hannah pulled her away into the crowd.

I moved closer to the circle of dancers. I watched them whirl by in pairs at a giddy pace. One particularly happy couple spun past, smiling and laughing. I recognized them immediately. Denn and Cora Lynn.

How many dances had they shared already? How many more would follow? Cora Lynn danced like a fairy – light and graceful, her feet hardly touching the ground. Her hair was coiled at the top of her head in the style all the older girls wore these days. She looked more grown up than I'd ever seen her. The flame of discontent blazed hot in my chest. I would never look like that, no matter how many baths I took, or how many rags I put in my hair. It wasn't fair.

Finding I could not bear to look at Cora Lynn's perfect beauty any more, I glanced at the long table beside me, piled high with food of every kind. Though I'd not eaten since breakfast, I found I had no appetite.

A sudden movement across the circle of dancers caught my attention. The Roscoe brothers stood facing me at the opposite edge of the crowd, their necks craning at strange angles as if to find someone particular among the many twirling couples. The eldest Roscoe's eyes happened by chance to meet mine. He froze. Nudging his brother he pointed in my direction. They started whispering again. My heart thudded in my chest. Were they planning to pull some embarrassing prank right here in front of everyone? Not if I could help it.

The eldest Roscoe brother squared his shoulders, smoothed out his shirt and started in my direction with a purposeful stride. With a swish of my blue skirt, I fled into the crowd, pushing my way up the path towards the edge of the orchard. I burst through the small picket gate and threaded my way through the shadows of the fruit trees, glancing nervously over my shoulder from time to time. Neither Roscoe brother was anywhere to be seen.

As I approached the other side of the orchard, I heard voices. Breaking the edge of the trees, I saw that I had reached the manor house itself. The newly married couple stood under a wooden arch decorated with delicate white flowers and ivy. Tall candelabras laden with dripping candles were planted in the grass all around them.

I was hesitant to approach any closer. The bride's family had sailed over from the mainland for the wedding. Only those of the highest standing had been invited to attend the private ceremony performed by the minister earlier that morning.

From the shadow of a large apple tree, I watched them greet their other guests. Lady Amelia, the beautiful young bride, could not have been more than two years older than me. She stood gowned in white, her pale blonde hair falling well past her waist.

With her long eyelashes, sweet rosebud lips and fair porcelain skin, she was a glowing angel in the warm light of the candles around her. It was little wonder Lord Graham had fallen in love with her.

Had the ill-fated Lady Lauretta looked like that? Why would the Windwaithe Mermaid bother with a little girl like Cecily when young ladies like this one existed in the world?

Icy chills ran down my spine. My right wrist prickled beneath the long sleeves of Mama's dress. Could the mermaid sense when I thought about her? I tried to shake off the unsettling idea.

Lady Amelia laughed at something one of the guests said, drawing my attention back to the bride. The sound of her voice rang out as silvery as the church bells in the night air. Her beautiful eyes shone, full of joy and happiness I could not even begin to imagine.

Thinking how I must look in comparison to her, I fingered my short hair and tried to smooth out a wrinkle in Mama's dress. They would no more care to see me than a bedraggled tide drifter. I shrank back into the trees, wandering aimlessly back towards the sound of the music.

"Adrianne!" Cecily skipped up through the orchard shadows with Hannah in tow. "We thought we saw you rushing in this direction."

Trey silently melted out of the dusk behind them, chewing his way through a large chicken leg (with most of the thigh still attached) as fast as his bulging cheeks would let him. As he finally got a good look at me, a peculiar expression came over his features. Swallowing hard, he squinted at me through the shadows of the fruit trees. He spoke thickly around the chicken still stuffed in his mouth.

"There's something's different about you tonight. Did you take a bath or something?"

Hannah jabbed her brother hard with her elbow. Trey yelped and rubbed at the spot with an injured air.

"How's Lark?" I asked to change the subject.

"Mama said it wouldn't be proper to bring a dog to a wedding feast. Lark howled like anything when we tied her up," Hannah said.

"I don't see why we couldn't bring her. This is only a celebration, not the real wedding," Trey said.

"I heard Mama talking to Mrs Rousay," Hannah said in excitement. "Mama said Lord Graham and Lady Amelia want Papa to sail them to the mainland for their wedding tour on Lord Durran's finest schooner. Mama says it's a great compliment to Papa that they want him to be the one to carry them. They plan to stay at the manor house and wait for his return."

"Wedding tours – who needs them?" Trey wrinkled his freckled nose in disgust. Hannah shot her older brother a scornful look.

"Did you hear?" Cecily asked, turning to me. "Lord Durran paid a fortune-teller to tell everyone's fortunes tonight."

"They say she can even tell you about the man you will marry someday," Hannah said with big eyes.

Trey gave a rude snort. The girls ignored him.

"Can I go if Hannah goes with me?" Cecily asked.

"Not me." Hannah shook her fluffy head, her eyes huge, dark pools on her pale face. "I'd probably step on her foot, and she'd put a curse on me to make all my hair fall out."

"What difference does it make if you're bald? With your looks, you'll never get a husband anyway," Trey said, taking another bite of his chicken.

Hannah took a swing, but missed as her brother stepped out of the way. Trey had probably learned that trick watching Denn keep out of my way over the years. He swallowed the last of the food in his mouth and threw the rest of the chicken leg over his shoulder. Hannah made a disgusted noise between her large front teeth. Trey ignored her.

"I don't know why you're in such a hurry, Cecily." Trey turned to my sister with a cocky grin. "The fortune-teller has agreed to stay on the island for a whole month. Besides, you're too young to be thinking about marriage anyway."

Even in the low lantern light I could see Cecily's soft, round cheeks filling up with a rosy pink colour. Little did Trey realize, Cecily hoped the fortune-teller would tell her it was him she would someday marry. My sister turned away to cover her embarrassment.

"You'll go with me, won't you, Adrianne? I don't want to go alone," Cecily said.

"Auntie Minnah would fly into a fury if she ever found out we'd anything to do with a fortune-teller," I said.

"But they say she can tell your future. Don't you want to know who – I mean – what will happen to you someday?" I was grateful to Cecily for not finishing her original thought.

"Come on." Cecily pulled on my sleeve.

I had to admit I was curious to see what a fortune-teller might have to say about *my* dismal future. After saying goodbye to Trey and Hannah, Cecily led me reluctantly past the festivities and revellers to a dark corner where a small canvas tent stood off by itself. It was draped with colourful paper lanterns and sheer material that billowed with every warm night-time breeze. As we approached, Rose and Heather Dunst burst from the tent opening, whispering in excitement and clinging to each other's hands. Flustered, but smiling, they hurried away into the night. Obviously *their* futures hadn't been so bad.

Cecily stopped before the shimmering cloth door, dancing nervously from one foot to the other.

I glanced at her. "Are you coming or not?"

She nodded, but when she started forward again her pace was much slower.

Inside the tent, dim candlelight flickered over black drapery covering the walls from floor to ceiling. Strings of dried flowers and herbs dangled from the ceiling, along with a couple of dead birds and a bat. A cloyingly sweet smell in the air made my head feel strange. A small table and three stools stood in the middle of the tent. And a great black candle sat in the table's centre, half melted but unlit.

Cecily clutched my arm so hard it went numb beneath her fingertips. I prised her loose with one hand – she immediately began crushing the bones in my fingers.

"Come in, good daughters of Windwaithe."

Cecily jumped as the black candle suddenly sputtered to life on the table. She clung to me with both hands, trembling. A small figure, dressed in brown, stood not three feet away from us. She had long, black hair plaited in a thick braid down her back. She was a young woman with a smooth, round face – not beautiful exactly, but arresting in her own way. Her eyes made me uneasy. I told myself they must be a very dark brown, but in the light of the candles they looked bottomless black, with no pupil at all. I began to wonder if coming here was such a good idea.

"I know what it is you seek," she said in spectral tones. "Be seated and I will tell you of your deepest desires." She smiled secretively, as if she knew something we didn't that greatly amused her.

Cecily and I sat on two of the stools. The woman sat across the table from us in the third. She took Cecily's hand gently in hers, turning it palm upwards for closer inspection. After studying it a moment, she looked deep into my sister's eyes.

"Ahhh." The sound was like the sigh of hot ash whispering among dying embers of a flame. "You have much to look forward to. I see you, prettier than a summer's day and beloved by all the young men in the village. You will live in a large, elegant house and never want for the good things in life."

I was quickly losing faith in the woman's powers of sight. Cecily wanted for the good things every day of her life, and as far as I could see she always would.

"What about my true love? Can you see him?" Cecily asked in dead earnest. I could tell by her wide eyes she was soaking it in like a rag.

"There *is* a young man." The woman looked deeper into Cecily's eyes. "I see him. He is fair to look upon, with a high, noble brow."

Trey? A high and noble brow? I snorted and quickly coughed to cover it. The woman froze, her unnatural, dark eyes shifting towards me. She hadn't been fooled one bit.

"You." The sorceress's voice was barely a whisper. Her liquid black gaze was now hard and cold. "It is your turn now."

I could tell my future would be nowhere near as cheerful as Cecily's.

"But what about me? You didn't finish," my little sister cried.

The fortune-teller ignored Cecily. Taking my hand in a biting grip, she jerked it towards her. My sleeve caught on the table's edge, dragging the cuff roughly back over the still-raw welts on my wrist. I let out a small gasp of pain. She glanced down and froze – staring at the ugly scars that were revealed.

Her lips parted and a strangled sound came from her throat.

She leaped to her feet and drew back from me so fast she knocked over the stool. It fell to the earthen floor with a heavy thud.

"You bear the mark," she cried in a high, shrill voice – all pretense of spooky mysticism forgotten.

My heart pounded heavily in my chest and the palms of my hands became slippery with cold perspiration. I tried to hide my wrist behind the folds of my skirt. "What do you mean?" I asked in a faltering voice.

"You bear the mark of the Windwaithe Mermaid! Just like Lady Lauretta one hundred years ago." With a trembling hand, the fortune-teller hastily made a sign that was supposed to protect one against evil. "God help you now, for there are no earthly powers that can."

Cecily's eyes widened. "A mermaid?"

I clutched at Cecily's shoulder, trying to silence what I knew would come next. It was too late.

"I saw a mermaid," my little sister said. "I talked to her."

The woman's dark eyes widened with horror beneath her winglike eyebrows. "Then you are both cursed. Get out. Leave this place and never come back. You will mean the death of us all!" The young woman's voice rose to a shriek that filled the canvas walls.

I grabbed Cecily's hand, yanked her off the stool and dragged her out of the tent with me. The hysterical screams of the fortune-teller filled the night behind us. People stopped to stare as Cecily and I rushed past, trying to get as far from the fortune-teller as possible. My sister wept in terror as I dragged her stumbling and wailing at my heels. We made quite a spectacle. Some of the boys cried out catcalls in our wake, and I thought I heard someone calling my name as we flew past the circle of dancers. I didn't stop to find out who it was. Down the path we fled, the cheerful music lilting away in the air around us.

I ran and ran, but I knew I could not escape the dark magic closing slowly in on me.

Fourteen

Auntie Minnah was furious when she saw the state of our best shoes after we walked all the way home from the wedding feast in them. In my haste to get away from the screaming fortune-teller, I'd forgotten to stop and collect our boots.

Auntie refused to speak to me the rest of the night, and first thing in the morning she announced her intention of going into town to run the weekly errands herself. She wanted me to know she no longer trusted me to do anything, much less go into town. I was, in fact, relieved to have her out of the house for a few hours. I needed time to think things through properly.

If Auntie thought she was angry now, she would be livid when she discovered the rest of what went on at the wedding feast. I knew better than to pray that no one would tell Auntie about the fortune-teller's hysterics after our visit to her tent. It was what the fortune-teller might say in defence of her actions that worried me most. If she told even one person about the mermaid's mark upon my wrist, my family and I were doomed.

For all I knew, at this very moment mobs might be gathering, intent on coming here to drag me from my home and throw me into the ocean as an offering to appease the mermaid's wrath. Feeling weary, I sat down on a stool and rested my head in my hands.

"Please let the fortune-teller keep quiet," I whispered softly to God, hoping Mama would not hear me in the other room. "I'll do anything, if you'll just help her stay silent about this. Anything at all."

Knowing there was nothing more I could do, I got to my feet and began my morning chores. Denn came over in the afternoon to deliver some fresh-baked bread from his mother and to return our missing boots, which he'd discovered under a tree the night of the feast. Lark came with him, and Cecily met the dog with lots of hugs and kisses just outside the door. Denn continued into the house with me, where I immediately sat down to put on my boots.

"What happened to you last night?" Denn asked, fiddling with his cap. "I called out as you and Cecily went racing by but I guess you couldn't hear me over all the racket. What ailed the fortune-telling woman, anyway? They said she was the one we could hear screaming all over the island."

"She didn't like my future," I said, tightening up my bootlace.

Denn laughed and mussed my short hair as if I'd made some clever joke. I glanced up at his grinning face and took some courage. If mobs were forming all over Windwaithe Island, Denn would not be acting so nonchalant about the whole thing.

"Trey went on and on about how nice you looked – all made up like a real girl, he said. You rushed past so fast last night, I'm afraid I missed it." Denn gave me one of those winks I hated because they meant absolutely nothing.

Cecily dashed into the house, Lark at her heels. She looked pale and frightened.

"What is it?" I stood up, rubbing nervously at the welts beneath my sleeve. I'd decided I was through with bandages.

"A-Auntie's coming," Cecily stammered. I surmised immediately that Auntie Minnah was not in a good mood. Denn must have come to the same conclusion, and made his goodbyes as quickly as he could. Auntie ignored Denn's jaunty greeting as he and Lark left, disappearing up the path. Cecily stood anxiously back as Auntie stomped up the front path, her face a thunderstorm in the making. Marching up to me, she planted her hands upon her hips, her dark eyes glittering in the bright sun. I braced myself for the worst.

"I've just come from the village," Auntie said. "Everyone is talking about some fortune-teller, and you making a complete spectacle of yourself at the wedding feast."

"It was the fortune-teller who made most of the fuss," I said.

"What were you doing in the tent of the devil's own in the first place?" Auntie demanded of me.

"Getting our fortunes told."

"*Our* fortunes?" Auntie Minnah's eyes became narrow and dangerous. "Are you telling me you took your innocent little sister into a den of dark magic on purpose?"

I figured there was no safe answer to such a question and remained stubbornly silent. Deep inside me the flame of hope rekindled. If the fortune-teller had told anyone about the mermaid's mark, surely Auntie Minnah would have heard about it in town. Was it really possible that my secret was still safe?

Seeing I was unmoved by her anger, Auntie Minnah decided to change tactics. She heaved a big sigh to show how much I tested her beyond all measure. Her voice was light, as if the vicious words she spoke held no weight. "I should know by now not to expect better than this from you, Adrianne. You'll never amount to anything, so why do I even bother reasoning with you? You do these things without a care for how anyone else will be affected by your actions. You're wicked through and through."

"Just like you." Even as the harsh words left my mouth I hardly understood what I was saying.

Auntie Minnah's eyes grew wide. For one brief moment, an expression of horror twitched across the surface of her surprised face. Then she slapped me so hard it resounded through the yard. Cecily gasped.

I clutched at my cheek, the pain driving tears to my eyes. As I stood hunched over, trying to catch my breath, the first hint of understanding trickled through my numb mind.

I was the plain, second-best, older daughter. I was expected to work, sacrifice, and live a hard life of poverty while others received better. Just like Auntie Minnah when she was a girl. Exactly like Auntie Minnah.

Involuntarily, I remembered the haunted look on her face as she watched Mama give Grandmama's locket to Cecily, taunted by the memories of her own days as a plain, second-best, older daughter. Poor, unappreciated, unloved Auntie Minnah. We shared the same fate, she and I. Destined to be treated like every other poor, unlovely girl born into this unforgiving world.

I looked up into her sallow, wrinkled face and saw the hatred burning behind her savage eyes.

I was just like her – and she *hated* me for it.

This knowledge was too much. I turned and ran from the house, almost bumping into Cecily as I pelted past. I ran, blinded with tears, not caring where I went. My chest hurt and my legs wanted to collapse, but I couldn't stop.

My heart pounded, ready to burst, till I fell against a large rock and lay there waiting for my lungs to stop their burning. I looked around me in a daze and found myself not far from the shore. Warm, damp sand shifted beneath my feet. The sparkling waves rolled before my view. The roar of the sea pounded in my ears. The bright sun reflected off the ocean into my tear-filled eyes.

I'd always believed deep down that if I just worked hard enough and behaved myself better, I might one day win Auntie Minnah's respect. I knew better now. Auntie Minnah would always hate me. The same way she hated the life fate had dealt her.

I sank down on to the sand, my head pressed against the rough, pitted stone, and gave myself up to sorrow. Not just for myself, but for all the miserable creatures that walked the world nursing invisible wounds inflicted by unfortunate circumstance, the thoughtlessness of others, and the ache of desperate need.

I tried to hate Auntie Minnah for all the horrible, mean-spirited things she'd done to me, for all the things she would do to me in the years to come. But I couldn't stop thinking about *why* she did it.

The overwhelming wretchedness that poisoned my own soul, day after day, was the very same twisted force that drove Auntie Minnah to be so vicious and cruel to me. The venom of discontent that burned inside me now had seeped into Auntie for many, many empty years – silently tearing at her from the inside out. Papa's and Grandmama's love had not been enough to staunch the bleeding of her heart. Time had not been enough to heal the damage done – the wounds she suffered were too deep and festering. Now that I understood, I could not hate. I could only weep with pity.

I don't know how long I sat there, staring out over the ocean before me. Something about the eternal rise and fall of the murmuring tide soothed me into a daze of numbness. Pulling off my heavy boots and placing them beside a large rock, I buried my bare feet deep in the sand, letting the warmth seep into my shivering body.

I stood up and carefully picked my way over the beach. The ocean winds buffeted me from every side. I felt strangely lightheaded – as if everything inside me had been scrubbed away, clean as one of Auntie Minnah's pots. As I walked, I looked out at the waves, wondering if the mermaid was out there waiting for me to venture closer to the water. Closer to her. I rubbed at my wrist, feeling the swollen furrows beneath my fingertips.

"Never," I whispered into the breeze. "I can outlast you."

"Well, well. If it isn't the village idiot come to pay us a visit," the drawling voice of Marcus Stebbs spoke somewhere behind me.

I whirled around to find him and Cora Lynn sitting on a large grey boulder. The rocky outcropping had hidden them from my sight before. I glanced back and forth between them, wondering what they were doing out here in such a cozy, private spot. I decided I didn't want to know.

Cora Lynn smiled at me. "Adrianne, darling, how is your family?" she asked. "Is your mother feeling better these days? I heard she was deathly ill." Cora Lynn squinted as if to get a closer look at my face. I knew my eyes must be swollen with crying and my cheek a mottled red from Auntie's slap. Out of habit, I dropped my gaze.

"Mama is better," I said in a careful voice.

"I'm *so* glad to hear it," Cora Lynn said.

Why was she being so nice? Perhaps she thought Denn was somewhere nearby. I drew in the sand with my toes, refusing to say any more. Marcus slipped off the rock and came towards me. I fell back a few steps in alarm. Marcus smirked over my reaction.

"My, don't you look nice this morning, Adrianne. Is that a new skirt?" Marcus asked in a polite voice. The dress was the oldest and most ragged thing I owned.

Cora Lynn tried to stifle a giggle but failed. She buried her face behind her hands as if she thought I was too stupid to see what she was really doing. Her laughter made Marcus even worse.

"So, Adrianne, been handing out any strawberry tarts to deserving tide drifters lately – like some noble queen?" Marcus said.

Cora Lynn giggled all the more behind her splayed fingers. I stiffened, but held my tongue. I had no desire to be thrown in the tide with the mermaid still out there, waiting for her chance.

"Don't you know that feeding the riff-raff only makes more of them come to the island?" Marcus said, sticking his face right up into my own. "If Windwaithe gets overrun with drifters, I'll be forced to report to the constable that it's all your fault, Adrianne."

"No need for that," Cora Lynn said, appearing from behind her hands, a pleased smile on her lips. "Papa spoke to the constable yesterday about what happened to me. He arrested that terrible woman. She was sent off to the prison on the mainland early this morning."

I looked up, staring unflinchingly into Cora Lynn's perfect blue eyes. Horrible nausea roiled up inside my stomach. "The constable arrested her?"

"Oh, yes." Cora Lynn nodded her pretty blonde head. "She was completely out of her mind – screaming and raving all the way down to the docks. It took two men just to drag her on board the ship."

If my stomach had not been empty already I might have disgraced myself right there on the beach. I could not believe Cora Lynn could sit there and calmly tell of the torment of another human being as if it were no more than village gossip.

"What about her little girls? One was so sick." The words came out as barely a whisper.

Cora Lynn gave a careless shrug of her delicate shoulders. "They were sent along to prison with her, I dare say."

I looked at beautiful Cora Lynn, in her perfect white dress, with her fashionable new boots of kid leather, and a wave of overpowering disgust washed over me, leaving me trembling with a righteous rage I'd never known. Why had I ever felt I wanted to be like her? She was ugly – so revolting I wanted to spit at the very sight of her.

"How could you?" My voice started low, rising as emotion built inside me. "How is it possible that you, who have everything, cannot find it in your heart to have pity on one wretched creature who has nothing – absolutely nothing in the whole world!" I stared at Cora Lynn, her face now pale with horror. "You're a vicious, filthy *monster*."

Marcus seized me tightly by the collar of my dress and shook me so hard my teeth clattered together. He swung me around to face him. "Don't you dare talk to Miss Dunst like that, you ugly guttersnipe – or I'll have the constable throw you off the island with the rest of the rubbish."

Before I could even think about what I was doing, I spit in his eye. Blinded, he roared in disgust. Cora Lynn screamed. I jerked free of his grasp and bolted up the beach as fast as my bare feet could carry me.

Shouting and cursing everything around him, Marcus came thundering after me. I could hear his boots pounding the sand, gaining on me every second. In desperation, I turned towards the Rumbles, hoping to lose him across the rocks. Even with bare feet, I scampered across them with the agility born of years of experience.

Although Marcus was not as familiar with the Rumbles as I, his determination to get even with me lent him more speed than

I'd counted on. I reached the furthest rock and had to stop. No place left to go but into the sea. The pounding surf sprayed up against the rocks at my feet, sending cold droplets against my toes. Before I could think of what to do, Marcus grabbed my left wrist and yanked me sideways. We struggled towards the edge. I stumbled and for a split second my foot plunged into the shocking, cold surf, but Marcus jerked backwards hard, pulling me back on to the rock beside him. He spun us both around, putting his body between the sea and me, as if he were afraid I might try to jump in and escape.

"You're not going anywhere, Adrianne Keynnman," Marcus sneered in my face.

I thought of slapping him, but he grabbed my other wrist before I could move. I looked down at his feet, but knew that my bare heel would have no effect on the thick leather boots he wore. As I watched Marcus's foot, which lay precariously near the edge of the Rumble Stone, I saw something break the surface of the water. Smooth and dark green, a shapely hand rose up and wrapped itself around his ankle. Marcus glanced down to see what had a hold of him, and was so startled he let go of me. The mermaid's hand jerked hard, causing him to lose his footing. With a yell of terror, he toppled into the water and disappeared beneath the foamy sea.

I stared, rooted with fear. Marcus thrashed about beneath the waves, fighting for his life. For one moment, his head broke the surface, his arms flailing about him like a drowning child.

"Adrianne!" He gasped out my name only once before being dragged under again.

I knew it was not Marcus the mermaid wanted. If I jumped in, she would pull me down into the darkness instead of him. If I didn't, Marcus would die in my place.

Trembling, with fists clenched at my sides, I leaped into the sea, diving deep into its icy embrace. A flame of warmth burst to life within my chest. It expanded outward, driving back the cold. With the heat came my newfound sight, clearing faster this time.

I looked down and saw the mermaid, her hand gripping Marcus's leg as he fought madly to escape. Her purple bodice and golden tail glimmered in the shifting light of the water. Her long braids floated all around her, coiling and uncoiling like living creatures. I could see the gold crown above her forehead, and the startling golden eyes that turned to look into my own. With great deliberation, the mermaid let go of Marcus and he shot past me to the surface. I was left alone to face her.

For the third time, I was struck by the serene look upon her face. How could someone who tried to kill so coolly one moment, look so gentle and unthreatening the next? Her powerful gaze held me in place.

She reached one graceful hand out to beckon me. The glove-like sleeves that covered all but her upper arm seemed to be made of the same shimmering purple material as her sleeveless bodice.

Come.

Her lips did not move, but the word was strongly imprinted inside my head.

I opened my mouth; quiet bubbles drifted upwards. If I tried to move she would lunge and bring me back. I'd seen how fast she moved through the water. Even though I was closer to the surface, I would never be able to outswim her.

Come to me, Adrianne of Windwaithe. She gave me one of her curious smiles. I shook my head. I did not trust her.

Why didn't my lungs burn for air? How was it that I was not numb with cold? What spell had she etched into my skin with her long fingernails? Would she be able to use this same spell to make me do what she wanted? I had to get to land now or it would be too late. Kicking my legs, I churned upwards as fast as possible – half expecting to feel strong fingers clamping down on my leg to pull me back. But I swam on unhindered and broke the surface. Blindly, I tried to pull my clumsy body from the surf, and fell back, too weak. She would be on me any moment. I could not understand why she hadn't grabbed me already.

My wrist was seized by a strong hand. I fought against it, but found I had no strength left. I was yanked from the water and flung across the wet rocks, the breath knocked from me. Gasping for air, I scrambled as far from the edge as possible. I forced my blurry eyes to focus on a dripping-wet Marcus. He stood bent over me, his face whiter than I'd ever seen it, his eyes burnt red with salty ocean. I realized, with a shock, he was the one who had pulled me from the water.

"What in the devil's name was that thing?" Marcus's voice was barely a whisper. "It had fingers like a woman, but the strength of a demon."

I looked up into his eyes, forcing my shaky voice to speak steadily. "It was a mermaid."

Marcus's face turned a shade paler, his voice softer when he spoke. "Why am I not dead?"

"It wasn't you she wanted." I looked out over the water, but found no sign of her among the waves.

Marcus drew away from me, a look of true fear growing in his eyes. I couldn't blame him. Only a fool would want anything to do with a girl hunted by the Windwaithe Mermaid.

Fifteen

I sensed the change the moment our family stepped into the church. The usual gossiping voices that fluttered softly around the chapel died away in an unnatural hush. All eyes turned in our direction.

In *my* direction.

I could see them eyeing the marks on my wrist. I'd been growing so much lately that a good two and a half inches of scarred skin showed beneath the hem of my sleeve. If only I'd thought to wear a bandage that day. If only I'd stayed away from the fortune-teller's tent or gone anywhere but to the beach the day Auntie Minnah slapped me. If only, if only, if only.

Had I really believed that Marcus would keep the encounter with the mermaid to himself? I'd been a fool to think that those few moments of common purpose we'd shared fighting the Windwaithe Mermaid would change Marcus in any way. I should have known it would only be a matter of hours before the whole island knew everything about it – but I'd hoped. First the fuss with the fortune-teller and now this. In the eyes of my neighbours, the evidence against me looked grave indeed.

Mama looked around at the blatant stares, and gave some of them a nervous smile. People turned away, as if ashamed. Some hurried past us, as if the welts on my wrist might be catching. The Dunsts came in behind us. Cora Lynn gave me one furious glare before stalking past me with her nose in the air. The rest of her family avoided our eyes while making their way to their seats.

The only person who bothered to greet us was Mrs Rousay, who pointedly approached us amid stunned silence. Mrs Rousay asked kindly after Mama's health as pleasantly as she would have without dozens of disapproving ears listening to every word she said. Only then did she lead her three-year-old daughter away to their regular seats up front.

"Let's go sit down," I whispered, determined to keep my back to the suspicious glances.

I took Mama's arm, thinking to help her to her seat. The ancient wood of the chapel floor creaked ominously beneath our feet, begrudging us each step we took. Cecily rushed ahead to greet three girls her own age as they sat whispering together at the end of a long pew. One of them giggled behind her hand as

Cecily came near. My sister smiled, but they pretended not to see. Cecily stood there in silence, her big brown eyes blinking uncertainly. Auntie Minnah grabbed Cecily's arm and rushed my sister up the aisle so fast she almost tripped.

Auntie's tense face told me she knew something was wrong, but she hadn't yet figured out what. It would only be a matter of time before she'd think to blame me for it.

We took our seats. The pews on either side of ours were conspicuously empty. I would have given anything to see Denn's teasing grin in the sea of hostile faces. The Youngs had sent their empty carriage to our cottage with a message telling us they would not be attending with us as they usually did. The two youngest were sick and Denn and his mother would be staying home to nurse them. Mr Stebbs had not allowed his family to darken the church doors for years. Without Marcus there, I was left to face the accusing congregation alone.

Auntie Minnah sat as tall and rigid as a tree, her eyes staring straight ahead. Mama glanced around, a bewildered look on her face. Meg Lyre, the tavern maid, passed by and made a quick sign against evil, peering darkly at me. Though I pretended not to notice, there was no denying my family had seen her make the gesture. Auntie Minnah's accusing gaze bored into me.

I ignored her by pretending to carefully study the large stained-glass window behind the pulpit. It depicted an avenging angel standing against a sea of clouds, a splendid figure dressed in flowing robes. His great, feathered wings stretched behind him like those of an eagle in flight. He had a drawn sword in his hand, as if he were about to deal out death and punishment on the unsuspecting members of the congregation below. I was greatly relieved when the service began.

The minister came in and stood at the pulpit; his eyes swept the congregation till they fell on me. He gave me a barely perceptible smile and winked to show he didn't believe a word of the gossip he'd heard about me.

Every word he preached that day spoke against belief in strange superstitions and wild stories. I suppose he meant to be helpful, but everyone in the congregation got the opposite message. My involvement with a mermaid made me guilty of exactly what he spoke of. Every time the minister made a particularly strong argument, Mrs Dethers, in the row behind us, rapped her cane against the back of my seat, taking great pains I should notice. I ground my teeth together, forcing myself to ignore them all.

Mama put her trembling hand on my wrist. Did she mean to comfort me – or herself, I wondered? Her fingers brushed my scar and the skin burned dully beneath her touch. The pain reminded me of the horrified face of the fortune-teller when she first saw marks in my flesh. Was it pure fear that had kept the woman from telling anyone about the marks and their significance?

The fortune-teller!

Why had I not thought of her before? The very sight of the marks had terrified her. She knew something about them. I had to find out what. Somehow, I had to make her listen and answer my questions. Hadn't Hannah said the fortune-teller was staying on the island for a month? Would her tent still be staked at the bottom of the orchard? It had to be.

As soon as the final prayer was said, I leaped to my feet and pushed my way down the aisle toward the doors leading out of the church. Mama called my name, but I pretended not to hear.

I was numb the whole trip, not thinking or caring about anything but getting to the fortune-teller as quickly as possible. When I finally found myself standing outside her tent, I looked it over while trying to catch my breath. The colourful tent silks billowed in the gusting winds from the sea. I pulled my shawl tighter around me, brushing a lock of my short hair out of my eyes. What would I do if she screamed and carried on as she had the night of the wedding feast? Taking a deep gulp of air, I stepped inside.

I'd caught the fortune-teller packing. She had her back to me, so she didn't notice my arrival. I watched in silence as she tore each strange item from its place and flung it into a heavy wooden trunk sitting in one corner. Dried bundles of herbs, shimmering scarves, and the rigid bodies of dead animals all quickly disappeared into its dark depths.

"You're leaving before the month is up?" I asked.

She froze, a long silken scarf dangling limply from one hand. Her chest heaved with fear beneath her dark brown robes.

"I knew you'd be back." She didn't bother turning around as

she spoke. "The moment I heard the story of what happened to the boy from the village I knew you would come back here."

Slowly she turned around, her eyes solid pools of black glaring up at me from under thick, dark lashes. "I can do nothing to help you. Leave me in peace."

"You must tell me all you know about this mark." I pulled back the long sleeve of my dress to show the scars. She stared at them, fascination and terror fighting in the depths of her black eyes.

"The one who gave you that – did she have skin the colour of jade and such beauty it was almost terrible to look upon?" She spoke as one caught in a trance.

I nodded, still holding out my wrist.

"The mark you bear is one of powerful magic. Lady Lauretta had one just like it, put upon her wrist by the hand of the Windwaithe Mermaid."

"How do you know this?"

She looked up at me, her bottomless black eyes unblinking. "My great-grandmother was a maid in the house of Old Lord Durran. She was there the night Lady Lauretta came back to tell her father she would leave him for ever. I know everything that transpired that wretched night."

"The mermaid tried to take my little sister. Tell me what I must do to make her go away." My voice sounded like that of a desperate child.

"You can't make her go away. Not once she has made up her

mind to take a victim." The fortune-teller eyed my scars. "Answer me this. If the mermaid is after your sister, as you say, why did she mark *your* wrist?"

"I – I'm not sure." I blinked against the tears of frustration burning at my eyes. I didn't want this cold young woman to see my weakness. "One night, during a storm, the mermaid tried to take my sister. When I interrupted her, she grabbed my arm and tried to drown me. She hurt my wrist before I could get away."

The fortune-teller widened her eyes, her nostrils flared like that of a frightened horse. "Foolish girl. Do you realize what you've done? You came between a mermaid and her prey, and by so doing, have cursed yourself."

I jerked back my arm as if I'd been bitten.

"She will wait for as long as it takes to seek her revenge on you," she said.

I felt as though I was spiralling down a dark well. Everything inside me felt cold and slippery. "There must be some way to get rid of her," I whispered.

"Lady Lauretta's father tried to get rid of the mermaid. It only brought her ire down on the whole island. It is only a matter of time before she uses her powers again. That is why I leave tonight. This island and all the people on it are doomed."

"There must be something that can be done to stop her!" I cried.

"There is." The fortune-teller looked deep into my eyes. "You can sacrifice yourself, just as Lady Lauretta did. Your death would satisfy her."

"Death?" My body turned cold around me. "Lady Lauretta didn't die, she married the Sea Prince."

The fortune-teller laughed, a hard, cheerless sound that filled the canvas enclosure. "Sea Prince. There was no Sea Prince. Those stories were nothing but lies to lure Lady Lauretta willingly to her fate. My great-grandmother saw Lauretta the night she came home to say goodbye. Chilled and soaking wet, the young woman's eyes sparkled with feverish joy as she repeated the stories the mermaid told her of a handsome prince living in a golden castle beneath the sea."

The fortune-teller spat on the floor as if speaking about it gave her a foul taste. "The mermaid had spun spells so strong, the girl was convinced she had seen this place with her own eyes. She claimed she could breathe seawater like air. Even her own father could not convince her of the truth. For weeks he fought against the mermaid's influence, but the magic was too strong – etched as it was into her very skin. The girl was so deeply under the spell she dreamed she could hear the mermaid calling her, even when she was awake. She spoke strange words no one could understand while she slept."

I stared at her, horror spreading through my body like ice. Lady Lauretta's story was only too familiar.

"In the end, she begged her father to let her go," the fortune-teller went on. "Told him she wanted to go – the bewitched fool – even tried to sneak out in the middle of the night. She wept from sunrise to sunset and finally refused to eat. In the end, the villagers came in an angry mob and forced him to let her go. It almost killed him."

I could barely get the words out now. "If there is no prince, what did the mermaid want with Lady Lauretta?"

"Mermaids take those of the land for only one reason." The dark eyes flashed at me. "To sacrifice them to the ancient demons they worship. It gives them more power."

My breathing came in small, shallow gasps. Was that really what the mermaid wanted with my sister? A willing human sacrifice?

"Never." The whispered word came from my throat, but it sounded nothing like my own voice. My shoulders fell back and my spine straightened. The fortune-teller cringed, afraid of something she saw in my face.

"It will be different this time," I said. "What happened to Lady Lauretta will not happen again. I swear by all that is good, she will not have my sister. The Windwaithe Mermaid will have to deal with me first."

"Idiot girl," the fortune-teller woman said in a subdued voice. "The Windwaithe Mermaid cares nothing for your sister now. It is *you* she has marked as her victim. And she will let nothing stand in her way."

Sixteen

Dirt and gravel crunched beneath my heels as I made my way gingerly down a rocky path along the western slope. The words of the fortune-teller swept around inside my head like a whirlwind.

Demons. Evil magic spells. Lady Lauretta wanting to go to the sea. She'd wept and begged to go. My steps lagged slower and slower the more I thought about it. If the mermaid could cast such a powerful spell over Lady Lauretta, why hadn't she done so to me – or to Cecily? She had, in fact, managed to convince my sister never to go near the water again for fear of sharks.

The fortune-teller believed I was now the one the Windwaithe Mermaid meant to kill, but if that were true why did the mermaid grab Cecily, rather than me, the day the skiff overturned? None of it made sense.

Perhaps this mermaid was a different one who had no powers of persuasion. But she did have powers. I remembered the fateful day on the Rumbles. For a moment, I'd felt myself falling into a state of complacency that I'd only just shaken out of in time. Why hadn't the mermaid used those powers then? And why did she go away when Denn came? Couldn't she have drowned him as easily as she wanted to drown me? Why didn't her wrath extend to him?

I gave my head a fierce shake. Nothing made sense any more.

A sudden movement up the hill shifted my attention back to the moment at hand. I had reached Cormy's Wood. The northern slope was covered with large masses of living green. Craning my neck, I tried to catch a glimpse of what creature might be moving among the dense tree growth. The throaty neigh of a horse came from just out of sight. I stopped short in surprise.

There were no pastures this far out and the only riding anyone did on the Sabbath was to and from church, with occasional wagon-drawn visits between neighbours in the cool evenings. I would have heard a rider or wagon approaching long before now.

Hesitating only a moment, I stepped from the road and made my way up the rocky, tree-covered hill that ran along the edge of the main path. I found it rough going at first; the loose pebbles and steep grassy banks made scrabbling up its side difficult. As

I fought my way through the thick underbrush, I saw the powerful, dark form of my old friend, Dartemore, the manor stallion standing before me. His sharp ears pricked at the sound of my steps and he swivelled his head in my direction. Sensitive nostrils inhaled my scent and, recognizing me, he gave a warm, welcoming whicker.

I stared at him in complete bewilderment. He was tacked up in saddle and bridle, but his reins lay limp across a lichen-covered log – the massive tree it had fallen from bore scorch marks down both its sides, attesting to a lightning strike a long time ago.

Dartemore's saddle sat empty.

A foreboding chill shivered through my body. I rubbed at the gooseflesh rising along my arms and was filled with nameless horror. I had done this before. Stood like this, with the warm sun beating down on my head, the steamy smell of horseflesh filling my nostrils. A lone horse standing riderless on the grassy banks of a hill just like this one.

No, I couldn't think about that day! I would not let myself be overwhelmed by the mere memory of it.

Dartemore tried to come to me, but was pulled up short by one of the reins tangled in the branches of the log. He threw his head and snorted as if to ask what was taking me so long to loose him. Every part of me screamed to run, to get away as fast as possible. Still, I could not leave the stallion standing there helpless.

I forced myself to walk to his side, made myself work the leather strap free with clumsy, shaking fingers. He nuzzled me in thanks.

I spoke aloud to the horse, hoping the sound of my own voice would break the icy spell that had come over me. "What are you doing so far from the manor?"

Dartemore had no answer to give me. Gathering his reins in one hand, I turned him about, thinking to lead him back on foot. The stallion followed docilely at my side.

I stumbled wildly over something hidden in the tall grass. I looked down and saw the boot. A man's black riding boot.

As if in a nightmare, I found I could not look away. My gaze followed the boot to the rest of Master Wickliff, where he lay, pale and lifeless in the grass, wildflowers waving lazily around him.

A strangled sound came from my constricted throat. Darkness drew close around me, making it hard to breathe. Two long years rolled back from my life in the span of a few seconds, dragging me to that day so long ago. I looked down at Papa's body, deathly still at the bottom of the gully. The landscape whirled, sucking me down into its heavy blackness.

No! I staggered, trying to break out of the memory's crushing grip. I fell heavily against Dartemore's solid, warm side, catching at his mane with my groping fingers. The stallion's wet muzzle touched my face in concern. His comforting, hot breath melted away some of the panic that had frozen my insides.

I would not let the fear take me this time. I couldn't give in.

Taking a few trembling steps, I forced myself to move closer to Master Wickliff's side. I had to know the worst. I had to be sure he really was dead. I could not leave until I knew for certain. Putting out my shaking hand, I held it hesitantly above the man's mouth and nose. At first I felt nothing – then a shallow breath warmed my fingertips.

He lived!

There was still time to save him.

Save him the way I had never had a chance to save Papa. I glanced helplessly around me until my eyes fell on Dartemore, waiting patiently where I'd left him.

I couldn't ride ever again, part of me whispered. If I'd never learned to ride in the first place, Papa would still be alive.

I had to ride.

No, I couldn't do it. Never again. I'd promised!

Master Wickliff would die, just like Papa.

I couldn't do it. I couldn't, couldn't, couldn't! My fingernails dug painfully into my scalp as I clawed through my hair with grasping fingers.

You have to do it.

Something calmer and greater rose up in me. I was the only one who could get help in time – get help the way I should have two years ago.

My foot was in the stirrup before I even knew what was happening.

Run for help. The thought was a command this time.

I swung myself on to Dartemore's back. The unbroken stallion half reared, but years of experience made my seat confident and my hands firm as I reined him in. He threw his head and danced sideways. I'd forgotten how tall it felt to sit upon the back of a horse. Raw power coiled beneath me, ready to spring into action at the slightest cause. I forced myself not to think, but to ride as Papa taught me, to bend a mount's will to mine.

Using my calves and legs, I urged Dartemore gently forward. He responded by bursting into a wild trot, almost unseating me. I barely had time to recover my balance when he broke into a canter, then a flying gallop. We swept over the land as if we were no longer bound to the earth, only to each other. I let him go, crouched low over his neck, settling myself into his pounding stride. We were one creature, thundering along together, gaining speed I'd never imagined possible. My heart and his hooves beat in time. It was magic. Like waking from a long sleep, I was more alive than I'd ever been. There was no fear, only sweeping exhilaration and breathless wonder. How much I had missed the freedom of riding!

We leaped a ditch without missing a step. A sweet wind rushed past my face, whipping at my short hair. My mind was clear. I could hear Dartemore's breath rushing in and out of his great lungs as he stretched himself out again and again, eating up the distance with his powerful legs. Matching my breath to his, I kept my arms in rhythm with his surging neck. We careened over the island fields, two creatures gone mad with joy.

A fence loomed before us. I felt Dartemore ready himself for the jump. I gathered myself in the stirrups. We sailed over as if we had wings upon our backs. I didn't have to direct him. He sensed getting me to the manor was the most important task in the world.

Someone sent up a cry of alarm as we tore up the hill almost to the very door of the manor house. Shifting my seat deep into the saddle and pulling back on the reins, I forced Dartemore to check his speed. Two stable hands ran to meet me, shouting in loud angry voices to dismount at once. I ignored them, all my attention on Dartemore, who plunged and reared, ears pinned flat against the sides of his head, clearly upset by all the confusion. I caught sight of Mr Chatsworth, the head groom, racing towards us from the stable.

"Go get the doctor immediately!" I shouted at him. "Master Wickliff has fallen and is badly hurt!"

Mr Chatsworth's mouth fell open. Without a word he turned himself about and sped off towards the manor.

A rough hand grabbed my left wrist and dragged me from the saddle to the ground. "Are you mad, girl?" the stableman restraining me yelled. "Lord Durran will have all our jobs if he learns you rode that stallion without permission!"

Dartemore screamed in fury and lunged at the man holding me. We barely made it out of the way of the stallion's flashing teeth. Two men moved to block the stallion. Dartemore reared, striking at them with his hooves.

I strained to get closer, but the stableman dragged me backward, forcing me further from Dartemore's side. More men rushed to help corner the stallion. The whites of his eyes showing, Dartemore turned his haunches to them and struck out at the nearest man.

"Stop it!" I screamed at them. "You're making him worse!"

"WHAT is going on here?" The voice of command broke through the bedlam like a cracking whip. Lord Durran strode up, his steel gaze cutting through the crowd till he found me. The hands that held me fell away. Even Dartemore fell silent as he danced at the end of his reins.

I looked into Lord Durran's calm face. Opening my mouth I tried to speak but my voice came out unsteady. "M-Master Wickliff . . . f-fallen."

His dark eyebrows drew sharply together. He spoke only one word. "Where?"

"The western slope of Cormy's Wood. Under the tree once struck by lightning."

"Chatsworth, I'll need a mount saddled at once," Lord Durran said. The head groom and four other men took off towards the stable at a dead run.

Something about Lord Durran's calm, no-nonsense manner caused all the tension to leak from my body, leaving me weak and lightheaded. I knew I should go with them, to show the way. I tried to take a step forward. My knees felt as if they were made of the same unsubstantial material as jellyfish. Next thing I knew, I was face down in the grass, everything spiralling about me.

Someone called out in alarm. Dartemore's shrill neigh echoed inside my whirling head. It sounded so far away. I sank into a shadowy place of blessed silence.

Seventeen

My eyelids felt like they had been tied shut. I groaned, blindly touching a hesitant hand to my still-spinning head. I sensed myself lying on some kind of sofa, a goose-down pillow beneath my head.

"I think she's coming around, my lady," said an older woman's voice.

"That's all right, Mrs Grenall. You can put the tea down on the table and go back to your work. I will see to her myself." The voice that spoke was as soft and sweet as a child's. It could have belonged to an angelic being. For one mad moment, I thought I must have died.

Forcing my eyes open, I found myself staring up into the fair, delicate face of Lord Graham's young bride, Lady Amelia. The middle-aged housekeeper at her side gave her mistress a curious look and curtsied before letting herself out of the room. I watched her go with a sinking feeling. A lady of the manor never waited on someone beneath her. What was going on?

"Are you feeling better, dear?" Lady Amelia asked, her gentle blue eyes filled with concern.

To my left appeared a handsome young man who couldn't have been more than nineteen years of age. It was Lord Graham himself. I remembered vaguely that Hannah had mentioned something about the bridal couple putting off their wedding tour till Captain Young could return, but my muddled mind made details hard to grasp.

Lord Graham put an arm around the shoulders of his pretty wife, but looked at me as he spoke. "Back in the land of the living, are we?"

I glanced around, noting that I seemed to be in some kind of fancy sitting room. Even the ceiling was sculpted over with intricately carved vines of blooming roses.

"Where am I, my lord?" I could hardly find my voice. They talked to me as if I were of their standing. I was at a loss as to how to respond.

"You're in the manor house, by Father's order, of course," Lord Graham said.

My heart leaped into my throat and stuck there. "What am I doing here?" I asked. Had I been brought into the manor house to be punished for my recklessness in riding Dartemore without permission?

"Father said you were to be kept here and treated with great care till he returned from dealing with his erstwhile horse master. And I, being the dutiful son that I am, have done exactly as commanded." Lord Graham gave me a mischievous grin. It only served to make me even more uneasy.

"Erstwhile? I'm afraid I don't understand, my lord," I said.

"Graham, stop teasing her," Lady Amelia said in a voice not unlike a pouting child. "Can't you see she's been through enough already?" Lady Amelia slid out from under her husband's hand and put a gentle arm around my shoulders to help me sit up. My head felt much steadier now.

"You've been very courageous. A true heroine, just like in the storybooks." The reverence in her voice calmed the fluttering in my stomach. She spoke as if what I had done raised me, temporarily, above the rules of class distinction. She smiled. It made her look so young I found it hard to remember she was not only a married woman, but also a lady of high standing.

"What happened to Master Wickliff?" I asked.

"He's got himself a right nasty bump on the head," Lord Graham said, flicking at some unseen bit of lint on his coat sleeve. "He's a little out of sorts right now, but the doctor says he'll recover in time, thanks to your quick thinking." He kept looking down at me with his head cocked to one side, as if I were some kind of strange new creature he'd never seen before.

Grudging admiration crept into the young lord's tone as he spoke. "How did you convince that wild beast of a stallion to let you up on his back? There isn't a man on this manor that hasn't tried and been thrown on his ear for his trouble. And yet, you not only got up on him, but you *rode* him all the way here, as pretty as you please. That will be one in the eye for all the good horsemen around here, won't it?" Lord Graham chuckled to himself, as if I had played an extremely good joke on them all.

"That is quite enough, Graham. This young woman needs rest, not more of your unceasing talk. Off with you now." She stood up and shooed him away with both hands. He grabbed one of them and kissed it, making her blush a pretty pink. Giving me a conspiring wink, Lord Graham left the room.

"Honestly, I don't know what comes over him sometimes." The amused smile playing about her lips suggested otherwise.

She sat down with such grace it could have been part of a dance. Trying to regain her composure, she arranged her long skirts with the air of a princess. "Your father was the horse master before Mr Wickliff, wasn't he?"

I stared down at the richly embroidered rug covering the floor and forced myself to nod in answer.

Lady Amelia turned to a silver tray beside her. On it sat a delicate, rose-spray teapot. She poured two matching cups full of steaming liquid and handed one to me. "My father-in-law has much good to say of your father. Much more than he has of that awful man, Mr Wickliff. It was a mistake hiring him, but that's going to be put to rights now."

"You mean he's been sacked?" I was so surprised I forgot

myself. She didn't seem to notice my rude behaviour.

"I should be surprised if he wasn't." I noticed her fiddling with the solid gold band on her left hand, as if she wasn't used to its weight yet. "After Lord Durran carried you into the house, he stormed out of here in quite a temper. He gave an order weeks ago for Wickliff not to try to break the stallion again. Obviously, Wickliff chose not to listen."

Lady Amelia took a graceful sip of her tea before going on. "Whatever could the man have been thinking, taking an unbroken horse out alone? And on the Sabbath, no less?" She shook her lovely little head back and forth in refined disbelief.

I stared down into my steaming teacup. Who would be the horse master now?

The sound of heavy boots crossing the threshold of the room startled me out of my train of thought. Lord Durran ducked slightly as he entered and Lord Graham followed right behind him. Hot tea spilled down the front of my dress. I put the cup down with a clatter, feeling very much as if I'd been caught helping myself without permission.

Lady Amelia rose gracefully to her feet to greet them. "Is everything all right?"

Lord Durran nodded before motioning with one hand for his daughter-in-law to be seated again.

"What happened?" Lady Amelia sat down beside me once more.

"Mr Wickliff is no longer under my employ. He will be

asked to leave the island as soon as he is fit to travel," Lord Durran said.

Lady Amelia gave an approving nod as she took another sip of her tea.

"And that only leaves you to deal with," Lord Durran's stone-coloured eyes turned to me. My stomach twisted itself into an uneasy knot. So, I was to be punished after all.

"Did your father let you ride Dartemore when you were young?" he asked in a soft voice. I was surprised by this question.

"No, my lord," I said. "Papa never let me ride any of the manor horses without asking your leave first."

Those eyes of his seemed to stare into my soul. I was positive he would spot any lie a person might try to utter in his presence. He nodded his head, as if making up his mind.

"I believe you," he said.

"But how did you manage to ride that beast without him throwing you?" Lord Graham asked with wide, unbelieving eyes.

I didn't answer. Lord Durran spoke with the gentle, steady tones I'd heard him use on many a spooked horse in his stable.

"Dartemore always favoured you, didn't he? Even as a colt he would only come when you called him, would only let himself be led by your hand."

"It would seem he still favours her," said Lord Graham with a chuckle.

"So it does." Lord Durran rubbed at his chin, his brow

furrowed as he contemplated me.

"I will be placing Chatsworth temporarily in charge of the horses. That will leave me shorthanded in the stables," Lord Durran's gaze was riveted to my face. "I would like it very much, Miss Keynnman, if you might consider helping me with Dartemore's training. You would be paid for your services, of course – the same wages as the other stable hands."

Out of the corner of my eye, I saw Lord Graham give a start. Lady Amelia's hand flew to her mouth and she gave a little gasp of shock. No fourteen-year-old girl had ever been paid a man's wages in all the history of Windwaithe. Lord Durran ignored his son's and daughter-in-law's reactions, looking only for mine.

"No man has been able to tame that horse. Perhaps it is time we let a woman try her hand at the job," he said.

I could only stare, my jaw slack with shock. A woman, he'd called me. And yet I'd never felt so young and afraid. How could I ride again after failing Papa?

Perhaps Lord Durran sensed something of my dilemma. "I think your father would have wanted you to do this," he said. "Those who have gone before would not want us to deny ourselves those things that bring simple pleasure. It will not help anyone, least of all them. You have a gift that should not be wasted. Do you not see that you are meant to do this?"

I thought about all the hard work I'd done and all the prayers I'd breathed out over the past two years, begging for a way to provide for my family. Was this the answer? It would not be an easy task. There would be many who would resent my being a girl. But if I took the job, my family would never want again. And I did miss riding so much.

"Will you do it?" Lord Durran asked.

My eyes stung, and my throat was so tight I couldn't speak. I dipped my head in assent. For the first time, I saw His Lordship's eyes crinkle up at the corners and his lips spread into a real smile.

"Done and done then," he said, putting out an immaculate, gloved hand. I reached out my dirt-soiled fingers and shook on the bargain.

Eighteen

The sun hung low in the rose-coloured sky when I finally started for home. I wondered if Mama would be worried about me yet. Of course, gossip being what it was on a small island like ours, she might have already heard of my adventures. Still I hastened my pace, anxious to reach home before it got dark.

Mr Stebbs and Marcus passed me on the road, driving their wagon towards home. I cordially stepped aside to let them pass. Mr Stebbs had the jowls of a bulldog and the build of a bull ox. It was said that Obadiah Stebbs was a brutal and heavy-handed taskmaster to those who worked beneath him. The glower he levelled in my direction made me wonder, for the first time, if perhaps he didn't employ these same cruel methods upon his wife and seven children. I glanced at Marcus in sudden curiosity.

He turned his head away, refusing to even look in my direction – but not before I saw the fear glittering in his eyes. The tips of his ears glowed as red as the glorious sunset behind him. Marcus Stebbs was afraid of me and his fear shamed him.

After they'd gone, I stood in the middle of the road and sighed. A different part of my life had now begun. I wasn't sure if it would be better or worse.

The wind stirred the leaves on the trees. Tendrils of my short hair tickled my forehead. Somewhere nearby a seagull screamed at the sky.

Laying a hand against my chest, I had the oddest sensation that my heart was being drawn out of me, lifted out across the land towards the surging surf shifting in the distance.

Come to me.

I stopped breathing, every part of me straining, waiting for the words to come again.

Come to me, Adrianne of Windwaithe. Meet me between moonlit rock and dark ocean.

My right wrist pulsed strangely – the welts swelling in and out as if they were part of a breathing creature. A vision rose up before my eyes, blotting out the world around me. Like ghostly spectres, the forms of hulking rocks sat glittering in the light of a full moon. Thundering surf pounded against them, engulfing everything in a glowing mist.

Between moonlit rock and dark ocean.

"Adri?"

I jerked back to the present so suddenly my teeth rattled. I spun around to find Denn standing not three feet from me. I hadn't even heard him approach.

He peered into my face, his brow furrowed in concern. "Are you all right?"

I forced myself to draw air into my lungs. "I – I'm not sure," I said, still shaky.

"Your mother got worried when you didn't come home. She sent me to find you." He took a step closer, one hand held out as if to catch me at any moment. "Are you ill? You're very pale."

I stepped back from him and folded my arms close to my body as if to drive out the sudden cold settling over me. "I'm fine."

"You don't look fine," Denn said.

I could see worry growing in the depths of his eyes. His concern made my throat constrict. I turned quickly from him, not wanting him to see me cry.

I noticed Lark was with him. The dog stood a few paces from us, her head cocked to one side, tail still and solemn. Denn put a hand on my shoulder. I clenched my teeth against the sobs that fought to rip free of my throat.

"I heard about what happened at church today, but you mustn't let Marcus win, Adri. This story he's made up is just another one of his ways to get at you. In time, everyone on the island will come around and see what foolish nonsense it is."

"It's not foolish nonsense!" I whirled on Denn, hot tears

beginning to sting my eyes.

Denn squinted in disbelief, studying me. "Are you saying Marcus's story is true?"

"As true as we're standing here."

Denn pulled off his cap and ran a hand through his unruly red curls before he stopped to regard me. I could hardly stand to look into those disbelieving green eyes any longer, so I turned towards the ocean. I could see it glimmering at the western edge of the island.

"She's still out there," I said. My voice sounded strangely distant. "She won't go away till she gets what she wants."

"Wait a minute," Denn said. "You really expect me to believe some mermaid tried to drown Marcus?"

"Marcus wasn't the one she wanted to kill – I was."

"You?" I'd never seen Denn look so flabbergasted. "But Marcus said she attacked him."

"She knew I would jump in to save him."

"There are no such things as mermaids and if there were, why would one want to kill *you*?"

I breathed in a slow sigh. "She tried to take Cecily that night at the Rumbles. When I tried to stop her, the mermaid grabbed my arm and tried to drown me instead. I barely got away with my life."

"I didn't see any mermaid that night," Denn said.

"She didn't want you to see her any more than she wanted you to see her the day she overturned your family's boat."

Denn's jaw fell open, his lips moved, but nothing came out of his mouth. His eyes darted to the welts on my wrist. Uncertainty clouded his features.

"She tried to drown Cecily that day, but I attacked her and made her let go. She was the one who grabbed my leg and tried to pull me under."

"Impossible." But he didn't sound so sure of himself this time. He'd felt the power that tried to take me. He'd fought against it with all the strength he possessed. Denn shook his head as if to clear it.

"Now you've got me half believing this nonsense," he said with a frown. "Encouraging this superstitious blather will only make things worse, Adrianne."

He was not going to accept the truth, no matter what proof I presented. This knowledge made my heart feel as if it were trapped in a hollow cavern. But I couldn't stop myself from talking now that I'd begun. Turning from him, I spoke as if to the air around me.

"I hear her all the time now." My voice was like a soft breath of wind. "She comes to me in my dreams at night and calls out across the land to me by day. She wants me to come to her, just as she wanted Lady Lauretta. She calls and calls, knowing eventually I'll go."

Denn grabbed my shoulders and shook me roughly to break me out of the daze I'd fallen into. I looked up at him. His face was pale, and fear had wiped all traces of humour from it. He looked more like a man than a boy that way.

"I'm taking you home to your mother. It's been a long day. You need some rest." He turned to the dog. "Come on, Lark, let's go."

The setter stood rooted to the spot. Denn slapped at his thigh and whistled. Lark's ears drooped and she let out a frightened whine. Still she would not come near. Her brown eyes were sad as she stared at me – her muzzle lifted, trembling in fear.

"She knows," I said.

Denn turned to me. "Knows? Knows what?"

"That I'm marked by the Windwaithe Mermaid."

Denn stared for a moment. He opened his mouth to speak just as a high voice called through the air.

"Yoo-hoo, De-enn."

Both of us looked back to see Cora Lynn Dunst mincing her way along the rocky path towards us. She waved at Denn. I turned away, determined not to let her see my swollen, red eyes. Denn looked at Cora Lynn, then back at me, clearly torn.

"Denn – I mean – Mr Young." Cora Lynn gave him a simpering smile as she stopped before us. "Papa saw you passing on the road in front of the house and sent me out to invite you in for supper. It's such a long way to your home from here. You must be famished."

"I – I, right now I need to—" Denn glanced in my direction.

Cora Lynn shot me a scathing look. "*She's* not invited. I'm not speaking to her again after the way she treated me at the beach the other day."

"Treated you?" Denn turned with narrowed eyes on Cora Lynn. "What has Adrianne ever done to you?"

Cora Lynn put her hands on her hips, her lips set in a delicate pout. "She called me a monster. She said I was horrible, and after I'd been so nice to her, too. And when Marcus tried to defend my honour, she went and called up a demon mermaid to kill him."

I'd heard quite enough. With a snort of disgust, I turned my back on her and started up the path for home. Lark scampered out of my way, tail between her legs. Denn called out to me.

"Let her go," I heard Cora Lynn say in a purring tone. "Everyone on the island knows what she is now. You wouldn't want to be seen with her. People might get the wrong idea about the two of you."

I lengthened my stride and walked along the dusty road, trying not to let myself feel a thing. A bubble of numbness encircled me, driving out all thoughts of Denn and what had happened that day. I refused to even glance at the Dunst cottage as I passed by it.

I hadn't gone more than a half mile when I heard Denn call out to me. Wonderful. All I needed was Cora Lynn to witness Denn yelling at me all over creation. I tried to pretend I didn't hear him, but his long strides soon caught him up to me.

"Adrianne, will you stop already? You're going to make yourself ill walking home at such a pace." I could hear Denn beginning to lose his temper again. I stopped but didn't face him.

"I told you not to go stomping off like that any more." Denn sounded like he was working himself into the mood for a real lecture. I turned to see if Cora Lynn was enjoying the show. Only a sheepish Lark stood on the path behind us, her tail tucked meekly between her legs.

"Adri, are you even listening to me?" Denn asked.

"Where's Cora Lynn?"

"Forget Cora Lynn. It's you I'm worried about. You're talking like a mad person."

"Aren't you going to go eat supper with the Dunsts?"

"No, I'm not eating with the Dunsts. And after the tongue lashing Cora Lynn just gave me for sticking up for you, I don't think she plans to ever ask me again."

I bit my lip till it hurt. Once again, I had let my own problems affect someone else's life. What kind of selfish friend was I, coming between Denn and the girl he loved most in the world?

"Go," I said, clasping my hands before me, begging Denn to listen. "Go after her as fast as you can. If you apologize right away she'll forgive you, I know she will."

Denn shook his head.

"Don't be a stubborn idiot. Don't you see she wants you to go after her? You can still have supper with her father if you leave now."

"I don't want to have supper with the Dunsts!" Denn shouted.

"And I won't apologize to Cora Lynn or anybody else who believes that pile of nonsense about you selling your soul to mermaids." He looked away from me, struggling to gain some control again. He spoke so softly I could barely hear him. "There are no such things as mermaids."

A shiver ran through my body. The cold of the evening seeped through my thin dress into my bones. I half expected Denn's words to bring the Windwaithe Mermaid's voice, calling my name on the breeze. Denn's warm touch settled on my shoulder. I turned my face to him. His eyes searched mine as if he thought he might find answers hidden there.

Why couldn't it have been me he loved? If I had even the smallest portion of Cora Lynn's power, I would have had the courage to tell him what I really felt for him. How much he meant to me.

"Don't look that way," Denn said, dropping his hand. He rubbed his fingers lightly against his pant leg as if trying to brush something off his skin.

"What way?" I asked.

He stopped rubbing, and hesitated before answering. "Sometimes your eyes get filled with such sadness. They're like those of a grown woman rather than a young girl." Denn's tone was so low I could hardly make out the words. "Those beautiful eyes haunt me – even when I'm asleep."

"Then don't look at them." I stepped away from him, but he grabbed my arm and hauled me back.

"Where do you think you're going?" he asked.

"Home, of course."

"Not to the beach?"

I tried to shake loose of his hold. Seeing it was useless, I gave him one of those wide-eyed looks of innocence Cecily always seemed to manage so well. "Why would I want to go to the beach?"

I must have overdone it. Denn pushed his face in close to mine. "Listen to me, Adrianne Keynnman. You're not to try anything rash or foolish before tomorrow morning, do you hear me? We'll figure out together what to do about all this gossip. Right now, I'm going to escort you home and if I find out that you set even one toenail out of doors this night, I will be very, very angry. Understand?"

I looked up at him. Our noses inches apart. "For someone who doesn't believe in mermaids, you seemed awfully edgy to me, Mr Young."

"Get going," Denn gave me a shove in the direction of home. "And don't forget, I'm right behind you."

He needn't have bothered. The ocean was the last place I wanted to go. Death lay waiting for me there.

Nineteen

I told Mama and Auntie Minnah about Master Wickliff's accident. I explained about the job Lord Durran had offered me as a reward for saving the man's life. Auntie Minnah stood before me the whole time, her dark eyes gleaming with a feverish light.

"So far I have heard you admit to desecrating God's holy day and placing yourself above your proper station, but not a single word about the wild stories spreading over the whole island," Auntie said with deathly calm.

I looked at her. My lips pressed tight together.

Auntie lost her patience first. "Did you, or did you not, entangle yourself with one of the most evil and vile creatures in all of God's creations?" she demanded.

"There are no such things as mermaids," I said.

Without a word, Auntie turned and marched into the bedroom. Mama gazed at me with frightened eyes.

I had no room left inside me for anger. I could not blame Auntie for feeling the way she did, nor could I hate her for doing so.

"She'll get over it in time," Mama said in a hesitant attempt to comfort me.

"No." My voice was trancelike. "Not over this."

I picked up a candle and walked slowly to the bedroom. Cecily, fully clothed, was fast asleep in our bed. It had been a long day for all of us. I slipped into my thin nightdress before putting out the light and climbing on to the straw pallet beside my sleeping sister.

I hadn't lain there long when I heard Mama and Auntie talking in the front of the house. Though I could not make out their conversation, I could hear the ugly sounds Auntie made, hissing and spitting out words like an angry cat.

I prayed Mama would be able to bear it. Her tears would only make Auntie worse than ever. As Auntie's temper grew, so did her voice. Soon I could hear them as clearly as if they were in the room with me.

"Minnah, please – calm yourself." Mama sounded tense.

"Calm myself? How can I be calm over something like this?" She took little trouble to lower her voice. I wondered if she wanted to make sure I heard her. I looked at Cecily's still form, grateful for her ability to sleep so deeply.

"What is to become of us all now?" Auntie continued. "The whole village knows of the evil thing your eldest daughter has entangled herself with. To hear Marcus Stebbs tell it, the devil himself is after Adrianne and will stop at nothing to get her. If anything bad happens after this, the whole island will blame us for protecting her. We'll lose everything!"

I curled myself into a tight ball, shivering beneath the shabby blankets. The blood pulsed uncomfortably in my right wrist. Cecily breathed deeply beside me as she slept. I forced myself to breathe in time with her. In and out. In and out. It didn't help. I was drowning.

"The gossip will die down in time. We must be patient till then." Mama's words carried no conviction.

"Die down? This will never die down," Auntie Minnah said. "Do you really think Adrianne will be able to live a normal life after this? Who will want anything to do with a girl like her – cursed as she is? Do you think Lord Durran will allow her to work with his precious horses when he finds out? What man in his right mind would want to marry such a girl? You'll be stuck with her for the rest of your life!"

A heavy silence followed. I held my breath waiting to hear Mama's answer. There seemed to be only one choice left to her. Would she really turn me over to the Windwaithe Mermaid just as Old Lord Durran had turned over his daughter? I could hear the tears when Mama spoke.

"I will not hand my eldest child over to a hysterical mob so she can be drowned in the ocean to appease some imaginary mermaid." Her tone was fierce and final.

"Imaginary, is she? Then what are you so frightened of? What is it that haunted this island a hundred years ago if not the Windwaithe Mermaid herself?"

"I don't know." Mama's voice faltered. "Be it superstition or a flesh and blood creature, I will not allow Adrianne to be harmed because of it. I'll die first."

"You'd protect her? The girl who lost your fortune and brought you nothing but shame and poverty?"

A long pause, taut as wet leather, stretched between them. A sick feeling lurched within me. I knew what would come next, as clearly as if it were written on a page I could read. No, she mustn't tell. Auntie Minnah would never understand. Please don't let Mama tell the truth – not now!

"Adrianne didn't do this to us." Mama's voice shook. "No one is to blame but me."

"You're talking nonsense now," Auntie Minnah said.

"Adrianne was only twelve years old when Richard died. She didn't know the first thing about running a large household. She'd never been trained."

"That's no excuse. She was the one left in charge while you were so ill. It's her fault."

"I wasn't ill."

My throat constricted painfully over the knot lodged there.

"What are you saying, Giselle?" Auntie sounded confused.

"If anyone is to blame for our poverty, it is I." Words of confession burst from Mama like water from a broken dam. "I was overcome with grief because of Richard's death. The sickness wasn't in my body or even my mind – but in my soul. I was too tired to go on. I took to my bed and refused to get up. I could have, but I didn't want to. I didn't want to go on living, so I gave up and left my poor Adrianne to do everything." Mama's words were choked into silence by a sob.

I remembered it well. Weeks and weeks of trying to get Mama to speak or even look at me. I begged. I shouted at her. I even wept, wailing for her to please tell me what to do. She wouldn't open her eyes, but I knew she was awake. I could sense it in her rigid body and the quickening of her breath. She listened to every word I said, but refused to shoulder the load that was rightfully hers. The servants had come to me, asking what they should do. I told them to do as they always had. I went on paying their wages and buying food as we'd always done, never realizing what I was doing – that the money I spent each day had to come from somewhere. The storekeepers let the bills get higher and higher, out of respect for Papa. By the time Auntie Minnah came and realized what had happened, it was too late.

Even Papa's savings had not been enough to cover our losses. There were months and months of debts to pay. If only I had known then what I knew now. If only I'd let the servants go and sold the house off right away. But I hadn't, and now we had nothing.

"Adrianne did her best. I see how she works so hard, day after day, trying to pay for what happened, even though the fault was mine. All mine."

"I refuse to follow you into this folly." Auntie Minnah's voice was tight with anger. "If you choose to protect her, I will not stay another day under your roof. My old friend Laura Mills once invited me to come live with her. I refused at the time, thinking to do my duty and help Richard's family, but I intend to accept her offer now. I will have Denn write a letter for me when he comes tomorrow and post it immediately. When the mobs come howling, I will not be here to receive them." Auntie's loud footsteps crossed the room, followed by the sound of a bedroom door crashing shut behind her.

A terrible quiet came from the front of the house. Then, ever so softly, Mama's sobbing began. I ached to go and comfort her, but it would only shame her more to know I'd heard everything. I lay awake for a long time after that, praying to know what to do.

Would the people of Windwaithe turn on me, the way Auntie said? What if this mermaid grew angry and drove away the fish, and brought down storms upon the island like she had before? Yes, I thought, they would come for me to protect their own families. It would only be a matter of time before they dragged me away and tossed me into the sea with their own hands.

There was but one thing left for me to do. I only prayed God would grant me the courage to do it.

Twenty

I lay awake a long time, listening, till the silence of deep sleep fell over the whole house. Careful not to wake Cecily, I crept from my bed and changed into my dress. Tiptoeing out of the bedroom, I made my way through the dark cottage to retrieve Mama's old work boots from under the bench in the kitchen. The drapes on one window stood drawn back, the milky light of a full moon fell through its murky glass to the floor below. I let out a startled gasp as I recognized Mama's sleeping form lying in the pool of light. She'd fixed herself a makeshift bed from a couple of blankets and a half-empty bag of meal propped beneath her head like a pillow. I couldn't blame her for not wanting to share a bed with Auntie Minnah after their quarrel. Her head lay next to her boots, one pale hand thrown across them in her sleep. I could not retrieve the shoes without waking her.

It made no difference. Barefoot or not, I would make my journey, probably to meet my death. A strange calmness settled over me once I'd made up my mind. If I had to die to save my family and all the people on the island of Windwaithe, so be it.

My naked feet made hardly a sound as I stepped lightly across the room to the front door. Mama did not stir as I carefully unlatched the door and stepped into the cool night. Tall grass tickled the soles of my feet and a limp breeze stirred my skirt. I'd never seen a moon so bright and full. It bathed everything in an otherworldly glow. I could see every blade of grass in the yard, every leaf on the shimmering trees. Every stone was like a shining pearl upon the ground.

"I knew you'd try something foolish."

I whirled about, startled by the sound of a human voice in this strange fairyland of night. I saw a figure, not five feet from where I stood, with arms folded tight across its chest.

"I knew when I looked into those half-wild eyes of yours, you would try something like this."

"Go away, Denn," I snapped. "This doesn't concern you."

"Doesn't concern me? Look at you, running around outside after all decent folk are in their beds – and barefoot, no less. I don't know how I could be more concerned. If I don't look after you, I don't know who will."

"What are you doing out here if all *decent folk* are in bed?"

"I'm here to make sure you don't do something stupid."

"It doesn't matter what you say – I must go. The fate of the whole island depends on it."

"Just listen to yourself, Adri. Those old tales are just *stories*. There's no such thing as a mermaid!" Denn's mouth was a tight line across his face.

"Fine, have it your way. There's no mermaid, so there's no reason I shouldn't go down to the beach tonight."

"You can't go out to the water this time of night. You could stumble and fall in the dark."

"Look around you, Denn. There's enough moonlight to see by. I'll be fine." Even as I said the words, I knew they weren't true. It was quite possible I would be dead before this night was over.

"You're determined to do this?" Denn asked.

"Yes."

"Then I'm coming with you – even if it is sheer foolishness."

A cold sensation crept over my skin. "You can't come. It's too dangerous."

"No more than it would be for you," Denn said, in that stubborn tone I knew only too well.

"She tried to kill Marcus."

"She won't expect two of us, will she? We'll have the element of surprise on our side." The words were spoken with a mocking sarcasm that sparked my temper.

"Fine, be that way," I snapped. "Whether you believe me or not, I'm still going – and I don't need you to protect me."

A strange stillness came over Denn. He sounded tired when he spoke. "I don't doubt that you can do anything you set your mind to, Adri – with or without my help – but why go alone when you have a friend willing to stand by your side?"

It was as if someone lit a candle in the darkness of my mind. I had always believed Denn was protective of me because he thought I was too weak to do things for myself. Was it possible his desire to help me was for another reason entirely? I looked at him standing there in silence, trying to figure out if he really meant it.

"All right, you can come," I said. "But only under one condition. You must stay hidden so if anything goes wrong, she won't be able to hurt you."

Denn scowled dubiously, so I rushed on. "It's probably all in my imagination anyway, so what is there to worry about, eh? If you're right, and the mermaid doesn't come to meet me, I'll come home without any arguments, all right?"

He frowned. "Where are you planning to go?" he asked.

I turned towards the shore. "To a place between moonlit rock and dark ocean. The place I first met her."

"The Rumbles," Denn murmured.

As we picked our way along the moonlit path, Denn kept up a steady stream of useless talk – as if he were afraid to let the silence overtake us even for a moment.

"You know," he said out of the blue. "Trey was talking about you the other day, yammering away. Half the time I couldn't figure out what he was on about. One minute he mentioned what a hard worker you were, the next minute he couldn't say enough about your cooking – said a man would be lucky to marry you when the time came." Denn laughed to himself over the memory. "I couldn't shut him up. I think he might be sweet on you."

I stopped dead, right there in the middle of the path. Denn took a few more steps before halting as well.

Trey, that idiot. Did he really think such transparent tactics would change his brother's feelings for me in any way?

Denn misunderstood my reaction. "I'm sure Trey only meant it as a compliment," he said.

I stared at Denn across the shadows, slowly shaking my head in disbelief.

"You can be such an idiot sometimes, Denn. Did you know that?" The words that should have been bitter came out gentle, almost sad. I started walking again, not trusting myself to say more. Denn quickened his pace to catch up with me.

"I'm an idiot again, am I? What did I do this time?" he demanded. I could hear the exasperation building in his voice.

"Trey didn't say those things because *he* wants to marry me; he said them because he wants *you* to marry me."

It was Denn's turn to stop walking. I turned towards him, amazed at how calm I felt after saying such a thing out loud.

What did it matter any more? This might be the last chance I had to speak, my last breathing moments in this haunting moon-lit world.

Denn swallowed and seemed to regain himself. "Why would Trey—" He stopped mid-sentence in confusion.

"Because it just so happens, Denn Young, that your sweet idiot of a brother is convinced that I'm wonderful – something really special. His devotion is touching. I'm quite a catch after all, with all my family's debts and my complete lack of dowry. And who could resist my moody, changeable disposition—" I was horrified when my voice actually broke, threatening to dissolve into tears at any moment. I quickly turned away, struggling for control. When I managed it, I turned and looked Denn square in the face.

"Trey may be ten years old, but even he can see that I'm in love with you." I waited for the flood of embarrassment and shame that should have followed such a bold declaration, but found to my amazement there was only ragged relief filling the empty cavern inside me.

Denn's stunned gaze searched mine in the darkness. His mouth opened, then closed again without a word coming out.

I laughed – a light, unnatural sound that echoed in the stillness. How could I laugh like that when all my dreams were being torn asunder?

"I tried not to love you, Denn," I said. "I really didn't want our friendship to end this way. I'm sorry." What had got into me? Had I gone completely mad? And yet, I found I could not wish the words unsaid.

"Adri, I never—" Denn's voice faded away.

"A fact of which I am only too aware." My voice was gentle with the final acceptance of that which can't be changed. "I suppose you can't help not loving me any more than I can help loving you. Such is the nature of things."

I walked away from him, wondering if he would follow. To my amazement he did.

We made the rest of the trip to the rocky shore in heavy silence. What was Denn thinking under that battered cap of his? Was he completely disgusted by my feelings for him? Did he plan to show up on Cora Lynn's doorstep and beg her forgiveness first thing tomorrow?

My bare feet made the trip longer, but the evening was comfortably warm. When we reached the shore, the water stretched out before us; a ribbon of bright moonlight painted the surface to the horizon. The Rumble Stones rose up out of the sea like ancient creatures of myth. I climbed gingerly on to the nearest one, my toes curled around the cold, wet rock. With a thundering roar, the ocean pounded at the Rumble Stone, causing it to shudder beneath my feet.

In the lull between waves, I could hear Denn scrambling over the rocks behind me. My eyes scanned the dark water around us, searching for any sign of a figure breaking the surface. Nothing but the crashing sea as far as the eye could see.

Carefully picking our way, Denn and I leaped from the top of one stone to the other till we reached the largest Rumble Stone. We paused as salt and spray burst against the rocks, settling beads of fine mist in our hair. Denn sidled closer to me.

"I don't see anything," he murmured somewhere near my ear, almost as if he were afraid of being overheard.

I didn't answer. What more was there to say?

I sensed him watching me. He was so close I could hear his steady breathing over the sound of the tide.

"You've changed," Denn said softly.

I waited, bracing myself for what would mean the end of our lifelong friendship. I knew it was better this way, but it hurt all the same.

"Sometimes, I think I don't even know who you are any more," Denn said.

The salty air danced through my short hair. All fear had left my body. I took a deep, measured breath and smiled at Denn.

"I am Adrianne of Windwaithe," I said like one in a dream. "The girl who chose to face the Windwaithe Mermaid."

Denn studied my face – like a stranger, seeing me for the first time. He opened his mouth to speak.

"Shhh!" My fingertips brushed momentarily against his lips, cutting off whatever he meant to say.

"What is it?" Denn's voice dropped to a whisper, the spell

between us broken. "Did you see something?"

Moonlight from above moved over the surface of the shifting water, flashing and changing in an eternal rhythm. The skin along my right wrist pulsed as if alive. My heart quickened.

"She's coming. You must hide."

"What do you mean? I don't see anything," Denn scowled at the open ocean.

"Trust me, Denn, she's coming. Hurry before it's too late."

Denn looked unconvinced, but decided to play along. Tugging firmly at his cap, he slipped into the shadows of a large outcropping of rocks and crouched just out of sight. I could feel his watchful gaze upon me as I walked away from him and stepped out on to the last of the Rumble Stones. I tiptoed across its slippery surface, which chilled the bottoms of my feet. Approaching the edge, I stopped. Golden moonlight trembled upon my skin like a tangible living thing. Waves lapped at the stones below, splashing my toes with droplets of icy sea.

An ocean breeze rushed from the open water to wash over me. I breathed in deep, holding the cold tang of it in my lungs. Everything around me had a crisp edge, almost too perfect to be real. Stillness came over the night. Even the waves seemed to pause in their restless rise and fall. I looked down into the black water. It quivered and broke as the head and shoulders of the Windwaithe Mermaid surfaced. Beads of water clung to her skin and hair, sparkling like gems in starlight.

Twenty-One

The mermaid was barely three feet from where I stood. I was not afraid of her. I was ready for death. What more could she do than kill me?

For the space of a dozen heartbeats we stood, regarding each other in the silence of night. I did not let my eyes stray to Denn's hiding place, but I could not help wondering what he thought about the reality of mermaids now. The Windwaithe Mermaid did not speak. She seemed to be waiting for me to begin.

"Who are you?" I was pleased with the steadiness of my voice.

The mermaid proudly lifted her chin. "My name is Jendayi, appointed ruler of the Caribbean Sea." Her words were rounded with a softly foreign sound, as if the language we spoke was not her native tongue.

My breath froze within my chest. Ruler? Had I heard correctly? "Are you the Sea Queen?"

"I am a queen, but not *the* Sea Queen, who is High Queen over all other kings and queens of the sea."

"Are you a descendant of the mermaid who came for Lady Lauretta a hundred years ago?" I demanded of her.

"No, not a descendant." Her voice was like a rich melody, smooth and deep. "I am the same."

I blinked in surprise. Could this exquisite creature really be over a hundred years old?

I decided the direct approach might be best in this situation, so I came right to the point. "Have you come to steal away my sister, Cecily?" I asked.

Jendayi's smooth expression softened into one of sadness. "There *is* merit to be found in your sister. It has grown with her desire to be more like you," the mermaid said, her voice like a breath of wind. "In truth, it is not your sister I have come for, Adrianne of Windwaithe, but you."

"Me?" The word came out a rasping whisper. The fortune-teller had been right all along. I straightened my back and braced myself for whatever she might try next. "You have come to kill me as punishment for getting in your way?"

Jendayi shook her head. The pale green braids swayed gracefully about her shoulders. "The gift of life is the most valuable of all

God's gifts. To take a life unnecessarily is the greatest of all crimes."

I was startled by her words. God? But what of the ancient demons the fortune-teller had spoken of? Was this another mermaid trick?

"You lie!" I said. "I saw you try to drown Marcus. Had you held him down any longer he would have died. What of his life? Or that of my sister the day you tipped us into the water? You held her under so long she almost drowned."

The mermaid's voice was full of gentle patience when she spoke. "It is impossible for men of the land to drown under the hand of a mermaid. Had either of them breathed in the sea, they would not have died."

Involuntarily, I remembered back to the day on the Rumbles. I saw again her green hand, clutched firmly around Marcus's kicking ankle. And what of Cecily? How easily the water had come from her lungs, as if it had been mere air rather than the salty sea. There had been no coughing or sputtering. Could the touch of a mermaid really allow someone to breathe water as easily as they did air?

"But what about all those years ago, when Lauretta's father wouldn't let her leave? You brought down storms upon the people of Windwaithe, destroyed their homes and their crops, and scared away all the fish."

"I did. But only to put fear in their hearts. Sometimes fear is the only tool that will force men to do what they know they should. Lauretta's father knew imprisoning his daughter was wrong. I helped him do what he knew was right."

The golden eyes held me in place. They were clear and open. I could not deny the truth reflected in them.

"The year that followed Lauretta's disappearance was one of great plenty," Jendayi continued. "Only gentle rains fell upon the face of the land. Crops grew in abundance. More fish leaped into the fishermen's nets than had ever been caught before – or since. They made enough wealth that year to rebuild all that had been destroyed, better than before. I repaid them for all I'd done by restoring all that had been lost and more. All without their knowing I helped them."

"What of Lady Lauretta? You cast a spell on her, forcing her to go with you."

"I cast no spell. The girl came with me of her own choice. I took her into the sea, showed her all the wonderful things that could be hers. She chose for herself to marry the Sea Prince."

I remembered the tale of the fortune-teller. Lady Lauretta had come home soaking wet the night she told her father she would leave him. Wet, as if she'd been bathing in the sea.

"But when she went back to her father," Jendayi continued, "he could not believe she wanted to leave him. He convinced himself evil magic was to blame and would not hear otherwise."

"How do I know you are telling me the truth?" I asked.

She looked up at me from beneath her long dark lashes. "Your heart will tell you. You have but to listen to the voice of truth deep within you."

I did know. Something about Lauretta's story had never seemed right. Too many contradictions and questions left unanswered. What of Lauretta's wet clothes the night she returned? Not one life had been lost in the storm the Windwaithe Mermaid had set upon the people of Windwaithe all those years ago. Only houses and crops had been destroyed. I looked into the mermaid's face and knew she was telling the truth. Truth that had been hidden all these years.

"If you don't mean to kill me, why have you forced me to come to you this night?" I asked in a quiet voice.

She smiled. For once, both corners of her mouth turned upwards. "It is you I have chosen, Adrianne of Windwaithe, to be the bride of the Sea Prince."

I gasped. Out of the corner of my eye I saw a sharp movement from the outcropping where Denn lay hidden. I suppose he was as shocked as I to hear this announcement.

"Me? But I don't understand. You tried to take Cecily the night of the storm."

"When I found your sister alone on the Rumbles, I knew if I kept her there you would come for her. Just as I knew you would come to rescue the boy, Marcus – ready to trade your life for his, despite all he's done to you."

"How do you know what Marcus has done to me?" I asked.

"I do not have to leave the sea to know what happens on the

land. It has always been such for my people. The hearts of men cannot be hidden from the folk of the sea."

What she said seemed impossible, yet it must be true. Somehow, her powers had reached out to me across the land.

"I have seen the hearts of every man, woman and child on this island – as well as in many other lands – but you are the one I have chosen."

It seemed like absolute madness. Part of me wanted to break into hysterical laughter over the absurdity of it.

"I – I can't help but think you've made some sort of a mistake." Not wanting to offend her, I fought to find the right words. "Surely the Sea Prince will not want a homely waif like me after being married to the beautiful and elegant Lady Lauretta."

Jendayi smiled again. I had the impression she was amused with me.

"Lady Lauretta lives, dear child. She is not a girl any more but a beautiful young woman, and someday she will rule at her husband's side."

"How can she still be alive? It's been over a hundred years."

"Time is different for those who live in the sea."

It certainly must be if this was indeed the same mermaid who came to Lady Lauretta over a hundred years before.

I shook my head, trying to clear away the confusion. "But you said you came to find a wife for the prince."

"It is not the eldest Sea Prince I've come for, but his younger brother." She cocked her head to one side, and her flowing braids shifted. "By the reckoning of age, he is not much older than you."

By the reckoning of age? He had to be over a hundred years old!

"There are girls on this island ten times more beautiful than I. Surely your Sea Prince would much rather have one of them."

A stern expression tightened Jendayi's beautiful features. Her voice trembled with a fierceness that frightened me. "I have seen these girls you speak of. I have looked into the deepest part of their hearts and seen the shabbiness of their souls as plainly as the tattered clothing the world sees when they look upon you. Do not compare yourself to them."

Was it my imagination, or did the mermaid's golden eyes flit for a moment towards Denn's hiding place? "Men are fools," she said. "They see only with their eyes, and are blinded to the truest treasures that stand before them dressed in the ordinary dust and sweat of hard life. Those other girls are no more worthy of the Sea Prince than blind worms wriggling in the mud."

Her voice rose till it roared all about me like thundering waves. "It is you, Adrianne of Windwaithe, who was struck down by great tragedy and circumstance, you who found the strength to stand again. You, and only you, loved those who were weak, and carried heavy burdens that rightfully belonged to others. You were the only one compassionate enough to see the needs of the hopeless, and strong enough to have hope when all was lost to you. You were the one who had the courage to stand up for what was right, even when others persecuted you for it, yet forgave them even as they did it. You are more of a woman than many who claim four times your years in age."

I sank to the ground, hugging my knees to my chest like Cecily did when she was overwhelmed. How did the mermaid know? How could she have seen what I'd striven so hard to hide?

Jendayi shook her head and thrashed her mighty tail as if she could not contain the emotion she felt. "The men and women of this island should beware, for they are pitiful creatures indeed when true greatness can be hidden from them by mere dirt and rags. They do not deserve you."

Jendayi drifted closer. Reaching up one of her long slender hands, she touched my face. The salt water on her fingertips mingled with the hot tears running down my cheeks.

"There are no tears in the ocean, Adrianne of Windwaithe. Leave this place. Come with me. See for yourself all that can be yours. As a princess, you will be seen for what you truly are and treated with the respect and honour that should be afforded someone of your greatness."

A spray of loose pebbles clattered somewhere behind me. I knew it was only a matter of moments before Denn would break from his hiding place and rush to save me.

I could barely find my voice. "If I go with you now and see what you speak of, can I still come back?"

"If you so wish." I could tell by the tone in her voice she believed I would not.

"Adri. No!" Denn's panicked voice echoed over the water.

Jendayi's eyes never left my face. She drifted away from the edge of the Rumble Stone, leaving me room to jump.

"ADRIANNE!" I heard Denn scrambling over the rocks.

Without looking back, I leaped into the air. The sea rushed to meet me. In an explosion of liquid and bubbles, I entered the icy water. It spilled into my ears and weighed down my clothes. A miraculous warmth rose up in my body to drive away the cold. I opened my eyes, but I could see nothing in the blackness below. Strong fingers encircled my wrist. A flash of gold scales in the murky moonlight dancing on the surface of the water told me Jendayi had joined me.

With a swish of her powerful tail, she shot forward at an alarming speed, pulling me along with her. I closed my eyes. After half a dozen thundering heartbeats, I breathed in. Icy seawater spilled into my lungs. I felt dizzy for a moment, but my throat did not sting, nor my lungs burn. I breathed in again – water rushed to fill my chest, clearing my mind.

I sensed Jendayi's smile, though I could not see it with my eyes. Without warning, she plunged downwards. Together we spiralled through the pitch-black waters, leaving the shores of Windwaithe far behind.

Twenty-Two

Light exploded before my eyes. I blinked against its brilliance, temporarily blinded. A glowing sphere hovered above Jendayi's cupped hand. She reached out and the ball floated away from her fingertips, flitting ahead of us to illuminate the way. Jendayi tightened her grip on my left hand, her powerful tail pumping at my side.

We swam impossibly fast, like two gulls sweeping over the ocean. My skirts streamed through the water, billowing about me as if caught by a chance breeze. The sphere danced ahead of us, trailing stars of light behind it.

I lost all sense of direction. Were we speeding towards the surface or diving deeper into the fathomless sea? Ghostly shapes materialized out of the darkness, as if drawn by the mermaid's magic. I turned my head and saw we'd been joined by a pod of dolphins. They spiralled around us as graceful as dancers on a stage before moving on. Large groups of fish darted to get out of our way. We could have been flying, the water pulling at our hair. Jendayi's braids streamed behind us like fluttering green ribbons as we sailed over the rocks and mountains that rose from the ocean floor.

The wreckage of an ancient ship passed beneath us, like the skeleton of some mammoth beast laid to rest in the murky depths. Colourful fish circled the tall wooden masts still standing against a liquid sky.

We continued on our journey, meeting with every kind of strange aquatic creature – giant turtles silently cutting their way through the water, an octopus with tentacles undulating about its bulbous head.

Jendayi's tail grew still, and we drifted to a slower speed. The mermaid looked back at me, her eyes aglow with excitement.

"The Sea Queen has sent messengers to greet you," Jendayi said. The water all around us made her voice sound as if she was speaking to me through crystal.

I turned, curious to see of what she spoke. The sphere of light flew ahead of us, shining on everything around it like a small sun. The light reflected up on to what looked like the hulls of great vessels drifting silently under the ocean. I blinked in astonishment. How could such boats sail under the water? No, not boats – but creatures of the deep, so massive they would have dwarfed even Lord Durran's prized schooner. They moved lazily, with great fluked tails propelling them forward.

Whales. I had seen them from a distance before, their gigantic tails crashing against the water before disappearing beneath the waves. But I had never seen them like this – in their full majesty. The closer we swam, the bigger they loomed. We drew next to the largest of them, so close I could see the barnacles crusting its flippers and the grooves running along its underside. Its black eye rolled in my direction. Compared to my own it was gigantic, but against its own great bulk the eye was a tiny black marble. I gulped in water, swallowing some by accident. My arms and legs were heavy with fear. I trembled. Jendayi pulled me close, comforting me with her nearness.

"They will not harm you. They know only gentleness and love. Touch him. Do not fear."

She started to let go of my wrist. I clutched at her like a frightened child, thinking I would drown if she let go. Jendayi smiled encouragingly, her white grin shining in the pulsing light of the magic sphere. "The mark upon your wrist helps you breathe without my help."

The pressure of her fingers lifted from my flesh. My lungs continued to pump the water in and out as easily as before. I kicked my feet and stroked my way closer to the whale. Had the creature really been sent to greet me by the Sea Queen herself? Me, the daughter of the town seamstress?

The whale regarded me with care as I drifted near its side. I'd never seen anything as gentle and wise as that unblinking eye. I could see it thinking, pondering what kind of strange little creature I might be. There were deep cracks and long scratches marring the surface of the beast's tough skin, a testament to the battles and danger it had faced in its long lifetime. I reached out my right hand and laid it against the whale's scarred side. My arm tingled.

The great eye moved as if to focus on me better. I could see my own awed face staring back at me from its dark surface. The whale let out a haunting cry that reverberated through my whole being. Like the music made when a bow is run along strings. It felt as though the strings were inside my heart. The song was so beautiful, I ached inside with its infinite sadness. Mourning for dreams that had never come true, for courage that went unsung, and for the spark of hope that refused to die – even in the darkness of a world that tried to smother it.

The song was mine. The whale keened my pain and sorrow for the entire ocean to hear. How many times, in lonely silence, had my heart made that exact same cry? Wailing at the emptiness, refusing to give up. Hot saltiness stung at my eyes, but quickly mingled with the vast coolness of the sea and was lost.

"There are no tears in the ocean. Only joy can last here," Jendayi said.

I removed my hand from the whale's side and swam back to Jendayi, who'd watched me from a distance. Taking hold of me once more, Jendayi left the whales far behind and delved down and down, faster and faster, to depths that frightened me.

Twenty-Three

We swam for what seemed like for ever. How many hours had passed – two, three? The darkness beyond the sphere of light was so complete I could see nothing. There was only Jendayi and me in a sea of black.

I looked at the mermaid at my side. She was such an alien creature – the way she moved, the way she looked – and yet, here I was fathoms below the surface with my life in her hands. Where was she taking me? Surely nothing could live this deep in the bowels of the sea. The weight of the whole ocean pushed down upon me, but the mermaid magic planted within my skin drove it back. I stared at the swollen furrows on my wrist that made it possible for me to do such amazing things.

"I'm sorry I hurt you that night," Jendayi's voice vibrated

gently within my water-filled ears. "The mark must go deep beneath the surface and into the blood, if the spell is to work."

"I'm sorry for pulling your hair when you were trying to save Cecily's life." It was hard to speak around the liquid in my throat. My voice came out sounding oddly hollow, as if I were talking with one of Auntie's large kettles over my head.

The mermaid's eyes crinkled in amusement. "I have no one to blame but myself. I went about everything all wrong. I only meant to get your attention, not startle you into overturning your boat. I went to aid your sister because I knew you could not drown with my mark upon you." Jendayi laughed softly to herself. "I should have known better than to turn my back on you – even for a moment."

I looked at Jendayi. "Why didn't you say something that first night at the Rumbles? You could have explained what you wanted."

The merwoman's tail stroked slower, her face thoughtful. "You were frightened. Fear makes the human mind like a cold wall of iron, impenetrable to reason. I thought if I forced you to breathe water you would see you could not drown and know I meant you no harm. I even tried drawing you into the water with a spell, but your will is like none I've ever known. Sheer force was the only thing that worked last time I dealt with men of the land. I thought it would work again."

Jendayi shook her head in a sad, graceful movement. "I was wrong. I should have reasoned with you as I did Lady Lauretta.

I let what happened a hundred years ago cloud my wisdom."

"You mean because Lauretta's father wouldn't let her come back?" I asked.

Frowning, Jendayi nodded, her braids bobbing in the current.

"Humankind fear what they cannot understand. Why, it was only a few weeks past that I tried to help a boy of your island by mending one of his traps and he threw a net over me. Sadly, I think I frightened him when I broke free. I admit I was somewhat angry by then. I may have been fiercer than necessary."

I tried not to smile. Lester, that idiot. Had he really thought he could catch a mermaid with a simple fishing net?

"The people of your world try my patience. It is sometimes hard to remember that not all your kind is that way, Adrianne of Windwaithe."

Even as she spoke these words, the most amazing sight opened before my eyes. Lights rose up out of the watery twilight, twinkling like a thousand bright stars. As we swam closer, the darkness drew back and the lights became a city nestled at the bottom of the ocean, its crystalline towers rising up in simple, elegant glory. It reminded me of a colourful, glowing coral reef growing up out of the sea floor.

I baulked, causing Jendayi to lose her grip on my arm.

"What is the matter?" she asked.

My pulse pounded in my ears, as I drew in icy water with gulping breaths.

"Where are you taking me?"

"To the underwater city of Siariah, kingdom of my cousin, Dakarai, High Queen of the Sea."

"Why are you taking me there?"

"Do you not wish to meet the Sea Prince before you make your choice? I informed him you might come tonight. He is waiting at the palace to be introduced to you. The youngest Sea Prince is as handsome as he is kindhearted. He is fairer than any upon your small island," Jendayi said. "Any" meaning Denn, I was sure.

I gave her a sharp look. "I thought what people looked like didn't matter to your kind."

Jendayi gave me a slow, mischievous smile in return. "It is not among the most important things – but it does not hurt when the rest is already said and done. Before the Sea Queen appointed me as a ruler in her realm, I was once the younger prince's private tutor. We are old friends, he and I." She paused a moment, an indulgent smile lingering over her lips. Her memories of the prince's youth must have been pleasant ones. But did I really want to go so far as to meet him face to face? Would I be expected to marry him if I did?

Jendayi must have sensed something of my uneasy thoughts. "Princess Lauretta also awaits you at the palace. She is most anxious to meet with another from her original home. It was she who asked me to visit your island in my searches."

Lady Lauretta! The beautiful but tragic figure of legend. Not only was she still alive, but she wanted to meet me. Still I hesitated. If I went on now, would I ever come back?

I floated in the water, the weight of the whole ocean pressing in upon me, my heart beating itself ragged against the inside of my chest. Jendayi waited patiently for me to make my choice, the gentle strokes of her tail causing my skirts to ripple about my legs in small eddies of current.

I thought of Denn and the awkward silence that had followed my declaration of love for him. My whole body turned hot with shame over the memory.

"Take me to the Sea Prince," I said firmly. "I'm ready to meet him."

Twenty-Four

The city of the merfolk was a wonder beyond imagining. Their homes were fantastic towering structures rising high into the watery sky. Unlike houses of the land, these complex buildings were not separate, but built one on top of the other, with beautifully pillared and arched doors on every level, even in the topmost towers. The merfolk swam in and out of these amazing edifices at their own will and pleasure, flitting about their business in much the same way people did back home in the village marketplace. Only instead of sticking close to the ground, the merfolk seemed to prefer swimming in and about the tops of the tallest towers – as though navigating between the trees of some giant, underwater forest. From below, I watched the merfolk gliding overhead like giant wheeling flocks of graceful sea birds. Their movements were hypnotic.

Every building in the underwater city was ablaze with the light of a thousand lanterns. In the heart of each lantern was a globe of light like the one Jendayi had called up to guide our way to the city. I noticed one curiously golden-skinned merman, dressed in long, red robes, making his way from lantern to lantern at the base of the building closest to us. He touched the magic globes within each lantern lightly with his finger as he passed, making them glow twice as bright as before. I put out my hand as we swam past one of the lights he had just renewed, expecting to feel heat radiating from its glowing centre like a flame. The water surrounding the ball of light was so icy cold it numbed my fingers – almost as if the light drew warmth from the water in order to feed its inner flame.

Noticing I had fallen behind, Jendayi stopped and beckoned for me to catch up. I kicked my legs and clumsily made my way towards her. It was frustratingly slow going and my lungs were pumping water hard by the time I reached her side.

"You are not used to so much swimming yet. You will exhaust yourself if you are not careful. Hold on to my arm. It will help," Jendayi said. She watched me absently massaging the welts on my wrist. They buzzed like a hundred bees were crawling over my swollen skin.

"All merfolk carry some form of magic within their blood," Jendayi informed me. "Because your mark is new, it reacts whenever someone draws near. The more power they have, the more intense the feeling will be."

I looked at the crowds of merfolk thronging the city's waterways above. That explained why the welts felt as though they were on fire.

I glanced at Jendayi, wondering why my wrist hadn't given me trouble on the way to the city. Her powers were so great the welts should have burned with fire long before now.

"As time passes, your body grows used to the magic of those near you and their powers' effects on the mark lessen while you are in their presence." Jendayi answered my inner thoughts with an ease that made me feel vulnerable.

Jendayi reached out and gently traced my welts with two of her slender fingers. The buzzing lessened considerably when she finished. "That should help for now, though you may have trouble if anyone comes too close."

"How does it work?" I asked, still staring at my scarred wrist in awe. "The magic, I mean."

"The elemental magic within our veins receives its strength from the water that surrounds us. We breathe it into our bodies and absorb it through our skin, transforming it into power. Everything we need to survive an underwater existence is provided by this drawing in of the sea's life-giving strength," Jendayi said.

I thought of the light pulling the warmth and life right out of the water around it.

Jendayi continued. "Just as the ocean is one great body of water extending from one end of the world to the other, so too are we who live within it connected. This connection is what allows me to pass my abilities on to you. It is also what makes your wrist burn when others with magic are near."

Linking her arm through mine, Jendayi towed me swiftly up into the crowded swirl of merfolk. While swimming, the people of the sea moved horizontally with their stomachs down and tails stroking powerfully behind them, but wherever we went the mermen and mermaids stopped to pull themselves upright, balancing with flapping tails beneath them, in order to let us pass. Many bowed formally to Jendayi as she swam by.

From what I could see, the merfolk of the city wore clothes much simpler in their design than Jendayi's royal attire. An unadorned blouse or tunic, tapered in at the waist in some way, seemed to be the fashion of choice. Tails were left free, showing off their brightly coloured scales to the best advantage.

The crowds of merfolk watched me pass with undisguised curiosity. I returned the compliment by gaping back at them in wide-eyed wonder.

Their beauty was beyond anything I could give name to, their skins the strangest shades of green, blue, purple and all other colours of the ocean. Here and there I caught sight of merfolk with skins closer in colour to those who lived upon the land, but they often had some shockingly bright shade of hair to go with it. One dark-skinned young mergirl swam by, her dazzling purple hair streaming gently behind her. She caught me staring and pulled herself up, her iridescent fin fluttering beneath her like a shimmering butterfly checked in flight. She gave me a timid wave. Hesitantly, I waved in return.

The more I looked about me, the more I realized that the city of the merfolk was not really so different from the world above. Two brawny, bare-chested mermen with impressive beards swam by, trawling a net filled to overflowing with seaweed in much the same way Windwaithe's fishermen might haul in the day's catch. A merwoman, holding a small bundle in her arms, hurried to get out of their way. As she darted aside, I saw that nestled within her bundle was a tiny merbaby, looking out at the world with curious little eyes. Beyond them a merman called up to a merwoman through an open window. She bent out and dropped some sort of heavy metal tool down to him. He caught it deftly with one hand and began working away on fixing a small break in the tower wall.

Jendayi slowed her pace as something up ahead of us caught her attention. My wrist tingled in silent warning. I followed her gaze and found a merman quickly making his way towards us through the crowd. I realized he must have quite a bit of magic in his blood to make my wrist burn in his presence the way it did.

Drawing himself upright, the merman fanned his tail and a pair of handsome tapered fins that ran the length of his lower hips in order to bring himself to a graceful hover before us. I noted that his tail was slightly smaller and more streamlined than Jendayi's. All the mermaids I'd seen in the passing crowd seemed to have larger and fancier tails than their male counterparts. Obviously it was a feminine trait.

This merman's skin was a light shade of violet and his tail the most stunning colour of aquamarine I had ever laid eyes on. He wore a sleeveless velvety brown tunic over a loose-fitting cream-coloured shirt that was gathered in at the wrists. Jewel-laden buttons and intricate embroidery adorned the front of his tunic. A simple gold sash was cinched about his waist with the loose ends floating artfully in the water behind him.

His black, close-cropped curls rippled lazily about his head as he moved to greet Jendayi. He spoke aloud, his mouth forming strange words I could not understand. The deeper tones of his pleasant voice purred within my ears like a contented cat.

When he had finished speaking, Jendayi turned to me. "This is Rriess, Royal Chamberlain in the court of my cousin the Sea Queen," she said by way of introduction.

I glanced up at Rriess, studying his masculine, clean-shaven face, which was completely purple. He graced me with a most charming smile, revealing a hidden dimple in one of his cheeks. I decided I liked Rriess.

He spoke again in his native tongue, addressing me directly this time. I shook my head to show I didn't understand.

"He says he is pleased to finally make your acquaintance, since he has heard so much about you," Jendayi translated for me.

"Heard about me? From where?" I asked in astonishment I could not hide.

"From me," Jendayi answered, with a hint of a smile playing about her lips.

I looked Rriess over again, this time with much greater care. My scrutiny made him give out a soft chuckle that tickled at my ears.

"Rriess needs to speak with me privately," Jendayi said. "You may indulge your curiosity by exploring the surrounding area, but do not wander too far; this will only take a few moments."

Glancing uncertainly between Jendayi and Rriess, I turned and swam slowly away from them, pretending to examine a rather large, ornate seahorse carved into the side of one of the nearest towers.

Sound in the ocean was not like sound upon the land. Though I was some distance from them now, when Rriess spoke to Jendayi I could still hear him as clearly as if he floated at my side. Too bad I couldn't understand a word he said. Reluctantly, I turned my attention to the passing merfolk around me.

Their voices vibrated hollowly within my ears as they hailed one another in greeting. Unlike on the land, judging relative distance by ear was nearly impossible. Noises near and far sounded much the same to me. Voices criss-crossed, tangling together like a badly woven piece of cloth. All of these voices seemed to be speaking the same cryptic language as Rriess.

Jendayi spoke my language so easily. It never occurred to me she might be an exception rather than the rule when it came to merkind. I glanced at the green-skinned mermaid who had brought me to this place. She floated in the water, her eyes modestly lowered, listening carefully to every word Rriess said to her. The merman and merwoman had drifted closer to one another as their conversation progressed. So close, Rriess's tail brushed lightly against Jendayi's for a moment. The gesture was so gentle, so fleetingly tender, it seemed as intimate as a kiss.

Feeling I had intruded on a supremely private moment, I turned quickly away from the pair and scanned the surrounding area for *anything* else to distract me.

Many of the merfolk stole glances at me as they passed by and then looked quickly away to make it seem as if they hadn't. A few nodded respectfully to me as if I were some kind of nobility. Did they know I was here to meet the Sea Prince? Thoroughly embarrassed, I scanned the area around me, pretending I was too busy taking in the sights to notice all the attention I was drawing.

There was a group of young mermen playing some sort of game not far from where I floated. I watched with great interest as they flitted about, laughing and calling to one another, passing a ball of light between them. The object of the game seemed to be hitting the light back and forth to one another using only their tails. The young mermen showed a great deal of skill in this pursuit, performing no end of impressive acrobatic manoeuvres to accomplish it. They would spin and dive, flipping backwards, head over fin, just at the right moment to strike the ball and send it speeding through the water towards an eagerly waiting teammate. Remembering the freezing cold of the magical light I'd explored earlier, I shivered over the mere thought of touching one. I figured merfolk tails must be better equipped for icy cold temperatures than my human hands were, even with magical help.

As I continued to watch the game before me, I noticed one youth who seemed particularly adept at it. He was like a graceful dolphin, darting and spiralling through the water at speeds that dizzied my mind. He didn't look much older than me, but was completely blue, from the top of his dark blue hair to the tip of his brilliant sapphire tail. Even the long-sleeved shirt he wore was a softer shade of powder blue, with a royal blue sash tied around its waist. I found myself wondering what colour the Sea Prince would be. Jendayi was green – did that mean he was, too?

One of the merboys noticed me watching and elbowed his blue friend, directing his attention towards me with a teasing grin. Deciding it would be best to brazen the situation out, I stared calmly back at him as he silently regarded me with as much blatant interest as I had shown in him.

An inviting smile spread slowly over his blue features and then, bold as you please, he winked at me. I think I blinked back in shock.

Merciful heavens! Did the young merman think I meant to

flirt with him? I realized how improper it would look for me to be seen swimming about in public with a handsome blue stranger when I was supposed to be on my way to meet the Sea Prince, to be introduced as his possible bride.

My wrist gave a small tingle as my bold blue friend started purposefully in my direction. Fortunately, Jendayi chose that moment to rejoin me. She swam between the two of us, her gaze locked upon the young merman. He fanned his hands and fins, and the looser part of his clothing gusted out around him as he came to a sudden halt. He glanced up at Jendayi's face and a look of horrified recognition swept over his features. Bowing low with respect, he backed away from the older merwoman as quickly as he could and swam a hasty retreat to rejoin his friends.

Jendayi turned to me, biting her bottom lip as if trying to keep from laughing at my expense.

I gave a mystified shrug of my shoulders. "All I did was watch them play their game."

"Humankind is something of a rarity down here. But you'll get used to that in time," Jendayi said in her careful way. "As for young mermen, I'm afraid, they are not known for their subtlety about such things."

From what I could tell, older mermen weren't much different. I glanced around to see if Jendayi's charming friend Rriess had been watching the whole amusing incident. He was nowhere to be found.

Once again, Jendayi understood my unspoken question.

"Rriess has gone on ahead to let the royal family know we are approaching the palace," Jendayi said. Slipping her arm through mine, she pulled me along with her.

I glanced over at the enigmatic merwoman, trying to interpret her mood in her smooth features. I wished I could read her mind the way she read mine.

"I think Rriess likes you," I said. Jendayi calmly continued to swim as if she hadn't heard. "I think you like him," I added recklessly.

Jendayi turned her full attention on me, her amber eyes searching my face. "I always thought you were a perceptive girl," Jendayi said, nodding her head. Her crown flashed, reflecting the light of the city in its polished gold surface. I waited for more, but she had already turned her attention back to her swimming. It would seem that was all the answer I would get out of her on *that* particular subject.

"The Sea Queen and her sons are planning to greet you in person when we reach the palace," Jendayi said. "I feel I must warn you ahead of time what to expect when meeting them face to face."

This was an ominous beginning for a new topic of conversation. I stayed silent, waiting for her to go on.

"The royal family holds the key to all the powers of mermagic in their blood. Their abilities are – great."

I had the feeling "great" might be something of an under-statement, but decided not to share my opinion out loud. Jendayi had probably read my thoughts anyway.

"Is the Sea Queen as powerful as you are?" I asked slowly.

"No one is more powerful than the High Queen and her royal heir," Jendayi said. "My own talents are a mere drop in a vast ocean by comparison."

And I was supposed to meet this almighty High Queen for the first time as a possible candidate for marrying her son? What if I decided I didn't want to marry the Sea Prince and his mother decided to smite me for it? This unpleasant idea made my heart beat hurriedly, as if attempting to flee my chest. Luckily, my ribcage managed to keep it safely in its proper place.

"The royal family's magical aura is stronger than most," Jendayi continued. "It can be a little overwhelming for those who are not accustomed to it. Everything about the queen and her sons emanates their power. The resonance of their voices, the force of their gazes, the very water that surrounds them." Jendayi looked into my face. "But you have no reason to fear their power. They carry only goodwill for you in their hearts."

Jendayi's grave words did nothing to calm my growing unease. What if the Sea Queen looked at me wrong and accidentally burned me to cinders? So sorry. Maybe the next potential bride will be a better-looking one.

"We are nearly to the palace now," Jendayi said with a flip of her mighty tail. "Come."

Twenty-Five

The luminous grandeur of the Sea Queen's underwater palace made Lord Durran's fine manor house look like nothing more than a squat little hovel in comparison. The palace's many splendid sparkling towers and turrets seemed to spiral up for ever overhead. And the size of it! Why, every man, woman, and child on the whole of Windwaithe Island could have lived comfortably beneath its roof with room to spare. There was a simple elegance about the line of its architecture, as if its many windows, doors and decorative arches had grown up out of the structure with the natural grace of a conch shell.

All of this was nothing compared to what the palace looked like on the inside. Jendayi brought me directly into the palace's cavernous main hall. There were at least a dozen or more jewelled chandeliers floating lazily about the ceilings at the end of large golden chains. These marvellous wonders bore many-layered tiers filled to the brim with hundreds of glowing spheres that cast their brilliant light down upon us. Somewhere out of sight, I could hear a single female voice singing a beautifully sad song that made me feel as if I had just entered the hallowed walls of a church.

Growing up from a floor of soft, white sand was a variety of water plants that reminded me of an underwater garden. As Jendayi and I swam over the many colourful fronds, they swayed and danced, the tallest ones brushing against my stomach and legs at times. To a person who had spent her whole life walking on the land, it felt more natural to me to swim closer to the ground. I appreciated Jendayi's willingness to accommodate me.

Inlaid into the smooth surface of the palace walls were intricate mosaic pictures, made up of many little tiles of coloured glass and seashells. Stunned by the sheer beauty of one particularly large mosaic picture, I slipped my arm from Jendayi's for a moment. I let my feet drop, pulling my body into a vertical position as I drifted closer to get a better look.

The mosaic depicted a strange scene. At the far right, a group of men and women raced towards the open swells of the ocean on two legs. The part of the group just entering the water seemed to be in the middle of a change, their skins brightly coloured and their legs sprouting scales and fins. The group on the far left of the mosaic was merkind, who used their tails to leap through the waves as they made their way out into the open ocean.

"What you see before you is the birth of our race." Jendayi had silently moved up by my side. As she hovered upright, the sway of her fanning tail sent silky soft currents flowing over my skirt and legs. The plants swirled and tangled beneath us.

"What do you mean? Haven't there always been mermaids living in the ocean?" I asked.

"Many centuries ago, our ancestors were like you. They lived on the land, breathing air and walking on two legs. Our people were peaceful. Men of other lands came to wage war against us, thinking to claim our island as their own.

"Our ancestors had no weapons, no means of driving away their enemies, so they fled to the ends of the earth. Finding all their boats destroyed and unable to go any further, they stood in the foaming sea, praying to their Creator to save them from certain death."

Jendayi's topaz eyes shifted in my direction. "And the Creator answered them. As the bloodthirsty men were about to fall upon them, our people found themselves changing – their legs becoming fins, their lungs burning for water instead of air. My people swam out to sea and left their enemies standing upon empty shores."

Jendayi gently took my hand in hers and squeezed it. "That is why our royal blood must be joined to those of the land every seventh generation," she said. "It is the Creator's way of reminding us of where we came from. Queen Dakarai's sons are the seventh generation. She charged me with finding human wives for them both."

"Why you?" I asked. "You've come a far distance just to play matchmaker."

"Her Majesty, my cousin, said I was the only one she trusted with the important task of finding brides for her sons." Jendayi's voice became warm and wistful as her thoughts turned to those she loved. "Because of my noble blood, I am, let us say, more adept than most of my kind at reading the hearts of men even while they are yet on the land."

"In other words, you're extremely powerful," I translated. "Are you saying not every mermaid can call up a storm?"

Jendayi smiled and shook her head modestly. "I found I could not say no to my cousin's one request. I am glad now that I agreed. You were meant to be a part of our world, as was Lauretta."

The increase in the intensity of the buzzing in my wrist should have been a warning to me, but I was too caught up in considering the story of the merfolk Jendayi had just told me. Before I knew it, the scars burned white hot. I gasped in pain, clutching at my wrist. Noticing my distress, Jendayi placed her hand over mine, instantly quelling the pain in my skin with her magical touch.

I looked up at Jendayi in silent confusion. She nodded at something over my shoulder. "They are here," she said simply.

Gooseflesh prickled down my neck and across the surface of my skin. Stroking with my hands, I turned myself slowly about and laid eyes upon the legendary lost Lady Lauretta for the first time.

Lauretta drifted a few yards above us, looking for all the world like a messenger descending from heaven. Watching me with bright, curious, blue eyes, she looked much too young to have been born over a hundred years ago – in her early twenties at the very most. Her masses of hair hovered about her shoulders in a lovely cloud of strawberry and gold even Cora Lynn would have envied. She wore an elaborate necklace of glowing beads draped over her shoulders and neck like strings of glimmering stars.

I could see the tips of her toes peeping from beneath the hem of her long, flowing dress, a cream-coloured confection that swirled about her body with a life of its own. She stroked the water back and forth with her hands to keep herself balanced upright. The movements were like a slow, elegant dance.

Lady Lauretta was not alone. An impressively tall merman swam up to her side and righted himself with a smooth ease I could never hope to accomplish with a hundred years of practise. I took one look at the newcomer and knew he was the one who had caused my wrist to burn like fire. Jendayi had warned me about the aura of the royal family, but nothing could have truly prepared me for the waves of power rolling off the remarkable being that now floated majestically before me. I felt like a tiny mouse cowering in the corner as a cat of incredible strength and beauty examined me at his leisure.

The regal merman wore the same style of dress Rriess had, only this tunic shimmered as if woven from a pattern of pure gold and had emerald buttons running the length of it. The merman had a brilliant, emerald-green tail and comely golden-blond hair, trimmed short. His skin was the same fair shade as Lauretta's and mine, but there was nothing remotely human about the rest of him. He had the same elfin eyes and pointed ears as all the other merfolk I'd seen in the city. He was so handsome he was almost angelic. I could not tear my gaze from his. Looking into his eyes was like tumbling into a well deeper than the ocean itself. I was sure he could see everything, down to the smallest and most selfish things I had ever done, things I had hidden within my private soul. I was so overcome, I forgot to tread water for a moment and began to drift off course. Lady Lauretta smiled at my reaction, a slow, blossoming expression that spread through her face, transforming every lovely feature with its sunny light.

Seeing I was too stunned to make the first move, Jendayi placed her hands on my shoulders and pushed me up through the water, forcing me closer to the couple. Lady Lauretta manoeuvred herself forward and slipped her hands into my own in warm greeting.

Her distinguished merman companion moved closer and the welts on my wrist swelled and pulsed in response. His power was alarmingly great indeed.

"I am Prince Dasarian, first son of the Sea Queen Dakarai and appointed ruler of the kingdom known to your kind as the Celtic Sea." The strength of the merman's voice vibrated within my very bones as he spoke to me. "This is my wife, Princess Lauretta of Windwaithe."

I could not stop myself from wincing over the force of his voice. Lady – or should I say – Princess Lauretta noticed it right away.

"You must rein in your influence a bit more, my love," Princess Lauretta said to the merman in gentle remonstration. She turned back to me, squeezing my hands encouragingly within her own. "My husband's magic can be a bit overwhelming at first. Don't worry, dearest one, as the change within you grows, the discomfort will soon lessen."

The change? What exactly was that? I wasn't sure I wanted to know.

"Princess—" I began.

"You may call me Lauretta," she said. "Being 'princessed' all the time makes me weary."

I turned my attention to Prince Dasarian, looking him over with increasing curiosity. This was, after all, the older brother of the Sea Prince I'd been brought here to meet.

"You have a question for me?" The crown prince's voice was softer this time, as if he were holding back the full strength of it for my sake. It still caused tingles to shiver through my spine.

"I thought you would be—" I stopped, realizing how

rude my comment might seem.

"You thought I'd be green," Prince Dasarian finished for me.

Obviously he could read minds as well.

I glanced sheepishly at dark green Jendayi, who floated silently at my side, then back at the prince. "Something like that."

Prince Dasarian studied me with a disconcerting amount of consideration before answering. "Being required to marry humans every seventh generation means their blood runs strong in our royal bloodline. It tends to resurface in the seventh generation. A gentle reminder that the eternal bonds between our worlds must not be broken."

"I think the tamer colouring helps the human brides be a bit more willing as well," Lauretta added with a very unprincess-like grin. "A green husband might be a nasty shock for some."

"Does this mean your brother isn't green?" I asked Prince Dasarian much too hopefully.

The prince shook his head, a warm smile spreading into the curve of his lips. In a flash, his irises changed from their original dark colour to a jewel-like green and a wave of warm, golden magic enveloped me. I think I might have started gaping again.

"Don't worry," Lauretta said to me. "You'll grow used to that particular trait in time. It is rather astonishing, though, isn't it? I remember being extremely distracted by the shifting colours the first time I met my husband. By the by, the green means you've amused him."

"Jendayi's eyes don't change colour," I said, glancing again at the merwoman in curiosity.

"Did you think everyone beneath the sea would be just as I am?" Jendayi asked with her one-sided smile.

"It is only the curse of those of the direct royal bloodline to have their every thought revealed in the colour of their eyes," Prince Dasarian said. "It is the inner will and emotions, you see, that help us to channel our magic."

"He's so bursting with power his slightest change of mood affects everything around him." Lauretta gave her husband a teasing smile.

"Luckily, most do not know the colour of my moods as well as my wife does." There was a hint of gentle banter beneath the surface of Prince Dasarian's reserved demeanour.

I realized how foolish it was for me to imagine all merfolk would be exactly like Jendayi. Humans differed vastly from one another. It stood to reason, merfolk would also. As for the younger Sea Prince, if he looked anything like Prince Dasarian, we were going to get along just fine.

"Is the Sea Prince coming to meet me soon?" I glanced up at Prince Dasarian hesitantly. Meeting his brother was the whole reason I came to this fantastic place. I was a little confused as to why he wasn't there to greet me.

"Yes, where *is* your brother, Dasarian?" Jendayi glanced around as if attempting to discover where the young Sea Prince might be hiding himself. "Why does he make Adrianne wait so long?"

Prince Dasarian and his wife exchanged a long, silent look.

"Our mother has gone to fetch him from his room," Prince Dasarian's eyes shifted to a muddy hazel colour as he spoke these words. The water around me turned clammy against my skin.

Jendayi was instantly suspicious. "He should be prepared by now. I sent for him hours ago."

"And our noble mother, the queen, has been with him since that time," Prince Dasarian replied.

Jendayi's golden tail began whipping back and forth, sending powerful currents of displeasure whooshing off in every direction. "He promised me he would behave tonight," she said in slow, deliberate tones. "He said he understood why things must be done this way."

"His resolve seems to have fled to his room along with him." Prince Dasarian's eyes flashed back to a cheery green as he fought a smile. The water was warm and pleasant once more.

"Don't fret." Lauretta moved quickly to calm Jendayi down. "The prince does understand. He just needs time to collect himself."

"He will give Adrianne the wrong idea." Jendayi waved her open hand in my direction, and angry sparks danced for a moment at the ends of her fingertips. The three of them turned to look at me. I tried not to look as upset as I felt. I don't think I quite managed it.

Prince Dasarian's eyes turned a burnished gold. I could feel invisible tendrils of his concern reaching out towards me through the water. His voice was filled with a gentle reassurance when he spoke. "You will have to forgive my brother, Lady Adrianne, but he is feeling a little—"

"Willful?" Jendayi supplied.

"Shy," Prince Dasarian amended.

"*Your* brother? Shy? Do not be absurd," Jendayi said.

"Now, Jendayi, you don't want to lose that royal temper of yours. You might frighten our guest," Prince Dasarian said, looking my way in warning. I prayed he was not serious.

As a child I had often pictured the Sea Queen to myself as Papa told me stories of her. Never would I have dared to imagine her doing anything as ordinary as trying to argue sense into a rebellious son hiding in his room.

"If the prince doesn't wish to meet me then maybe we shouldn't force him," I said, glancing uneasily at each of them in turn.

"It's not you the prince objects to." Jendayi folded her arms regally before her. "This is nothing more than his way of rebelling because I refused to let him help choose his bride."

Jendayi's braids snapped around behind her as she shook her head over the Sea Prince's unbelievable audacity. "It will be two human years before the marriage can take place. You and the prince will have plenty of time to grow comfortable in each other's company between now and then."

Her eyes softened for a moment as she looked at me. "In time he will grow to love you. He will not be able to help himself."

"Then you may be sure it will happen," Prince Dasarian said with firm finality. "Jendayi is always right about these things."

"She has the gift of foreseeing the future," Lauretta explained to me.

"Not the future," Jendayi amended. "Only the shadows of distant paths that might be taken." Jendayi glanced at Lauretta and Prince Dasarian. "Nothing is for certain until one acts."

"Which we did, corals of life be praised," Lauretta said, looking up at her extraordinary husband.

"Your brother is being stubborn simply to annoy me," Jendayi said.

"It seems to be working." Prince Dasarian broke into a small grin that sent sunny tingles skipping through the water.

Jendayi was not amused. Her tail beat at the water so hard by now I had a hard time fighting the current. Noticing my struggle, Lauretta slipped her arm through mine and kicked against the rush of water, helping anchor me in place. She was a much stronger swimmer than I, but her skirts kept tangling with my own as the currents whipped them about.

"Perhaps now would be a good time to show Adrianne to her dressing room," Lauretta said in serene tones that belied the strength of the currents swirling around her. "It will give the prince time to – collect himself."

Jendayi still looked extremely displeased, but did manage to get her tail temporarily under control as she realized the difficulty she was causing us. My and Lauretta's skirts settled themselves into a languid drifting once more.

Lauretta beckoned with her free hand to an older merwoman hovering near the roof. Since I wasn't adjusted to the idea of possibly having people floating *above* my head, I hadn't noticed her there before. She swam swiftly down to us after being summoned.

"This is Griette," Lauretta said by way of introduction.

Griette bobbed before me in the mermaid version of a curtsy. The merwoman was the eldest of the merfolk I'd seen so far. She had shockingly pale, silvery blue skin with fine-looking wrinkles, a pleasantly plump figure, and lots of strikingly white hair braided up into graceful coils on top of her head. She wore a high-necked, dark grey blouse that fell almost to her thighs. The material was gathered in at the waist with a simple drawstring.

"Griette is my own personal handmaid. Which means she is used to looking after the strange needs of us humans. She will help prepare you for your meeting with the Sea Prince," Lauretta said.

Prepare me? I wasn't sure I liked the sound of that.

Like a lost child who needed someone to hold her hand, I looked to Jendayi. "Will you come with me?"

"We have much to discuss with Jendayi while you are being dressed." Lauretta patted my arm reassuringly. "Griette will take good care of you, I promise."

Jendayi reached out to brush a strand of my short hair from

my forehead with two of her fingers. "I will be here when you return, Adrianne of Windwaithe. I am to act as the prince's interpreter."

"Doesn't he speak English?"

Jendayi slowly shook her head. "The prince speaks some of your language, but not enough to carry on a conversation, I am afraid."

I looked uncertainly at the three of them, trying to hide the disappointment I felt rushing to fill the empty space where hope had been. "You all speak English," I pointed out.

"I had an excellent teacher." As he smiled down at his lovely wife, Prince Dasarian's eyes changed to a deep, velvety brown that inexplicably made me feel like blushing.

"You spoke perfectly well before I ever met you. I only helped refine your skills a bit." Lauretta slipped her right arm through her husband's. Her left hand she placed on his upper shoulder in a somewhat intimate manner. Prince Dasarian pulled her in closer to him, his tail momentarily brushing against her skirts. Cecily would have said they were as spoony for each other as the day is long.

I could not help wondering why Prince Dasarian learned to speak English before meeting his bride when his younger brother hadn't. It seemed a bit odd, if you asked me. Especially since Jendayi had tutored the young prince herself.

Griette drifted closer and gently touched her mistress's shoulder in reminder. Reluctantly pulling herself from her husband's embrace, Lauretta turned her attention back to me.

"Griette, take Lady Adrianne to the dressing room and show her the lovely surprises we've prepared for her," Lauretta said.

I think that was the moment I began to panic.

Twenty-Six

The dressing room was on the second floor, but there were no stairs in the palace; you simply swam wherever you wanted to go. It was quite convenient really.

Griette pulled me through a winding maze of dim corridors with bare, sandy floors and many beautifully arched windows. I quickly discovered that none of these windows held glass when a large dark fish darted through one and nearly startled me out of my wits. Griette shooed the thing back out again as calmly as Mama would have shooed the hens from her garden.

Finally, Griette ushered me into a spacious room with pink walls that seemed to be made of many diamond-shaped coral tiles of various shades, fitted tightly together in decorative designs. I noticed that the ceilings in the palace were higher than those of houses on the land. I assumed this was to leave more room for swimming about.

Right away Griette introduced me to a pair of mergirls who looked only a few years older than myself. With merfolk, however, I knew looks were probably deceiving. The mergirls did not speak English, but I surmised from their similar attire and subordinate behavior to Griette that they were her assistants in the task of making me presentable.

Like Griette, the two younger mermaids had their hair coiled up into braids on top of their heads. I wondered if all female servants were required to wear their hair that way when working in the Sea Queen's palace. One assistant had bright red hair and skin the colour of creamy porcelain; the other had deeply tanned skin and tresses that looked like they were spun from pure silver. Both of them glided closer, examining me head to foot.

Murmuring to one another, they looked and pointed, curiosity written on their faces. For a moment, I thought the shabbiness of my dress had caught their attention and hot shame burned through me. I soon realized it was not my clothes they found so interesting, but my two bare feet, peeping beneath the drifting hem of my skirt. Curling my toes, I pulled up my knees in an attempt to hide them. The redhead gave a girlish giggle. Griette shushed her with a watery hiss, and then turned to me with a comforting smile.

"Come, we dress you," she said. Griette had a gentle speaking voice that was pleasant to the ears.

I figured "dressing me" would involve nothing more than my being forced to wear some embarrassingly fancy frock. I couldn't have been more mistaken.

The first thing Griette did was strip me down to the skin and give me a good, hard scrubbing from top to bottom with some sort of unpleasantly coarse sponge. She worked with the speed of a whirlwind, stirring up eddies of buffeting current in her wake as she attacked me on every side. The water around us soon grew murky with the two years' worth of ground-in dirt she managed to scrub out of my hair and skin.

While Griette practically flayed me alive, the redheaded assistant spirited away my tattered dress and underthings, wrinkling her nose over the soiled state of them as she left the dressing room.

After Griette finished scouring my flesh raw, she dressed me in a silky new shift and turned me over to the silver-haired assistant, who painfully dug the dirt out from under my broken fingernails and filed them into a more presentable shape with a small, flat stone.

When the redheaded assistant returned with the new dress, it was every bit as horrifically splendid as I imagined it would be. A deep, radiant blue creation with fancy beadwork and real gold embroidery stitched into the bodice and the cuffs of its sleeves. I was terrified to even touch the dress, but Griette (with quite a bit of help from her two younger assistants) managed to stuff me into the silly thing. I ran my fingers over the rich material of the skirt. It was slick and smooth and shimmered like the scales of a fish. It fitted my body a lot snugger than Auntie Minnah would have deemed proper – but just this once, I figured I was safe from my aunt's ire.

I thought about how much time it would have taken Mama to sew such a dress by hand. The merfolk would have had to start working on it months ago. How could they possibly have known I would come down to their world at all, much less what size I would be if I did? Perhaps Jendayi's foresight was sharper than I gave her credit for.

Griette swept me through the water over to a large balcony-like alcove jutting out from the chamber wall. Carved into the balcony floor was a fancy pink coral chair with elegant dolphin-shaped armrests and a shiny mother-of-pearl seat. Attached to the wall before the chair was a large, dark stone in the shape of an oval, with a fantastic decorative border carved into its outer edge. Its glassy surface seemed to be polished within an inch of its life. I looked into the stone's dark surface, amazed to see how clearly my own pale face reflected back at me in the golden light of the glowing lanterns mounted throughout the room.

A magical mirror made of stone. Would wonders never cease?

"Sit." Griette gestured to the chair with one silvery blue hand.

I tried to sit down and quickly found such a feat was not as easy as it sounds when one is underwater. I bumped about a bit, then slowly began to drift back out of the chair. Instinctively, I tried bracing my feet against the floor and managed to launch myself right up over Griette's head. The young redheaded assistant giggled, but her silver-haired companion quickly silenced her with a sharp elbow to the ribs.

Griette looked thoughtfully up at me floating above her and planted her hands on her round hips. "You float," Griette stated dryly.

Yes, I *had* noticed that little problem.

Griette pointed down at one of the dolphin-shaped arms of the chair. "For helding," she said.

Helding? What in heaven's name was helding?

Griette gripped the armrest with one hand and tugged against it.

"For helding," she repeated patiently.

Ah – for holding! She wanted me to hold myself down with the armrests. I swam back down and caught hold of the chair, manoeuvring myself deep into its seat. I anchored myself in place with both hands. Griette smiled and nodded her satisfaction.

She murmured some orders to her two assistants in the language of the merfolk, and they quickly set about brushing through my hair and fastening tiny golden combs in a row along the crown of my head. After they were finished, Griette deftly pinched my cheeks to rosy them. Auntie Minnah would have died a thousand deaths in horror.

Griette's assistants flitted from the room for a moment and quickly returned with another "surprise". It was a necklace. Not just any necklace, but a golden work of art. Its fine strands were seeded with flashing rows of tiny sapphires and woven into a delicate net, joined together in front by the largest, deep blue jewel imaginable. A present fit for a true princess.

I wanted nothing to do with it.

Trying to communicate my reluctance to wear the luxurious jewellery to my two devoted handmaids was another matter entirely. They couldn't understand a word of my protests, so they ignored them completely. In the end, the silver-haired maid held my arms down at my sides while the redhead draped the necklace around my neck without permission. All the while, Griette floated off to the side, hiding her bemused smiles unsuccessfully behind one plump hand.

The necklace was so heavy I knew it had to be made of pure gold. The ponderous weight helped to keep the necklace in its proper place, resting against my neck and chest, instead of floating up to obscure my vision whenever I moved about in the water. Griette and her two assistants waited expectantly as I looked over the final product of their labours in the stone mirror.

I wished deep within my heart that Denn could have seen me at that moment. The absence of dirt did wonders for the healthy glow of my skin. The elegant dress brought out gentle curves in my slender form that I hadn't even known existed before that moment. But then, I'd never had a dress that fitted me like a glove the way this one did. The tiny gold combs sparkled in my hair like a crown, making me look like someone important.

I thought I knew exactly who I was. Adrianne Keynnman, the poor, scrawny daughter of the village seamstress. A girl who had lost her family's fortune and always looked and smelled like something the cow had dragged through a muddy field. The girl looking out at me from the magical stone mirror in no way resembled that person.

She was not stunning or breathtaking like Cora Lynn, but quite attractive in her own right. The water gave her hair a fluffy clean look that framed her face quite nicely and brought out the true beauty of her eyes. This girl looked like something really special. A princess in the making.

She was a complete stranger to me.

I remembered Jendayi's words to me out on the Rumbles that night.

They see only with their eyes, and are blinded to the truest treasures that stand before them dressed in the ordinary dust and sweat of hard life.

I assumed she spoke of Denn and the others of our island, but now realized, perhaps, I was just as blind as the rest of them when it came to the way I viewed myself. The girl in the mirror had always been there – I just hadn't been able to see her.

Griette gave me an encouraging pat on the shoulder. I wondered if she caught some inkling of my inner thoughts as I sat there gaping at my own reflection.

"Come," she said softly. "Majesties wait you in hall."

I wondered if "majesties" included the younger Sea Prince. There was only one way to find out.

Letting loose of the arms of the chair, I let myself float upwards and dutifully allowed Griette to tow me back through the palace the way we had originally come. The silvery blue merwoman looked me over one last time before patting me fondly on the cheek and leaving me in the corridor just outside the entrance to the main hall.

Taking a deep breath, I waved my way closer to the open doorway, and peeked inside.

Lauretta, Prince Dasarian and Jendayi still floated halfway up in the middle of the room, exactly where I had left them. Prince Dasarian spoke the soothing, rounded tones of merlanguage as he attempted to reason with Jendayi, whose golden tail fanned open and shut like a blacksmith's bellows, feeding her inner flame.

It was Lauretta who first noticed my return. The other two were so caught up in their intense discussion they didn't see her slip away from the group. Arms at her sides and legs together, Lauretta used her whole body like a seal's to propel herself swiftly across the room to greet me. The tiny lights within the beads of her necklace seemed to glow even brighter as she passed from the well-lit hall into the dimmer shadows of the poorly lit corridor. She drifted to a stop, her skirts swirling about her in the water. The glowing necklace twinkled as it swung forward, then settled back into place against her chest.

Lauretta looked me over and cooed in quiet admiration over the results of Griette's hard work.

"I picked the design of that dress myself," Lauretta informed me. "But it was Jendayi who chose the colour. I'd say she got it just right, wouldn't you? The young prince will be overcome with admiration the moment he lays eyes on you."

That one look in the mirror back in the dressing room had been enough to convince me that she just might be right this time. Too self-conscious to admit it, however, I glanced over Lauretta's shoulder at Jendayi, who was now arguing back with Prince Dasarian in their native tongue. She seemed to be working herself up into an impressive state of royal displeasure.

Lauretta pressed a comforting hand on my shoulder. "Do not worry, everything will come right in the end. The first time Dasarian and I met was an utter disaster. I'd never learned to swim, you see. I wobbled and bobbed about like a cork on a fishing line trying to keep myself upright. I even flipped upside down while trying to curtsy to him." Lauretta laughed lightly to herself over the awful memory. The sound bubbled pleasantly within my ears.

"Would they really force the prince to marry me if he doesn't want to?" I asked. At the moment, Jendayi looked perfectly capable of forcing anyone to the altar, even a legendary Sea Prince. But I could not begin to imagine myself party to a marriage where the groom was dragged into it against his will.

"The marriage will not take place right away, of course. You're too young for that yet. It will take about two human years for the change within your body to be complete. During that time, you will continue to grow normally."

"This is the second time you've mentioned a change," I said. "What is this change exactly?"

"The magic placed in your blood by Jendayi has begun to alter you. Don't look so alarmed, dear one, you won't grow a tail, I promise you, but you will become more like the merfolk. Your aging will slow and your body will accustom itself to living underwater properly. During these two years of change, you will be taught many things, such as the language of merfolk and their history and customs."

Lauretta clasped her hands thoughtfully before her, making small movements with her legs to keep herself in place. "You must understand, the younger prince has no objection to marrying a human, only to being forced to marry a stranger he had no part in choosing."

Lauretta glanced towards Jendayi and her husband as they continued to "discuss" the problem at hand. "Ever since he first learned of his fate as a seventh-generation child, the young prince has always been a little rebellious about the idea of an arranged marriage. He stubbornly refused to learn the language of humans when he was younger. I suppose it was his way of keeping control of the situation."

If the prince couldn't communicate with his intended bride, then it would take even more time for a marriage to take place.

It was a very clever idea indeed. So clever I couldn't help but admire the Sea Prince's ingenuity.

"When he learned of you, the prince asked me all kinds of questions about the land of my birth," Lauretta continued. "He has pestered Jendayi with questions about you as well. The prince is true and kind and good. A gentleman through and through. Many a mermaid has lost her young heart to him, but he has held himself for his future human bride, as he knows he must. When he's finished his little protest, he will come down to meet you on his best behaviour, you will see."

"But what if he doesn't fall in love with me?" I asked. Denn hadn't. The very idea of it had struck him broadside like a whale barrelling into a ship.

"If Jendayi says he will love you one day, then it will be so. She sees true. That is why Queen Dakarai chose her for this errand. The prince knows it, but he has never liked being told what to do, even when he knows it is for his own good."

I began to think I might actually like this prince. He sounded blessedly normal. Not at all like those frighteningly perfect princes you hear about in fairy tales.

Lauretta paused a moment to consider me, her head to one side. The smile slipped from her lips for a moment as her gaze shifted from focus. I had the feeling she wasn't really seeing me any more – but some memory far distant.

"You remind me so much of myself when Jendayi first came for me." Her voice was barely a murmur, like the sigh of the sea.

"I, too, came from Windwaithe Island."

"There are stories about you," I said.

"Are there truly?" Lauretta laughed in soft surprise, as if she could not quite believe it. "Do the stories tell what a wilful, disobedient girl I was growing up?"

I shook my head. "They make you sound like a saint."

"The truth is, I was a holy terror, especially to my prim and proper governess." Lauretta paused thoughtfully. "I haven't thought of poor, overtaxed Miss Carvell in a very long time."

"The stories don't mention a governess," I said.

"I imagine not. You see, I did exactly as I pleased in those days, no matter how much it shocked those around me," Lauretta said. "My father always predicted I would get myself into real trouble someday. But he laughed whenever he said it."

She gave a small watery sigh. "I was only sixteen when Jendayi took me away," she said, almost more to herself than me.

Two years older than me. The same age Denn was now.

"Jendayi refuses to speak of the world above when I am about." Lauretta brushed her drifting hair aside with one hand while glancing over her shoulder at Jendayi before continuing. "She says much time has passed there, though it seems like only a few years to me. I think Jendayi is afraid dwelling on the past will bring me sadness, but not talking of it at all is worse. For then the happy memories are lost to me as well."

Lauretta's words trailed away for a moment as she seemed to be thinking some private thing I could not hear. Her gaze sharpened, all her attention suddenly directed at me. An arrow could not have pierced me so deep.

"Adrianne, do the stories say anything of my father and his fate after I left?" she asked.

No. Not that question. Anything but that, I thought in rising panic.

Lauretta waited for my answer. An answer I knew would bring great pain to those clear blue eyes. Her father held her a prisoner in her own home. He sacrificed her to a mermaid to protect the people on his island, and yet, a century later she could still not cast her love for him aside. "I know of you only from legend," I answered as carefully as I could. "The legends do not say what happened to your father."

Lauretta turned her face from me. I was glad I did not have to see the pain I knew she must be hiding there. "If I am naught but a legend, then of course my father must be dead and buried long ago," she said with a calm acceptance that must have taken a truly heroic effort to accomplish.

I tried to imagine what it would have been like to learn of Papa's death in such a way. It tore my heart apart even imagining it.

"I wish my father could have seen this place." Lauretta's words were gentle, but heavy with that which was lost to her for ever. "If only Father could have met Dasarian and spoken with him just once."

I moved to place a comforting hand on her shoulder. "If he

had, I'm sure he would have understood why you needed to go."

As I spoke these words, I could not help but think of my own family. Would they understand if I were to decide never to return? This question gave me pause. Up until that moment, I hadn't seriously considered the idea of not going back. What if I did not have to leave this underwater paradise? What if I decided to stay like Lauretta had?

It was as if the finger of providence reached down to touch my soul, stirring up the once-stagnant pool of my possibilities. What lay before me was paradise. The kind of place people of the land only dreamed of. The weight of exhaustion brought on by years of never-ending, back-breaking work would never touch me in this beautiful place. I wouldn't be chained down by the weakness or burdens of others. Never again would I know the gnawing pain of hunger. No sorrow. No disappointment. And to be loved. Cherished as a jewel beyond price. Never would I be overlooked or compared to another again. Being shown such possibilities felt like stepping into a light of blinding brilliance. I sat there gasping like a helpless fish swept unexpectedly from my element.

Would I really be happy marrying the Sea Prince? I began to wonder if I actually might.

"The prince – what does he look like? Does he have red hair?" I hadn't meant to speak that last part aloud. Even as the question fell from my lips I knew its significance. But Lauretta did not.

"The prince has fair hair, like my husband," she said absently, distracted by something going on in the hall.

I followed her gaze to find Jendayi and Prince Dasarian were no longer alone. The purple-skinned Rriess had joined them. Jendayi and the elder prince listened intently as Rriess spoke to them, gesturing at the ceiling with one of his hands.

"Something has happened. Would you excuse me one moment?" Lauretta swam like she'd been born to it. Her skirts billowed behind her as she flashed across the hall to rejoin the rest of the group. Rriess must have started to explain all over again, because Lauretta was completely absorbed in whatever it was he turned to say to her.

Just beyond the group, a figure appeared, swimming hesitantly through an arched doorway at the opposite end of the room. I took one look at the newcomer and knew it had to be him.

My prince.

The elusive Sea Prince was older than Denn – eighteen perhaps, well on his way to manhood. I could not tear my gaze from the perfect features of his face. He was like the ancient immortals of myth, otherworldly and *very* handsome indeed. More so than his older brother, if that is possible. A godling straight from the fairy realm.

The prince had a golden tail, slightly lighter in colour than Jendayi's, and hair so blond it shone like a creamy moon hanging in the night sky. His forehead bore a simple gold circlet, with a large cut sapphire set in its centre. His tunic was blue with gold embroidery, a perfect match to my new dress.

I understood then why Denn had been so dizzy with desire

for Cora Lynn. It would have been so easy to lose my heart to that oh-so-handsome face, to let all semblance of good sense wash away in the sheer delight of my bewildered senses.

Suddenly overcome by a bout of overwhelming shyness, I kicked my legs and stroked hurriedly backwards, drawing myself further into the shadows of the dim hallway so I wouldn't be spotted right away. Just like Lauretta predicted, the prince seemed to be on his best behaviour as he floated before his family and Rriess. It was Jendayi who seemed to be doing most of the talking now. I did not need to speak their tongue to understand how extremely displeased she was with the less than enthusiastic reception the prince had given our first meeting. As Jendayi scolded him in low, angry tones, the prince's eyes remained humbly lowered, listening patiently to every word of censure his mother's cousin felt called to lay upon his shoulders. Prince Dasarian gently interrupted Jendayi, speaking to her in calm, reasonable tones.

In that moment of respite, the younger prince looked up, his gaze flitting anxiously about the hall. I knew it had to be me he sought. Luckily he did not spy me hovering in the hallway like a frightened trout – not yet anyway. But he soon would.

The icy water within my lungs quickly turned warm as I forgot to refresh it. I think I might even have swallowed some. It was the salt burning at my throat as it went down that finally broke the trance I'd fallen under. Using my hands to stroke at the water, I whirled myself about and fled back down the shadowy corridor, cutting through the water as fast as I could.

Twenty-Seven

Slipping through the same window the fish had come through earlier, I escaped from the cheerier interior of the palace into the cold, darker waters of the wide-open sea outside. The glowing lanterns were fewer and far between, which made it harder to see. I kicked my legs and pumped my arms, cutting my way through the water and scattering a large school of colourful fish in my wake. Across the vast palace grounds I spied a small pavilion. Its fluted columns reminded me of a painting of a Grecian temple that once hung in Papa's study in our old home. Only the columns in this underwater structure were arranged side by side in a circle, not a square like in the painting. I made my way over to the edge of the pavilion and stopped to catch my watery breath. Glancing upwards, I saw there were no stars in the heights above, only inky blackness stretching up as far as the eye could see. With a shiver, I realized there was no way home for me without Jendayi.

With my knees tucked in tight so my skirts wouldn't float up into my face, I curled up in a dark, sandy corner of the pavilion and buried my head in my arms, willing myself not to break down sobbing. There may have been no tears in the ocean, but the pain was the same even without them.

What was I doing? By now Jendayi and the others would be madly searching the palace for me. Why had I run away from the Sea Prince? Wasn't my meeting with him the whole reason I'd come to this place at the bottom of the sea? How many times had I prayed for my problems to be magically taken away? So why was I now running away from my one chance to escape them?

If you go back, Adrianne, you will never return home, I thought. I don't know where my certainty of this knowledge came from, but I knew in my heart it was true. I needed time to think.

Much would be required of me if I chose to stay. I would have to learn a new language, not to mention the many customs and manners of the merfolk. I would also be required to negotiate a complicated relationship with a rebellious prince who wasn't exactly happy at the idea of marrying me. What if we disagreed and my all-powerful mother-in-law decided to take his side of the argument? I shuddered to think of the consequences.

Yet, being married to a fantastically handsome merman couldn't be all bad, could it? Jendayi said he would fall in love with me in time. I tried to picture myself being kissed by the young godling I'd glimpsed in the hall, but there imagination failed me. All I could see in my mind was me as a child throwing my small arms around Denn's neck and sneaking in a kiss.

I fiddled absently with the heavy necklace draped over my neck, then reached up and carefully pulled it over my head. Clutching it tightly in my hand, I stared down into the depths of its shimmering sapphires like one in a trance. This necklace made my grandmama's tiny locket seem like a cheap trinket in comparison – and yet, I would have given anything to see Grandmama's locket at that moment. Especially if it hung around my little sister's neck.

If I stayed here I would never again hear Cecily's childish giggling, or listen to Mama's soft voice singing over her work. I would never see Denn's grinning, freckled face or feel his encouraging hand upon my shoulder. Would any of them miss me? Or would they be glad to be rid of the one who brought them so much anguish?

Why should I not rush out to meet this new existence? What was there behind me that could not be replaced tenfold by what was ahead? Here I had everything a girl could desire: a handsome prince, riches beyond measure and clothes so fine they would have made even Cora Lynn Dunst drool with envy. So why did my heart feel like a lump of iron rusted deep within me?

The sapphire necklace slipped from my fingers and spiralled to the ground. Small clouds of silt and sand billowed upwards as it settled heavily to the bottom of the ocean.

What would happen to my family if I did not return? Who would milk the cow or make money for the tax? Even Auntie Minnah would be gone. Mama would be alone.

A memory floated to the surface of my thoughts. I could feel again Mama's gentle hand resting in mine. Her words a mere whisper. *Sometimes, I fancy if I hold you tight enough, some of your courage will seep into me and help me not to be so weak.*

And Cecily. I could still see her adoring eyes looking up into my own. *I think you're the best sister anyone could have. I want to be just like you when I grow older.*

My family would be better off without me, I reasoned within myself. If I went back now, I would only bring the wrath of every superstitious fool on the island of Windwaithe down upon them.

Still, something held me back – an invisible thread that resisted my desire to break free. Its very fibres wrapped tight around my heart, tugging at it in painful reminder.

My mind flitted momentarily back to the surface so far above. For the first time, I wondered what Denn had done after I disappeared into the water. How much time had passed? Had he gone to my family and told them what happened? Did they, even now, believe I was lost to them? Would Cecily cry like she did when Lark was sold? Would Mama take to her bed and refuse to eat or speak? Would Auntie Minnah still leave them in their distress and go live with her friend? If I never came back, would Denn miss me?

I would never know the answer to these questions if I stayed.

Having suffered so much, would I ever be able to forget the anguish and pain of those I would leave behind? They were my greatest trial because they needed me. That's what made me love them so much. A hundred years from now, would I, like Lauretta, still hold regret deep within my heart for those I had lost?

I understood why I asked that silly question about the prince having red hair. While I might enjoy looking at the Sea Prince for a very long time, in my deepest heart I would always long for the imperfect but lovable Denn, who had stood by me, even during the dark times. He might never learn to love me, but I loved him with all my heart. Part of me always would. We'd been through so much together.

There was so much more left to be done.

But would Her Royal Highness, the Sea Queen, even allow me to go home after I rudely rejected her son's hand in marriage? I had a hard time believing any mother would take this news calmly. Getting on the bad side of the all-powerful mermaid queen was definitely not a wise idea. What if she decided to strike Windwaithe Island down with a tidal wave in retaliation for such an insult? I shivered, hugging my knees even tighter.

The welts on my arm began to burn, warning me of someone

approaching. I clutched at my wrist in alarm. Was this the Sea Prince come to find me? What if the magic now flowing within my veins alerted him to my presence? Or worse yet, what if it was the Sea Queen herself come to hunt me down? How could I possibly face an onslaught of maternal wrath?

The welts swelled and tingled as whoever it was grew nearer. I held my liquid breath and waited.

Jendayi's elegant green form glided into view. She swam up and hovered before me, fanning her hands and fin. I had been away from her magic for a while. That must have been why her nearness affected my wrist.

I gazed silently at her – waiting.

"If you were trying to take revenge on the prince, I think your plan may have worked," Jendayi said gently. "He's feeling extremely guilty over having chased you off in this manner. By the time you return to the palace, he will be a jellyfish in your hands."

Still I did not speak. Jendayi tilted her head questioningly; her light green braids slithered about her shoulders with the movement. Noticing the necklace still lying in the silt at my feet, she swam forward and picked it up. She offered it to me, but I silently shook my head, refusing to take it. She dropped her hand to her side, the stones of the necklace glittering darkly between her fingers.

"If I were to stay here and marry the Sea Prince, would I ever see my mother and sister again?" I demanded of her.

Jendayi shook her head. "Once you are permanently joined to

the sea it is impossible for you to leave it again – just as I am barred from the land, so would you be."

"Might I bring my family down here with me?" I asked.

Even as I said the words, I knew what the answer would be. Jendayi silently shook her head again.

"I want to go home," I said.

"You are understandably upset under the circumstances," Jendayi began. "The prince did not make you feel welcome."

"I want to go home," I repeated stubbornly.

"You need time to get to know the prince better."

"You said I could go back home if I wanted to. I'm asking you to take me back, right now." I could feel my throat tightening dangerously. I would not cry. I refused to.

Jendayi peered at me with piercing amber eyes – reading the secrets of my heart as easily as she did all men of the land.

"Why do you want to go back?" she asked me. "Because you still hold affection in your heart for Denn Young, the redheaded boy you think of as your best friend?"

She knew his name. Just as she knew everything else about my life. I shivered involuntarily. Spending time with Jendayi the last few hours had made me forget what she truly was – an extremely powerful mermaid with powers unfathomable to my limited understanding.

"You deserve better," Jendayi said.

"There is no one better than Denn," I snapped back in fierce defence of my dearest friend.

Jendayi's tail began to sway dangerously. Her fingers tightened around the necklace in her hand. I'd seen enough of her displeasure with the prince to know I was quickly heading into stormy waters.

"Every day of your life on the land, you waited for your world to collapse around you. Every waking moment you worried about where your food or clothing would come from. Every day you had to listen to a small, bitter woman tear you apart and watch the boy you love pursue a beautiful but useless creature. Is that really the life you want to go back to?" Jendayi asked.

I swallowed the knot in my throat and nodded slowly. "Those I love are there."

The moment I felt the water turn cold around me, I knew I had pushed Jendayi too far. If I thought the rebellious Sea Prince made her lose her temper before, I was in for a rude awakening of biblical proportions.

Jendayi thrashed her tail in fury. Flashes of lightning-like energy crackled around her, making the icy water tingle against my numb skin. As the temperature dropped, Jendayi's amber eyes grew in intensity, their colour flickering and shifting like flames. Even her hair took on a life of its own. The pale green braids rose up around her, writhing like angry snakes.

This was the mermaid of my childhood legends, a wild and frightening creature with enough power to ravage an entire island with her wrathful fury. I curled myself into a tighter ball, cowering before her.

"Is it not enough?" Jendayi demanded, in a voice so powerful it made my ears ring. I covered them with my hands but still could not block the piercing sound. Jendayi gestured grandly about her with both hands, energy sparking from her splayed fingers.

"I have searched the ocean over to find you and bring you here. I have offered you everything. And still you wish to go back to a world overrun by greedy weaklings and short-sighted fools!"

She whirled on me, her eyes literally burning with rage. The water turned even icier, as she drew all the warmth from it into herself to fuel her magical fury. I began to shiver from cold as well as fear.

"Even if you were to return and spend all the short years of your life sacrificing for the happiness of others and carrying their burdens, they would still never see you for what you truly are," she said. "You will find no respect among your own kind. Those who sense the difference in you will be afraid, even hostile towards you. They will never know your true worth."

"I will know it!"

My desperate shout sent small tremors though the water. Even Jendayi's fiery temper was momentarily checked by the power of conviction in my voice. I let out a long watery breath, trying to regain control of my trembling body.

"You are right." I spoke the words as calmly as I could. "The world is a cold and merciless place. And Mama and Cecily will never survive in it without me."

Jendayi violently shook her head in denial of my words, but I continued on anyway.

"Didn't you say it was Cecily's desire to be like me that helped her become what she is? What if I'd not been there to influence her?"

Jendayi scowled down at me, her eyes still burning with the glowing flames of her power. The braids rippled and swayed in a hypnotic rhythm, as if waiting to strike.

"Look what happened to Mama when Papa died. How can I leave her alone to face an even worse fate? She will blame herself – you know she will."

"You are but a child yet. You do not understand the far-reaching consequences of your choice," Jendayi said coldly. "You will live a much longer and happier life here in the sea, Adrianne of Windwaithe, and your children after you. This is where you belong."

"You would keep me here against my will?" I could barely make myself speak the words aloud.

"If I must." The golden eyes softened for a moment as sadness touched the mermaid's dark green features, then hardened again with new resolve. "It is for your own good that I cannot let you go back," she said.

Now that I actually wanted to return to my old life, would I really be stuck here for ever? Dragged to the altar with an equally unwilling groom?

Slowly, I unfolded myself from the sea floor and drifted up so I might look directly into Jendayi's terrible but beautiful face. I was helpless against her. A poor, ordinary island girl shivering before one of the most powerful beings in all of creation.

"A hundred years ago, Lady Lauretta's father did everything in his power to stop his daughter from doing what her heart told her was right." My gaze did not falter from the mermaid's. "Would you do the same to me now?"

My words struck true. I watched as horrified recognition dawned within Jendayi's eyes, quenching the fiery flames in an instant. Her braids dropped back into their proper place as she clenched the necklace tight in her fist, struggling to gain control of her emotions. The warmth slowly returned to the water and her gaze faltered from my own, as the once-proud mermaid turned her face from me in shame.

"You are wiser than your years, little Adrianne of Windwaithe." Jendayi's voice dropped to a gentle murmur that did not hurt my ears. "For a century I have hated the man, Lord Durran, for what he did to Princess Lauretta, but today I have become no better than he was."

I put out a hand and softly rested it upon her shoulder. "You did it out of love."

"I suppose Lord Durran would have said the same," Jendayi said softly. Her tail was completely still as she opened her fingers and stared sadly at the beautiful sapphire necklace lying limply on her palm. She looked up again, her amber eyes meeting my own.

"Don't go." Her plea was barely a whisper of water stirring within my ears.

"This kingdom in the sea will go on being beautiful and peaceful whether I marry the Sea Prince or not," I said. "But those at home will have no beauty or peace if I leave them. They need me – and I need them."

Jendayi bowed her head, as if my choice were too heavy for her to bear.

"So be it," she said.

Twenty-Eight

When we reached the surface of the ocean, I released all the water from my lungs and took a deep breath of air. It felt strangely light and thin inside my chest. I was surprised to see the sky already turning the rosy hues of early dawn. I'd been gone all night.

I swam to the nearest Rumble Stone and pulled myself up, dripping, on to the solid rock. Water streamed from my dress, and my arms and legs felt as if hundred-pound boulders were tied to them. My body trembled beneath the weight.

Jendayi's graceful form surfaced silently beside the Rumble Stones. She hadn't spoken to me since I'd made the choice to return home. Now she lifted her powerful gaze to meet mine.

"You are sure of your choice?" she asked in her beautiful, foreign voice.

"Yes."

She closed her eyes, nodded, then opened them again. "Give me your right hand."

I placed my hand in hers. She stroked my welts with her slender fingers, massaging the swollen skin. Searing hot pain shot through my wrist and into my shoulder. As I watched, the welts withered like vines beneath her touch. Soon they were nothing but pale pink scars upon the surface.

"They will be completely healed by tomorrow," Jendayi said. "When they are gone, so too will be your ability to live beneath the water."

I nodded solemnly, with some regret, I must admit. Never again would I be able to enjoy the beauty of the world I'd glimpsed so briefly beneath the ocean.

I looked at Jendayi. Heaviness clung tight to a place inside my heart. "What will you do now? Where will you find a bride for the Sea Prince?"

"I will begin my search again and find another, though it will be hard to find one like you. But I have time. He is young yet."

"Not to mention it will give you an excuse to stay a little longer at the palace where Rriess is close by," I said with a mischievous grin. "I just hope he knows what he's getting himself into."

Jendayi smiled over this a moment, then reached out towards me. I bent down and let her touch my cheek. "You will not see me again, Adrianne of Windwaithe, but I will keep an eye on you –

and your daughters after you."

"If I have any." I could feel myself blushing to the roots of my short hair.

"Why not?" She shrugged her shoulders in a matter-of-fact gesture. "Why should one who is worthy of a Sea Prince not be able to charm one humble island boy?"

I shrugged in return, laughing out loud. She was right. Why not?

The mermaid smiled a private, knowing kind of smile, only one side of her mouth turning upwards. "There will be daughters – and possibly a son."

My laughter died away instantly. I blinked dumbly at her, not sure how to answer. What did she mean, possibly?

Jendayi drew away her hand. Her glorious golden eyes were a yellow flame in the approaching dawn. The light caught the metallic surface of her crown as she lifted her chin to look at me one last time. With a mighty heave of her tail she leaped back into the ocean and faded beneath the waves. A voice whispered inside my head.

Never forget, Adrianne of Windwaithe, that once you might have been a princess.

My eyes burned with a sadness I never would have imagined I could feel in saying goodbye to one I'd known so short a time. But her words lifted my spirits. I had almost been a princess. That would never change, no matter how the people of my village treated me.

Slowly, I made my way across the Rumble Stones and up the beach towards my home. My dress clung uncomfortably to my legs and the cold had sneaked back into my body. I rubbed my right wrist with regret.

I couldn't stop thinking about Denn. Where was he now? Had he run home to Mama and Auntie in a panic when I didn't return? I didn't know what to tell them if they asked me to account for where I'd been all night. The truth would be impossible.

There was a movement ahead of me on the sand. Cautiously, I drew closer.

I'd never seen anything as sad and pitiful as the battered-looking figure sitting on the damp beach, his back hunched, head buried against his knees. In an instant, I recognized the old cap and the mass of red curls hanging in wet ringlets about his head. His clothes were heavy and wet upon his body, as if he'd just come from the water.

"Denn?" I spoke softly, not wanting to startle him.

His head snapped upwards in surprise. He looked at me with blurry, red eyes, his freckled cheeks a raw pink. I stared in amazement. Had he been crying? Never in my whole life had I seen Denn Young cry. As I watched, his expression changed from one of complete wretchedness to utter amazement.

"Adri?" Denn said in a disbelieving whisper.

I nodded.

"ADRIANNE!"

Denn sprung up with the speed of a cat, sweeping me into

his arms. Encircling my waist, he lifted me high into the air, spinning me around and around. I clutched him around his neck in surprise. When we finally drifted to a stop I felt dizzy – not all of it due to spinning.

Denn set me on the ground and gripped me by the shoulders, as if to reassure himself I wasn't a figment of his imagination.

"Is it really you, Adri?" Denn's voice had a breathless quality, as if he'd been running a long distance. "How can it be? I jumped in – diving and searching for you for hours – but you were gone. Gone for ever. I couldn't go home and face your mother. I've been sitting here all night." He stopped dead, a troubled look rippling over his handsome features. "You're not going back, are you? I mean, it's not like Lady Lauretta?"

I looked into Denn's face and saw true fear lurking in his eyes. Fear of losing me. He'd missed me after all.

"I'm not going back, Denn. This is where I belong."

Denn hugged me against him, my chin pressed snug against his shoulder, his left hand cradling my head, the right hand pressed deep in the small of my back. His heart pounded hard against mine. Never had I been so close to Denn. Never had he touched me with such fierce tenderness, as if I were a treasure too valuable to let go. It felt so right.

I slipped my arms around his waist and let myself melt into his embrace, not caring what might happen next. For this one moment, Denn was completely mine.

I heard the familiar voice, a simple whisper in my mind.

Why not?

Denn jumped, jarring my chin painfully from its comfortable place. Drawing back from me, he looked around in confusion. I gazed up at him, my pulse racing. Had he heard Jendayi's voice, too?

"What's the matter?" I asked.

"It was nothing. I just—" He looked at me. A look unlike any he'd given me before – tender, full of possibilities. He rested his strong hands on my shoulders, squeezing them beneath his fingers. His eyes narrowed. Releasing me, he moved backwards a step, his gaze moving over me slowly from top to bottom. What was he looking so gobsmacked about all of a sudden? I looked down at myself and about swallowed my tongue.

Oh blessed day, I'd completely forgotten I was still trussed up in that horrifically fancy blue dress. Water dripped from its hem as it clung to my body in a most improper fashion. Denn tried not to stare but failed utterly. I touched the top of my head in alarm and discovered the golden combs were still in my hair as well. I must have looked like some sort of waterlogged royalty washed up from a shipwreck.

As if in a daze, Denn took off his hat and twisted it nervously between his hands. I'd always imagined Denn removing his hat for me someday, but now that it had happened I felt strangely nervous.

"The mermaid was right," Denn said, lowering his gaze. "I've been a fool."

"What else is new? Put your hat back on, Denn. I'm not Cora Lynn," I said.

He stared at his cap as if he'd never clapped eyes on it before, but he didn't put it back on. "No, you're not Cora Lynn. Putting on for her was so easy for me. That should have been my first clue something wasn't right. I need to have my head examined for being such a dashed idiot."

"You're not that much of an idiot. Cora Lynn is *awfully* beautiful."

"So are you." Denn risked another glance at me, his eyes lingering on my face. "I don't know why I couldn't see it before."

"It's this silly dress. It's gone and made you feverish in the brain. If you keep this up, Denn, you'll turn spoony on me. I don't think I could stand it. I've always loved you exactly as you are. No frills."

"I didn't exactly return the favour, did I?" Denn said.

"No. You never did." I could feel the traitorous unshed tears burning in my eyes.

Denn cupped my chin in his hand, tracing his fingers along my cheek. There was something new in his touch. Something I'd long given up hope of ever finding there. Now that it had come, I found myself trembling.

It was exciting but uncharted territory for Denn and me. Something inside us wanted to boldly sail forth, but neither of us quite knew how to begin.

Not yet, anyway.

Denn reluctantly dropped his hand. Fumbling awkwardly with his hat for a few moments, he placed it crookedly back on his head. Without thinking, I reached up and straightened it. Denn smiled down at me, ridiculously pleased. I knew then I would never be sorry for leaving behind the handsome Sea Prince in his perfect palace. He was not my Denn. My wonderful, redheaded best friend. We grinned at each other, as if the whole world was a brand-new, delightfully wonderful place.

Denn bowed low before me, his old teasing smile returning. "I will see you home, lovely lady."

I grinned mischievously up at him. "Yes, you *may* walk me home, Mr Young."

I watched as his ears turned pink. He looked a little uncertain as he spoke. "Uh, I meant – I mean – may I walk you home?"

"I said you could." I admit I enjoyed the moment far too much.

Denn lifted the edge of his cap for a moment to scratch at his head, completely baffled about how to proceed on such uncertain ground.

"You'll have to let me sneak inside the cottage alone, though," I said. "This dress will be hard enough to explain away. Can you imagine Auntie Minnah's reaction if I also had to try and explain why I was supposedly out with you all night?"

Denn blinked in dumbstruck silence. I don't think he'd

thought of it in quite that light before.

"Oh, come on, you dolt. Let's go before my family wakes up and finds me missing." With a playful toss of my head, I ran up the beach, my bare feet kicking up soft sand. Denn's heavier boots soon pounded after me.

I ran, laughing with pure joy into the salty wind. The sound of the ocean roared all around us. I felt like singing.

Finally I was where I'd always wanted to be.

Acknowledgements

My deepest and sincerest thanks to all those who helped to make this story a reality.

To my parents and family, who always believed this day would come and helped me to believe it also.

To Lisa Sandell, Karlene Browning, Christine Minch, Kristen Landon, and Donna Cardon, who worked tirelessly to help me create the best novel possible.

To all my wonderful friends and coworkers (past and present) at the Provo City Library, who supported me through every stage of writing this book.

And especially to Pinky, whose example and many years of unconditional friendship gave Adrianne her soul.

Author's note

As a very young child I was first introduced to the idea of mermaids through Hans Christian Andersen's classic fairy tale, "The Little Mermaid". I remember being delighted by the idea of mermaids who lived in the sea, but didn't like the way they were portrayed in traditional myths as dark, murderous creatures with absolutely no sense of fashion. Being the decisive and imaginative child that I was, I began to create in my mind a very different sort of world for my mermaids to inhabit. The underwater world in my story was born from those first youthful musings.

I received my BFA in children's illustration at Brigham Young University. I've been a children's librarian for over twelve years and counting. I currently live in Lehi, Utah, with my two pets, a tiny toy poodle and a parrot.

— Sheila A. Nielson
Lehi, Utah